Veiled Promises

Carol S. Lacey

Veiled Promises
© 2025 Carol S. Lacey

Distributed by Adriel Publishing

ISBN: 979-8-9865902-8-8

The New King James Version, © 1979 Thomas Nelson, Inc.

www.CarolLacey.com

What People Are Saying About "Veiled Promises"

"Carol Lacey is rapidly becoming my favorite author. Her latest endeavor, Veiled Promises, is brilliant. If you have ever thought of yourself as not good enough, this book is a must read. Carol will give you a whole new perspective and way of loving yourself, the way God loves you."

William Wieringa
Attorney and Counselor at Law

"To those who enjoy good historical fiction, and adventure, this book is a winner. This is my fourth novel of Carol Lacey's that I have read, and I am hooked. I enjoyed the details and smooth flow of the book. The story kept me riveted and returning again and again. As a lifelong reader I've read my fair share of books and can highly recommend this one. Veiled Promise is one you will want to collect and add to your library."

Tonya Nielsen
Stay-at-home mom and intercessor

"From the beginning of her story, Carol draws us into a picture of history, its customs and events, few are aware of. Though fiction, the author takes us along with her character into a dark time of the past and shows us a ray of light and escape from humanity."

Dianne Martine
Author of children's books

"Carol's book grabbed me from the first paragraph. I was drawn in and carried from one situation to the next as this young woman grapples with her identity, value and worth. Though different, I found myself identifying with challenges she faced. What she ultimately strives to discover is what we all need to recognize: a fulfilled life lies in God's plan for each of us in Christ Jesus. Read it and be inspired."

Mary Jane Mapes
Founder and President
The Aligned Leader Institute, LLC

"Veiled Promises transported me back in time to Ancient Greece. The story quickly pulled me into the tragic life of a young girl whose family rejected her. Left on her own, Carol follows Eunice's journey through disappointment and homelessness, in a city steeped with false gods. I cheered as an ordained encounter with a stranger, changed her life forever. This novel is definitely a page-turner!"

Pam Wellington
Bible Study Leader

"Veiled Promises is a fascinating journey of a young woman who has known nothing but rejection. Guilt from mistakes she makes, broken hopes of love, and unexpected kindness, flow throughout her search for unconditional love and family. Join me as Carol leads Eunice to discover that what we long for can spring from an unforeseen source."

Larry Mueller
Heartland Church
Fort Wayne, IN

"In Veiled Promises, readers will feel Eunice's desperation - to belong, to be loved, to be cherished, as well as the desperation in the choices that she makes. But hearts will sing when Eunice discovers that love and belonging can be packaged differently than one expects."

Lisa Mackinder
Writer for magazines &
Chicken Soup for the Soul books

"Once again, Carol has written a beautiful and moving story that reflects the human condition of rejection, helplessness, imperfection, and emptiness that can only be overcome by Abba's love. As the reader journeys with Eunice, in a detailed 1st Century setting of Roman-controlled Corinth, one recognizes the pain of loneliness and love, unfilled. This is a story of redemption and hope. It is the gospel... the good news. Eunice and the characters are alive on these pages and very relatable. We tremble with her and feel despair. We rejoice when hope and light overcome loss, deception, and defeat. Carol is a gifted storyteller. She illustrates the gospel with characters of the past that parallel the present. Again, what a beautiful story!"

Mary Scott
Intercessor, counselor, short-term
missionary with Iris Global Ministries
Chicken Soup for the Soul books

DEDICATION

I dedicate this book to every soul who has suffered rejection as a child, as an adult, as a spouse, or a parent. May Eunice's story, while fiction, give you hope that your heavenly Father sees you and knows your name. He promises to bring you into His family through His Son's sacrifice, and you will never be alone or rejected by the one who loves you with an everlasting love.

ACKNOWLEDGEMENTS

I am so grateful to the Lord for giving me enough years to fulfill my dream of writing fiction. Each book has come from my heart, guided by the input of His precious Holy Spirit, without whom I could do nothing. My greatest joy is hearing it has touched a heart, and my prayer is each book will reach someone who needs to hear there is a God ready and waiting to receive them into His fold, today and for eternity.

I am also thankful to Mary Scott who donates hours of her time to perfect my writing, my grandson, who does my covers, my readers critique group, Liz Lawless, my patient publisher, and all those who pray for and encourage me along the way. I couldn't do it alone. Thank you.

Note: I have included a Character List at the end of this book for rreader's who enjoy that detail.

Prologue

Red welts on the girl's arms and legs signaled a fresh beating. Her bruised face and crumpled form looked like she had yet to eclipse thirteen summers. Each jagged sob shredded my heart. The sound tore like rents in the tunic that barely clung to her body. I knew that sound: helpless despair. It echoed from my past and I could not leave her.

I bent beside her. "There, there, Little One. Let me help you up." Since Rome had taken over and rebuilt the city, it was not uncommon to find a girl beaten and tossed aside on the streets of Corinth. Parents, husbands, lovers, or clients that paid for favors, thought little of meting out punishment as they saw fit.

The girl pulled her knees and arms tightly to her chest and wailed like one in mourning. "Leave me.I tried. I truly tried. The man demanded I... he wanted me to...I just could not. I offered to return his money but he, he..." Her failure to explain things brought more sobs.

I lifted the girl's head into my lap and stroked her cheek. As best I could, I pulled her tunic over her half-naked body and whispered words of hope and encouragement. Her shudders ended like the reluctant sigh of a toddler denied its mother's breast.

The girl opened her eyes and pushed herself upright. She eyed me with horrified surprise. "You're not Friona."

"No. My name is Eunice. Can I help you get home?" The question was futile, the colors of the garment signified a temple prostitute. "Is Friona your mentor or friend?" She moaned into her fingers. "Oh, no one will be my friend now. Friona said if I messed up again, I should leave for good." Her shoulders shook. "What can I do? Where can I go? I cannot go home. I have been shamed. No decent man would have me."

"Come stay with me for a while. I have a small place where you can heal and rest until you decide what to do. Relief lit her eyes as I helped her up. My arm circled her tiny waist. Once home, I cleaned her wounds and scrapes. I found a spare tunic and tucked her into my bed, then arranged a makeshift mat for myself on the floor.

In the near dark, the girl turned toward me. "Why are you being so kind? You do not even know me."

I smiled to myself. "I have been where you are. Let me tell you my story."

Chapter One

I was about six when my mother called out, "Eunice, get in here and clean up the kitchen, and this time do not forget to sweep the floor."

I longed to rejoin the children I had been at play with. That day was the first time no one teased me about my face. I hurried inside to avoid another beating. My mother scowled as I passed. She cuddled Chara in her lap and crooned words of love to my little sister, who though almost three, was treated as if she were a helpless infant. My eyes are dark, but everyone admires Chara's beautiful blue eyes. Her name fits: happiness, a joy to us all.

On my bed mat in the dark, sometimes I pretend my mother loves me like that. I imagine her gently brushing the stubborn tangles from my curly hair or kissing me goodnight.

Reality crashes at dawn, like the broom with which she often hits me. Each morning, she screams for me to rise and go fetch water. The pot is heavy for my small frame, but she becomes irate if it teeters and I spill some. My two older brothers are the joy of my father, but he too finds no delight in me.

My older brother likes to taunt me and point at the ugly stain on the right side of my face, calling out, "Daughter of an evil god,"

"Born in the depths of the earth," the younger is quick to add.

Once, I begged, "Father, please make them stop," then slunk away as he agreed with them, citing the dark blemish as an undeniable sign that evil dwells in me. I do not understand. I do not feel like I am evil. Would I not know it if I were? Is evil my lot for something I did? Why have I been cursed? Did a god plant evil in me because he knew I snuck that extra chunk of bread the time I was so hungry? Or did he curse me because I cursed that boy who tripped me and held my face in the mud?

Sometimes Father criticizes my mother and then me for what he deems a careless slipup or purposeful neglect. Each time, I am denied the evening meal. My mother is afraid of him. So, to please him and redirect his ire, she swats at me with whatever is in her hand.

At our noon meal, when I was about twelve, my father made an announcement. "The Isthmian games start tomorrow." He gestured to my brothers. "Today we will clean and finish the items we have shaped so we can attend the festival."

Shouts of joy rang from my brothers. The games were the highlight of everyone's year. Damian, the older, asked, "But what of all the black-figure pottery in the kiln? Father, can we leave them?

"Yes. The iron will be fully reduced, and the kindling completed by this evening. I will temper the fire so it will diminish gradually and allow the vessels to cool slowly." We all knew from past failures that the shiny black-slipped surface, so desired by their buyers, must be carefully coaxed to a perfect finish.

Adonis, the younger, jumped to his feet. "And what of the perfume bottles we have fashioned from the cream-colored clay we dug last week, Father?"

"When we return, they will be placed on the middle shelf where the heat rises through smaller holes. That allows the perfect temperature to complete the firing of those more delicate vessels.

I listened in wonder at my father's detailed explanations. Why was he so patient with my brothers and so impatient with me?

My mother often sent me to the kilns to bring lunch to him and my brothers. It fascinated me to stare into the intense fire at the bottom of the circular structure. Large, limestone slabs supported the pear-shaped ovens, and bricks, connected by ceramic clay, rose all the way to the top. Heat that billowed from the open chimney could burn a hand, carelessly placed, in seconds.

My father said people of Ammon tossed their infants into that kind of a blaze as a sacrificed to the god, Molech. I shuddered. No one could survive that kind of heat. Were all gods that cruel?

Father finished his lunch and addressed my brothers. "Your mother will prepare what we need to take. Come. We need to ready all those bottles to fire, immediately, upon our return. They pushed from the table, their excitement heard until they were well past the homes of several neighbors.

I turned my attention to my mother. "Will you go to the games with them?" I hoped she would, and I would be left to care for Chara by myself. I loved my little sister. She followed me everywhere but was seldom left alone with me for more than a short time.

Mother snapped at me. "Do not be foolish. Women are not allowed at the games. Take Chara with you and go into the market and buy some dried fish for their trip. Do not let her out of your sight."

Chara took my hand. She danced with joy at being allowed to go along. We walked around the many stalls that surrounded the beama. Today, no speakers touted opinions on the platform, but crowds filled the stoa that wound from stall to stall through the market. Chara pointed out each item. She wanted to see everything. I told her to stay in a stall with pretty linens while I went across the stoa to buy the fish. When I returned, she was gone.

I checked the nearby stalls, perturbed that she would have wandered off. I called her name. Panic rose, like a sudden squall over the gulf, when she did not answer. I called louder as I ran from booth to booth. People began to stare.

My eyes grew wild as I begged each one. "My little sister, have you seen her?" I placed one side of my hand at the middle of my chest. "She is about this tall, with dark hair and blue eyes." Heads shook with compassion, but no one responded to my cry.

I ran back to the linen stall. "My little sister was here and now she is gone. Did you see her? It was just minutes ago."

The couple who owned the booth said they were sorry, but they had been very busy and had not noticed a young girl by herself. I was frantic. I ran the whole of the long stoa several times. I searched for her in every stall and called out, between sobs. Exhausted, I found a grassy knoll where I could see people that passed.

My only girl friend's mother once spoke to us of being cautious around strange men and the dangers of being alone in a public place. The memory flashed and the thought of Chara in the hands of an evil man turned my stomach.

I sat and scrutinized every person, but none looked suspicious. At length, a man in a ragged tunic sauntered by. He wore a long, dark himation draped over his head. Could he have taken Chara?

I jumped to my feet and followed him, disappointed when he joined his wife at a stall that sold seafood. Once again, I searched every booth. Twilight descended and shop owners began to pack up their wares. What should I do? I could not go home without my sister. My mother would be devastated at the loss of the love of her life, and my father...my father might very well kill me.

At last, I trudged homeward. What did it matter? Chara had been the only bright spot in my life. At home, I tried to explain but it was worse than I imagined. My mother screamed at me and called me names I had never heard, then collapsed in hysterics. My father yanked my arm and made me run with him and my brothers back to the deserted market.

His face was purple with rage. "Show me exactly. Where did you last see her?"

They looked on every side of the stoa, around the beama and the buildings that surrounded it, but did not find her. Hate spilled from my father's eyes as he grabbed my hair and pulled me all the way home. I cried out in pain, but my cries were ignored. My heart pounded as he dragged me into the shed behind our house and reached for a long leather strap. My father had beaten me before, but this time I feared he would never stop.

I staggered into the house and crawled onto my bed mat, certain I was about to die. My back bled through my tunic and my face was so swollen I could not lie on either side. The authorities my father notified, came by midmorning to question me. They did not comment on my bruised body. Nothing I could tell them seemed to help. I shivered as they told my father that Chara was one of several young girls recently abducted in broad daylight at the market. They promised to search for her, but their underlying message was she would not be found.

My family treated me like a leper after that. Father would not even look at me and my mother took out her pain and anger with such violence I feared for my life. My brothers were especially angry that my carelessness had spoiled their opportunity to go to the games.

Their cruel accusations did not compare with my own.

Chapter Two

A few months after Chara disappeared, my mother seemed obsessed with a desire we clean every part of our home. I did my best to complete each task but was never fast enough nor finished any room to her satisfaction. I was not told the reason for her frenzy.

From outside, her shrill tone grated on my ears. "Adonis, your grandfather would not be pleased with the looks of our courtyard. Get out there and pull every weed and sweep the stones from the path."

My younger brother groused, sure it should be my job, not his, but I didn't care. Grandfather was on his way! He was the only relative, or adult, who treated me like a person and showed me affection. His home was in Argos, south of us in the Peloponnese. I wondered how he could travel that far since he was very old. Surely, it would take several days for him to arrive. My mother was the daughter of his second wife. He had outlived three.

I loved the stories of his city and wished I could go and live there with him. He often said, "It is the oldest, continuously inhabited city in Greece. Its fertile plains feed half our country."

Delighted to have someone to talk with, I would beg, "Tell me again how you reared your horses and of your city's rivalry with Sparta." He spent hours on all the recent contests. I loved the descriptions of his horses or newest foal. Once, he told me of an ancient king who had created military innovations right there in Argos. He loved the theater. "It is the largest theater in Greece, you know. It has 20,000 seats." As he described the story and costumes of the latest play for me, I would imagine myself a participant of the glamorous scene.

The day before he was due, I tried extra hard to please my mother. What would she tell him about Chara? Would he join those she turned against me with her tales of how I deliberately neglected to keep her by my side? Each time thoughts bombarded my soul with paralyzing daydreams, Mother scolded me or hit me with whatever she held. If grandfather condemned me, I would not be able to bare it.

He arrived and though my mother resented the time he spent with me, he found a way to appease her and off we went. The bluffs that overlooked the Saronic Gulf were our special spot. I treasured those times when I had him all to myself. He became winded as we climbed, so I suggested we sit on the rocks and rest for a while.

He turned his face to mine, his watery blue eyes the color of Chara's. "Eunice, I have heard what happened to your sister, but I want to hear it from you."

Sobs, I had held too long, poured out as I spoke. He listened, nodded, and sometimes shook his head. I finished and he stretched out his arms. I plunged into his embrace and sank into his stream of love. Like an animal denied life-giving water, I gulped and gulped and refused to let go.

He held me, then cupped my face with his hands. "Eunice, it was an unfortunate incident that you never intended to let happen. You are strong and you will survive, but you must not carry this guilt. It will destroy you. You must choose to put this behind you and rise above it. The decision is yours. His eyes pierced mine. "Do you understand?"

I gazed into the face of kindness and nodded. At the moment, I believed him.

Two weeks after he left, we received word of his death. I mourned for months but never saw my mother shed a tear.

Later that summer, I became aware of changes in my body. My tunics fit more snugly over my chest and hips. I caught Damian eyeing me when he thought I did not notice. His stares made me uncomfortable. But that was not the worst of it. While I washed my face one morning, the dark side felt prickly. In the days that followed, I rubbed my hand across it several times. What was happening? Within a month the little hairs grew out like a man's beard, stiff and wiry. I cried. My ugly blemish was now more obvious than ever.

Even Iola, a girl a few houses from mine, stared afresh at the sight of my face. We had grown up together and on rare occasions, when I could get away, she would invite me into her courtyard to play. Her home felt like a different world. Her mother actually smiled at me and sometimes invited me to eat with them. I stared in wonder as she instructed Iola on how to hang laundry or set the table. She didn't scream or belittle, only encouraged. I wished Iola's family were mine. I wished I would be treated like that.

To escape the stares of people and the hostility of my family, I sometimes walked alone to the bluffs that overlooked the Gulf.

Large, witches-broom bushes lined the path. Their bright yellow flowers were unable to lighten my additional heartache. Despite grandfather's advice, I could not seem to forgive myself for leaving Chara alone in that linen booth. With both of them gone, loneliness became my persistent companion. No decent man would choose a wife who had a beard on one side of her face. The future held only endless years of abuse and rejection.

On a day in early autumn, I sat on the bluff and stared at whitecaps that brushed the shore. Footsteps rustled the newly fallen leaves behind me. I turned and saw Damian come toward me. I jumped to my feet, sure my mother had sent him to look for me.

He waved his hand. "It is just me. You do not have to hurry back. What are you looking at?" He sat close to the edge of the bluff and seemed to want to talk.

He had never given me any attention. He was six years older than I and two years older than Adonis. They were always together, and I was not welcomed into any of their play or conversations. My spirits lifted at this small gesture of friendship, so I sat back down, touched that he had decided to talk to me.

He pointed to the horizon. "Can you see that ship on its way to the Cenchrean Port?" I strained but could not see a ship. He moved closer and pointed again "See, right under that grey cloud."

I was so intent on finding the ship I did not notice he had placed his arm behind me.

He lifted his hand to my shoulder and jerked me to his chest. I was too shocked to react until his other hand reached into my tunic and fumbled for my breast.

I yelled, "Stop that!" and struggled to free myself. "Get away from me!"

He laughed, pulled me closer and ran his hand up my leg.

"Stop!Llet go or I will tell Father. I will—"

"Oh, really? And what do you think Father will do? I will tell him you asked me to meet you here. Who do you think he will believe?" He pushed me to the ground and pinned one arm behind my back. I scratched his face but he held me down with his chest while he lifted my tunic and tore at my undergarments.

Rocks dug into my back as I fought as hard as I could to free myself, but he was stronger. I pushed at his chest, even bit his arm but his weight was too much for me. I cried and screamed in pain and begged him to stop but he would not.

When he had satisfied his lust, he stood up and adjusted his clothing. He leered down at me and sneered. "I would think hard before you tell anyone about this. Everyone knows you are evil and could easily have tricked me into lying with you. No one will believe your story, and I would deny it ever happened."

I trembled as he left, too dazed and shamed to think straight. When I arrived home, I told my mother I was sick and did not want supper. I crawled into my bed, cried, and shook with fear. What would I do if his seed produced a child? I had not yet had my first blood, but was too terrified to ask if it were possible to conceive before one reached that milestone.

I stayed close to home from then on and ventured no farther than the well. My mother eyed me with suspicion, aware something was wrong, but did not bother to question me. Her contempt for me had not wavered. Daily, she made it clear she held me wholly responsible for Chara's disappearance. I knew my grandfather had reasoned with her about it, but nothing changed. I sensed it pleased her to see me suffer.

Six weeks passed with no sign I carried a child. I began to relax and awoke days later with blood on my night tunic. I told my mother and without a word she handed me some old cloths. She did not ask if I understood the changes in my body nor did she explain anything. It did not matter. A neighbor girl, a few years older than I, had already violated the unspoken rule of secrecy that concerned such things.

A month later, after I finished the dinner cleanup, my father called me to join him in the courtyard. I hurried as he almost never talked to me. What had I done now?

He eyed me strangely and gestured with his head for me to come near.

In an emotionless, matter-of-fact tone, he said, "Eunice, no one will ever want you for a wife and it is time for you to earn your keep. I have hired you out to a landowner with orchards in the Peloponnese. You will work for him there, and the man will send your earnings back to me.

Panic seared chest. Sent away? From my home? My family?

"But I do everything you or mother ask of me. What more do you—"

"Enough. The arrangements have been made. You are to be ready first thing in the morning." With that he spun on his heel and returned to the house.

What would it be like to work in an orchard? I stayed outside and looked up at the stars. I loved my access to the sea. But what else would I miss about home? I came up with nothing.

Chapter Three

Very early the next day, the orchard owner's laborer arrived to fetch me. I gathered my few belongings into a small woven bag. At the rock wall that surrounded our courtyard, I looked back. No one waved or watched me leave.

The farther south we traveled, the more I hoped we would be near Grandfather's former estate. I had no idea who might live there now or how I might recognize it, so I watched for a place with horses. Did I have aunts and uncles or cousins in the area? How I wished Grandfather were still alive. He would have welcomed my news.

Hidden in the bottom of my bag was a small, carved statue of a horse he once brought to our home. He had held it with pride. "This is an exact replica of Surbo, my favorite foal. In his later years, he sired some of my best horses."

I had carefully wrapped it in a nightdress so the legs wouldn't be broken. It was not really mine, but I took it because I knew Grandfather would want me to have it, and I did not know if I would ever return.

Acres of unsettled land amazed me. Some were fenced with a house in the middle, their nearest neighbor miles away. Herds of sheep wandered hillsides, but no shepherds appeared.

To the east, the already harvested trees we passed bore evening shadows. As we drove farther into the owner's estate, ripe fruit hung in other sections. They swayed in the breeze like jilted lovers who waited patiently for someone to come claim them.

Storage barns surrounded a busy area apart from the master's home. The house's exterior was brick. It was two stories high with large windows that overlooked the orchards. The driver took me to a door at the rear of the house and told me someone would direct me from there.

Two boys, about four years old, saw me. They stopped their play and ran into the house. Their voices carried as they told their mother about me. A woman, not much older than I, came to the door. The hair on top of her head was knotted so tightly it was a wonder she could close her eyes. The boys clung to her legs.

She did not smile. "I am Thera. I assume you are Eunice."

I nodded and she introduced me to her twin sons, Belen and Bemus, then motioned for me to come inside. I followed her through the kitchen to a small storage room.

"This will be yours, once those seed bags are removed. The master will send someone to gather them as soon as possible. We are short handed right now and the fruit must come first."

I thought she would direct me to the orchards to help pick, but instead she told me to come with her. I lay down my bag and followed her through the spotless house. She pointed out exactly where things were to be kept. I made mental notes of all she said.

The master's room was on the main floor while hers and the boys' were on the second floor. When we reached the top of the stairs she grabbed the rail, gasped, and clutched her chest. I didn't know what to do. My arms lurched at her, but she did not fall. Her face was ashen and black circles wreathed her eyes.

My heart pounded. "Can I help you...get you some water or something?"

She gulped air, shook her head, and pushed herself upright. Still breathing hard, she said she was fine. A few moments later, as if nothing had happened, she showed me her room and the section where her boys slept.

Back in the kitchen, she sat on a stool and stared at me. I knew she wondered about my face but she did not ask.

She pointed at a cupboard with tall doors. "That is the pantry. I was told you are able to cook and clean. Is that right?" Her tone reflected doubt.

I could only nod, surprised to learn I was hired to help in the house. My father had implied I would work in the orchards. Disappointment rose but I shook it off. I had welcomed the opportunity to be engaged with something other than housework. But at least my mother's critical voice would not taunt me.

"Yes, I have helped my mother since I was a small child."

"Good. You will rise before light and make breakfast. I will inform you, daily, what I plan for dinner. Then you can wash the clothes and clean until it is time to prepare the evening meal. I will manage the midday meal...unless, I tell you differently."

By then, my room had been cleared. She brought me a mat and blankets and told me to rest until time to make dinner. I lay down but grew restless. My thoughts churned. Why had she nearly collapsed? Would she be hard to please? Would I measure up to her expectations?

I slipped out the door where I expected to see the twins, but they were not around. Later, I learned she and the twins rested each afternoon at this hour. I wandered toward the orchard closest to the house. The aroma of ripe fruit teased my senses. I reached for a golden peach. The blush smeared beneath its fuzz-covered surface resembled a sunrise over the gulf. I rubbed it on my tunic and took a bite. To my delight, a sweet nectar filled my mouth and ran down my chin,

A voice called from behind the tree, "And who is the lovely goddess that steals my fruit?

I froze and dropped the fruit. "I am sorry, I should have asked permission. I..."

A lazy chuckle sprang from a man whose hands and tunic were badly stained and dirty. A large smudge remained where he had swiped his forehead. It left his handsome face a bit comical. A grin lit up his eyes. "I am the sorry one. I did not mean to startle you. You are most welcome to eat our fruit. Who are you? I do not recall ever seeing you."

His glance took in my face, but he did not seem offended by it. He reached up and pulled another peach from farther up the tree, rubbed off the fuzz, and handed it to me. He was much taller than my father or older brother.

"My name is Eunice. I just arrived." Who was this man? Should I tell him I had been hired to help the master's wife cook and clean?

"Oh yes, the girl we brought down from Corinth to help with the house. How was your trip?"

"It was..." We brought down? How was it this worker knew I had been hired and what I was here for?

He smiled and pointed at the peach. "Take a bite. We have had a great season. The harvest has been abundant.

I lifted the fruit to my lips and bit into it, aware he watched. "It's very sweet. I have never been to the Peloponnese, so I enjoyed all I saw." He didn't respond and I searched my mind for a reason to leave. "Excuse me. I need to get back."

"And did you meet my sons Belen and Bemus? They can be a handful, but they are good boys."

His sons? This was the master? A man who had been hard at work in the orchards? I was so surprised I did not know what to say. Back home, men of prominence did not do manual labor. I assumed he must have inherited the estate from his father as he looked no more than thirty.

"Yes. Fine boys." To please him, I took another bite and admired its sweetness. His eyes remained fixed on mine. It sent color to my face.

He asked about my life in Corinth. Besides my grandfather,I had never met a man with such a kindly manner. I told him that I had two brothers and had lost a sister, about my father's pottery business, and my love of the sea.

He listened and nodded. I suspected that somehow, he knew there was more to tell, but he did not pry.

An awkward moment followed, broken by the sounds of noisy children. "Father, Mother sent us to ask if you will be finished in time to have dinner with us tonight?"

He scooped up both boys and snuggled them to his chest. "Tell her yes, I just need to check on the pickers in the north orchard and then I will be done for the day." The twins peeked around his broad arms and eyed me until he tickled them with his whiskers. The familiar ruse sent them into fits of laughter before they wriggled from his arms and ran back to their mother.

"I had best hurry. I need to prepare dinner."

Beyond that, I needed to escape those dark eyes that promised to haunt me and drew out a longing I did not understand but could not deny.

Chapter Four

My days at the estate were filled with duties learned back home. I cooked and baked bread, prepared vegetables, meat and dishes with spiced peaches or nectarines. I cleaned rooms that were never used, scrubbed the kitchen, mopped floors, and washed clothes. That chore included pails of blood-soaked rags Thera no longer hid from me. Often, I was asked to supervise the twins. They had warmed to me and constantly sparred for my attention.

I loved time with them. It brought back memories of Chara at that age. The master's young wife no longer hovered as she saw how hard I worked and that I would see to all she asked. Each day, I followed her routine and stopped at mid afternoon while she and the boys rested. For an hour or so, I was free to do as I pleased, walk or explore, as long as dinner was underway on time.

I often went to the orchards. I enjoyed changes each season thrust upon the trees. They shifted from branches heavy with fruit, to leaves bright with color. Leaves, driven to the ground, left branches as intricate shapes, exposed and naked. As the days grew colder, I simply walked and speculated about my family. It had been months, and I had not heard from them. Did they ever think of me?

Late one morning, Thera stopped me. "Eunice, I need to rest a bit earlier today. I want you to prepare lunch for the master and the boys."

I assured her I would, concerned with how pale she had grown. The foul cloths she left to soak, oozed with more blood each day. Yorgos, the master, arrived at midday. He stopped at the well to wash up and splashed water on Bemus as he finished. His son squealed with delight, and soon, Belen joined in the fun.

I hardly ever saw Yorgos as I did not have meals with the family. Surprised to see me lay out the meal, he asked, "Where is my wife?"

"The Mistress is at rest. She asked me to..."

Before I could finish, he was halfway up the stairs. The boys started to follow, but I stopped them with the assurance their father would be right back.

The door had not yet closed when I heard Thera's voice. "Really, Yorgos, you need not hover over me. I am doing well and..."

Her tone had been sharp. Why would she disdain his concern?

Yorgos returned soon after. He looked hurt and baffled but addressed me kindly. "Please see to it that she does not leave her bed, at any time, for the rest of this day." He ignored the food I had laid out, headed for the door, and stopped. "Thera tells me you are doing well here. Can you see to the boys, make them rest, and prepare the evening meal without her?"

Worry lined his brow. I told him we would manage and suggested he take some food along with him. That did not seem to register. He simply nodded and hurried through the door.

How would it feel to have someone care that much about you? I told the boys their mother needed time to rest, they were to nap quietly, and later could play outside. They complied when I promised to join them after I saw to their mother and cleaned up from lunch. I fixed a tray of broth, some fruit, and bread and knocked softly on Thera's door.

Her reply barely reached my ears. "Yes. What is it?"

I pushed open the door and entered before she was able to hide her tears. "Would you like to eat something?"

"Oh, thank you. It smells wonderful."

I set the tray on a table within her reach. "It is broth I made from bones left from the lamb we roasted yesterday. My mother said it will strengthen your blood." My hand flew to my lips. "I am sorry, I should not have — "

She pushed herself into a sitting position. "It is all right, Eunice. You could not have missed that I have a... a condition. I am grateful you took over for me." Her voice caught, "I am afraid I may need to depend on you more in time." She wiped her eyes with the cloth from her tray.

"Please, do not hesitate to ask anything of me."

"I have known, for a while, that my days will be short. Yorgos, my husband is a good man, but he refuses to accept the inevitable." Her eyes filled again. "The worst part is to leave my boys. They are my life."

What could I say? I wanted to comfort her, but I could not deny what she knew to be true. The irony of it struck like a sudden earthquake. Here was a woman who had everything but no hope of a future, and here I was who owned nothing, but had the likelihood of healthy years to come. She would not live to enjoy what she had, and my prognosis was a life void of love and security.

Then and there, I vowed to make her last days fulfilled in any way open to me.

"Let me help you make the best of the time you have. I will watch over the boys and bring them to you whenever you feel you can bear their boundless energy."

She smiled. "Thank you, Eunice. You have been a great blessing to me."

I handed her the broth and she ate most of it. "Umm...that was good. Maybe it will help me sleep."

I took the bowl but left the figs and grapes for her to eat, later.

You have been a great blessing. Her words whirled in my mind and brought tears to my eyes. No one had ever spoken of me as a blessing, quite the opposite. Joy flooded my heart as I joined the boys in the courtyard.

Belen delighted when Bemus scooped up the five stones that lay before him on the ground but missed the one he tossed into the air. "You missed. You missed!"

Bemus conceded that Belen had won that round of jackstones. "I almost made it." They insisted I try. When I failed on the third stone, they doubled over in laughter.

Bemus addressed me in the way his mother had taught him. "Miss Eunice, why do you have whiskers on the side of your face? Father has whiskers, but not mother."

He caught me off guard. No one had ever been bold enough to ask me that, outright.

I searched for an answer he could understand. "Honestly, I do not know. When I was born that side of my face had a dark reddish stain. When I grew up, whiskers grew from it."

Belen studied my face. "Do you like to have whiskers?"

I touched the clear side of my face. "No, I wish it were like this side." Bemus drew closer. "Can we feel them?"

"Of course." I bent down beside them.

Each one gently stroked my face. Both agreed they were not as stiff as their fathers and were quick to return to their game. I marveled at their curiosity and acceptance.

That evening, I called the boys to wash up for dinner, then made up a tray and took it to Thera. She was asleep, so I left it on her table. I was nervous as I served the boys and their father, shortly after. Normally, I laid out the food and left it for Thera to dish out. Now, all eyes were on me.

Yorgos soon signaled that they were finished and left to join Thera. I oversaw the boys' bedtime routine, impressed with their zeal to follow their mother's nightly directions.

Belen finished first. "Miss Eunice, Mother always tells us a story. Will you tell us a story?"

A story? My mother had never bothered with what she considered "nonsense." What could I say? Tell them about Grandfather popped into my head. I told them to wait a moment and left to fetch the statue he had given our family. I held up the replica for them to see.

"This belonged to my beloved grandfather. The horse's name was Surbo, and he was Grandfather's favorite foal." Each begged to hold it. I agreed but warned of the need to be very gentle. They lay back on their bed mats and listened as I told of my grandfather's horse ranch, his adventures, and that he had lived not far from them.

I tucked them in and promised to tell them more tales of my grandfather and of his visits to my home near the gulf. I blew out their lamps and left, startled to realize their father had listened just outside their door.

He seemed embarrassed and said, "I always come and say good night to them."

He backed up enough for me to ease around him. I returned to the kitchen to put the leftovers away and washed the dishes, embarrassed that I nurtured his scent in the hidden chambers of my heart.

Chapter Five

Yorgos stuck his head through the kitchen door. "Thank you for your kindness to Thera and the boys, Eunice. I am afraid she will not be able to do much for a while. I will try to find someone to help you."

I loved the way he said my name but grieved the pain that shadowed his words. "Please, do not be concerned. I have learned how the household runs. To manage the work and the boys will be no trouble."

I waited for his reaction, but he said no more. He simply stared at me with those dark eyes that held such mystery.

For the next few weeks, Thera was able to be up for short periods, but it was obvious to us all that her strength had greatly diminished. I checked on her several times a day. When she was awake, I stayed and listened to her reminisce about memories dear to her heart which included details of the boys' birth and their antics as toddlers.

I struggled to keep up with the household demands-to clean, bake, and do the extra laundry her condition brought about. Each day, I helped her bathe and took on more and more decisions about meals and what needed to be done.

"Eunice," she said after I had changed her gown and bedding for the second time that morning. "You never talk about yourself or your family. Was your home a great distance from here? Do you ever long to see them?"

How should I answer? She was burdened enough without my tales of woe. I sat close to her and told of my life in Corinth. I shared about those who were in my family and of my grandfather, but nothing of my heartache.

She leaned back in her pillows and sighed. "Sounds like you and your grandfather had a wonderfully deep connection. That does not happen in everyone's life."

"But you have Yorgos..." My face flushed. "I mean, the master. And I have seen how much he cares for you. Surely, you have known such love."

Thera gazed out her window. "He is a kind man and he treats me well. When I was just thirteen there was a young man that worked for my father. We saw each other every day and talked when I brought him and the others water. I cannot put it in words, but something stronger than ourselves drew us to one another."

She closed her eyes and did not add anymore to her story. I thought she had fallen asleep. I planned to tiptoe out, when suddenly, she opened her eyes. They were wet as she poured out her heart. I sensed a need for someone to understand the loss she had suffered, before it was too late.

"I never told anyone, but after my parents were asleep, I would sneak out of my house to meet him. We would talk for hours and one night he kissed me. We knew there was no chance my father would give me to him, but our love would not let us give up.

"One night, my father acted upon his suspicions and followed me. He found us, and in a rage, commanded I return to the house. I never saw my beloved again. The next week, my father betrothed me to Yorgos."

I did not know how to respond. Part of me grieved her lost love, while another part wanted to shake her. Obviously, she only tolerated Yorgos, a man I would give my all to have love me like he loved her.

When I said nothing, she turned and faced me. "Have you ever known love, Eunice? Have you ever been with a man?"

My face colored. "No, not really." My voice betrayed the partial lie.

She whispered, "I am sorry, I did not mean to pry. Tell me about your face. Were you born like that?"

I explained how it developed and had affected my life. As I spoke of the memories of rejection, especially from my family, tears fell in an emotional release that broke through my resolve to never share my biggest shame with anyone.

I sobbed into my hands. "The worst thing was when my older brother took advantage of my low status and raped me. I had no one to tell who cared enough to commiserate with me."

Thera put her hand on my arm, her tears spilled with mine. "Eunice, you have a lot of love to give, and it is my hope you will find someone who deserves it."

From that day forth, we were like how I imagined sisters would be. Each day, we shared our hopes and regrets as well as our sorrows. Nothing was off limits...except my deepest longing.

***

Except for when we passed briefly at breakfast, the only time I saw Yorgos was when I served dinner. One night before I left for the kitchen, he stopped me. "Eunice, it is not necessary for you to take your food to the kitchen. Stay here and eat with us."

The boys chimed in. "Yes, Miss Eunice. Eat with us."

I laid my plate back on the table and pulled up a chair. Could he see how nervous I was? Did people who owned huge estates behave differently at meals than my family had?

I was awed at the interaction between the twins and their father. They talked and enjoyed one another's company. After a few nights, they drew me into their conversations. The boys asked me questions while they talked of their imaginary conquests, often at the same time. Yorgos spoke, mostly, of the progress he and his help made as they pruned and trimmed the trees for winter's long rest. I loved that he aimed his discourse at me.

Thera never left her bed that spring. Despite the supervision required to produce a bountiful crop, Yorgos spent as much time with her as he could. The boys missed their mother. On her better days, I took them in to see her in short spurts. In time, she was too weak to respond to their chatter, and they ceased to beg to see her.

I moved my bed mat into a corner of her room so I could hear her call in the night. One morning, long before dawn, I awoke and realized I had not heard her for hours. I rushed to her side and found she was gone. Her fight was over. The strain on her face had evaporated like a morning fog and left no witness to the battle she had endured.

I dressed, ran, and knocked on Yorgos' door. He opened it, confused at the hour. "Eunice? What is it?"

My tears spoke for me. He rushed past me, up the stairs. I wondered how he would explain the loss to the boys.

Yorgos did not return for nearly an hour. He did not look directly at me, but his puffy, red eyes and slumped shoulders spoke loudly of his grief and genuine love for Thera.

His voice trembled. "Eunice, I need...I mean, would you prepare Thera's body for burial? She was so fond of you. Her family lives somewhat north of Corinth. I will send word and they should arrive in a couple of days."

I wanted to hug him, to relieve his pain. Did he know he was not Thera's true love? I assured him I would attend to Thera's preparation and have beds and the house ready.

To lay Thera to rest was a quiet process. I washed and dressed her in her finest tunic and, arranged her hair in soft swirls around her face. I cooked and baked well into the night so there would be plenty of food for the family, houseguests and mourners. Her family arrived and the funeral was held the day after.

I stole a look at her father and tried to picture how he ordered Thera to leave the man she loved. Her mother was dressed in drab, colorless clothing. She trailed behind and said little, but shed many tears. I wept with her. Surely, she loved her daughter. Did she know of Thera's first love or ever had one of her own?

The gloom that followed the weeks after Thera's death was as drab as a sunless winter. Time hung beneath its cloudbank and refused to hurry the season of mourning. Yorgos spent every moment he could with the twins and tried to satisfy questions that had no answers.

Where was their mother? Would she ever come back? Could they go visit her?

Before the sweet cherries began to ripen, Yorgos often left on unexplained, overnight ventures. I had come to meet the boys' needs of a mother so well, he no longer bothered to inform me not to expect him for meals.

On a beautiful, late spring afternoon I walked in the orchards while the boys rested, used to the routine their mother had established. The sweet cherries had been harvested but the bright red sour variety hung in clusters that begged to be picked. They looked almost transparent as the afternoon sun glistened off the plump fruit.

To reach these irresistible beauties, I climbed onto a shiny, dark branch that hung low to the ground. I braced myself in a roomy crotch and plucked a few. A little higher, many more waved in the breeze. I climbed farther to reach them, and soon the lap of my tunic was full. I needed to get down.

A voice brimmed with mirth. "And how do you propose to climb down from there with a lap full of cherries?"

My face turned as red as the cherries. It was Yorgos.

"Here, let me help you." He lifted a small container high enough for me to fill it. I hung onto a branch with one hand and eased the fruit into the pail with the other. While he settled the bucket on the ground, my foot slipped. He rose just in time to prevent me from hitting the ground.

"Whoa!" His grin spread from ear to ear. "If you cannot pick cherries without the risk of a fall, maybe you should stick to baking desserts with them,"

I hardly heard, aware only of his closeness and the strong arms that held me. Concern replaced his grin as he set me on my feet. "Are you all right?"

I rubbed my elbow where it had scraped the tree. "I am sorry. I am fine. I should not have—"

"No, I am glad you wanted to pick some. Few can resist these colorful treats. Let me see your arm. Are you sure you are all right?" He took my hand and turned my arm to look. "It is not much but you probably should clean it before long and rub some salve on it."

I thanked him and said I had better see to the boys and dinner. My heart fluttered so hard I forgot the cherries.

The boys had awaited my return. I joined them in the courtyard for a while then excused myself to start dinner, my mind far from their constant chatter. That night,I lay awake and relived the feel of Yorgos' arms around me, the closeness of his body and his tender concern.

I heard him softly call my name, sure it was part of my fantasy. It was not.

Chapter Six

It was raining so hard, that when Yorgos called again, I almost missed him. My mind ran to the many reasons why he might be at my door. Were the twins all right? Had there been an accident or a problem in the orchards? Hope that he desired time with me bloomed brightly in my imagination.

I jumped up, put on my cover, and opened the door. He wore a himation that covered down to his boots, the hood already pulled over his head.

"I am so sorry to wake you, but I wanted you to know I will be away for about three days. If any problems arise, ask my overseer and he will help you. I forgot to tell the boys, but they are so fond of you they will hardly miss me."

The smile he added rippled my heart. I hid my disappointment, assured him we would manage, and wished him safe travel.

Hope beckoned as he turned and faced me. "I believe it is time to clear out Thera's room. Would you remove all that remains of things her mother did not take, and see that it is ready for use again?"

I told him I would see to it. My eyes filled at the prospect of his being ready to move on.

He left and I lay back on my mat. What was important enough to draw him out at night in such a storm?

Just as Yorgos predicted, at breakfast the boys asked why their father had not joined them, and promptly dropped the subject in favor of their plans for the day. The first day, I cleared out and cleaned Thera's room.

I envisioned it becoming mine.

The next day, I busied myself with routine work and laundry but finished early. Time dragged. I invited the twins to assist me while I baked. They jumped at the chance of something new. Before long, flour dust covered the counter, the floor, and them.

I kept dinner simple, sausage with tangenites. Covered with honey, the flour and oil mixture fried with crisp edges was the boys' favorite. At bedtime, I told them more of the adventures of my grandfather. What would I conjure up when my memories ran out?

Bemus eyed me shyly. "Miss Eunice, are you going to be our mother now?"

I felt a flush rise from my neck to my face. Had the desire of my heart been so obvious a child discerned it?

"Bemus, what made you think such a thing?"

"Well, Father told us he was going to get us a new mother one day."

My heart leapt for joy. Yorgos was ready to take another wife, a mother for the twins.

"I think you will have to wait and see. Maybe it will be soon." I tucked them in, kissed them goodnight, and blew out their lamp.

I floated to the kitchen. Could it really happen? Would Yorgos see me as a fit wife? Chills of hope ran up my arms.

The days that followed were the longest I had ever known. I tried to stay busy, keep the boys occupied, and dismiss persistent images of being Yorgos' wife. The someday spoken to the boys could be months or years away.

I sighed. I would wait forever for such a life.

We had just finished dinner the third night, when Belen ran to the door. "I hear Father's carriage! He is home." In a flash, Bemus joined in his dash out the door.

I followed them out, delighted to watch Yorgos gather both boys into his arms. He set them down and led them to the door of the carriage where he took the hand of a young woman and helped her down. She brushed her long brown curls back over her shoulders, fluttered innocent eyes at him, and smiled.

From that moment on, things moved in slow motion. The woman bent over and hugged each of the boys. Her petite frame hardly eclipsed theirs. I could not see their faces, but recognized their stiff reactions. Yorgos tousled their heads, "Come on. Let us go introduce her to Eunice."

I wanted to run, to hide. I wanted to scream, to cry, "No! This cannot be. This is not what I dreamed of or hoped for." It was too late. They were at the door.

Yorgos took the lady's arm. "Eunice, "I want you to meet my wife, Amara. We were married yesterday in a small city this side of Corinth. You probably passed it on the way here."

My stomach threatened to lose its contents. I pasted a smile on my face and willed my lips not to tremble. "How nice to meet you. I am sure you will be happy here."

Her smile was genuine. "I have heard so much about you. I hope I can be as good a mother to the boys as Yorgos tells me you have been."

Gracious words aside, I wanted to take hold of her, drag her back to the carriage, and swat the horse into a gallop. The glow of peace and joy on her face should have been mine. Instead, her happiness stamped, *dream never to be, across my heart.*

I was greatly relieved when Bemus asked if he could show her his rock collection. Belen added a request and the three of them hurried up the stairs. I could not look at Yorgos. I needed the sanctuary of my room before I lost all pretense of being happy for him.

He asked me for a moment. My escape delayed, I clutched my nails to transfer my pain. "Eunice, you have done such a wonderful job with the boys and our home. I want to thank you and to let you know I have informed your father that the money you earn here from now on will be given to you, not sent to him."

My jaw dropped. I pictured my father's angry face at such a decision. But Yorgos was right. I was the one who did the work.

I tried not to stammer. "Thank you. I believe I will turn in now." I could not bear to announce that Thera's room was ready for his new wife.

"One more thing. My wife is from a wealthy family with many servants and will need help to learn how to run a household. I would appreciate it if you would teach her how things are done here."

I nodded, "Of course," and quickly shut my door.

Soon, the house was quiet. The injustice of life brought sobs to my pillow. Rivers of blame and self-pity joined to choke all hope of a future. The squeak of stairs magnified my pain. The bride had descended to her husband's chambers.

A cry from my childhood accused, What did you expect? Did you really think a man like Yorgos would choose a girl with a beard for his wife? No decent man will ever want you.

The message crashed like porcelain bowls in an earthquake. How could I have let my heart lead me to think otherwise? I had to leave. I could not bear to stay and watch his new bride revel in all the joys I expected to be mine. But where would I go? Certainly not back to my family.

I determined to survive this painful loss. People like my grandfather, who would not judge me unfit because I had hair on my face, had to be out there. A plan formulated in my mind. I would stay long enough to save money and go back to Corinth and make a new life for myself.

The next morning, I rose, determined to ignore the many incidents that fed my despair. And they came. Each day, the new wife swept into the dining room all primped for the day. She looked like she had found buried treasure. Yorgos arrived and beamed at her. One of the twins referred to her as "Mother."

I put on a cheerful demeanor and made breakfast. That everyone seemed pleased with the changes, made it harder to hide my resentment. How could they be totally oblivious to my pain?

For a month, I endured the intolerable situation. I avoided Yorgos and carefully horded the drachmas he gave me. I helped his new bride learn to manage the house and the boys. To make the transition easier and help them warm to each other, I encouraged Amara and the twins to ask questions about their lives and dreams.

At first, I did not know how I would manage to leave without questions as to why, but an idea grew into a plan. I asked Yorgos if his carriage driver could take me back for a visit to the place where my grandfather had lived.

He was very receptive to my request. He grinned, "The boys told me about your stories of your grandfather and of the little colt you showed them. You deserve a day off, and I would be more than happy for my driver to take you."

To leave proved harder than I expected. My few possessions were easy to bundle and hide in the carriage. I tracked down the boys in the side yard to say goodbye.

Bemus pouted, "But why can we not come with you, Eunice?"

I covered my tears with a fictitious tale of how next time I would include them, but first I had to ask permission of Grandfather's heirs.

Belen nodded, "Tell him we love the stories about his horses,"

I was so touched that they both wished to accompany me that tears mingled with my goodbye kisses.

When the driver arrived in an area where there were horse ranches, I told him to stop at a large villa along the way. At the door, I spoke to a servant with the pretense of asking if she knew my grandfather. She did not. I thanked her and returned to the carriage.

I lied to the driver. "This is the home of some of my relatives. They invited me to stay the night so you can return for me tomorrow afternoon."

The driver looked skeptical. "The master did not say —"

"Oh, I know. But he told me if I wanted to stay over, he would not mind."

Finally, he shrugged. "All right. I will return for you tomorrow." With that, he turned the carriage and left.

I picked up my parcel and pretended to walk back to the house. When he was out of sight, I turned and began the journey to Corinth.

Chapter Seven

It took many days to walk to Corinth. Sometimes, a peddler offered me a ride on his cart. Most had only two wheels, so they tipped up and down with each rise in the road. Still, it was a welcome relief. I rode in the back where my feet dangled in my broken sandals, inches from the ground. I vowed to buy new ones at the market.

To keep from being seen by those who preyed on lone travelers, I slept under bushes well away from the road, grateful it was summer. Even the smaller villages had public wells where I could get water and, sometimes, buy food from a vendor.

Once I left the Peloponnese, I chose roads that would take me far from my family's home. The sky darkened as the outskirts of Corinth came into view. What should I do? I went into the marketplace to buy food, but the stalls were empty.

I stopped at the fountain and drank deeply. Maybe it would satiate my hunger. A more permanent booth enclosed on three sides was deserted so I laid my spare tunic on the floor and fell asleep.

To avoid the owner, I left early the next morning, splashed water on my face at the fountain, and bought some bread and cheese from the first vendor to arrive. I had never been into the city and the farther I wandered into the heart of it, the more apprehensive I became. I had no idea it was so big or filled with so many people determined to reach destinations, beyond my imagination .

Few glanced my way as they rushed to their many temples, monuments, and homes.

I found a quiet bench next to a Roman temple and watched them hasten by, hoping...for what? Like the flames in my father's kilns, my bravado began to die. I had no idea what I wanted, where to go, or how to get what I needed.

Back at the market, once again, after the merchants left for the day, I found a place to sleep. By the second evening, I had no more of a plan than before. I crept into the booth I had found the first night and sank to the floor. A fitful night left me still asleep when the owner of the booth arrived in the morning.

The man shouted, "What are you doing here? This is not an inn." I grabbed my things. "Who are you? Have you no home to sleep in?"

My heart raced. Would he call the soldiers? "I am so sorry. I will not come again."

He blocked the door, arms across his chest. "Why have you slept in my booth? Where is your family?" His tone had switched to curiosity.

"I have no family," It was not a lie. My family did not want me.

He cocked his head and peered intently at me. His gaze settled on my face. "What happened to your face?"

My cheeks burned and I tried not to whimper. Would he, too, consider it a sign of evil? "The darkness was there at my birth."

For a moment, he simply stared. He was very tall and heavy, much bigger than my father. I knew I would not survive if he decided to beat me.

He thrust a cloth and a broom at me. "Here, you can sweep and clean some to pay for a night in my booth." I went to work and soon had the place clean and swept. He busied himself, but I knew he had his eye on me.

An hour passed, and he asked me my name. "I am Ophelos. I sell wool in this stall, and my wife is large with child. I need someone to watch over her and to help me here when I must be gone. I will give you food and a safe place to sleep if you promise to do what I say."

I could not restrain tears that welled in my eyes. Unable to hide my eagerness, I nodded, "Yes. I will work hard and do whatever you need me to do."

He motioned for me to follow, and for the next half hour I helped him bring the wool from his cart and arrange it on the shelves. When we finished, he gave me a mixture of potatoes, carrots, and lamb wrapped in grape leaves.

"He handed me a piece of cloth. "Here, take this and use some strands of the wool to fashion a veil for that side of your face. No need for the customers' attention to be distracted with unwelcome curiosity."

I was glad he did not say drive the customers away. I did as he said. Why had I not ever thought to hide my disfigurement that way? He left me alone in his booth for short times that morning and for nearly an hour that afternoon, while he went home to check on his wife. I marveled at his trust in a stranger. He taught me the different values of the wool he sold, how he priced it according to texture and quality, and whether it was loose or carded.

I paid close attention to how he dealt with customers. He showed them what he had and suggested what would best suit their needs. Near the end of the day, he told me to wait on a woman who looked for a soft, lightweight wool for her expected baby. I showed her what was available and when she decided to buy it, he insisted I wrap it up and take her money.

We packed his cart, ready to leave for the day. I was so grateful to have won his trust, that before he asked, I found his broom, swept the floor and dusted the shelves again. We had worked well together, and I knew he was pleased.

He pushed his cart and motioned for me to follow. We walked about a mile from the city in the direction of the gulf. His house was larger than my family's home had been, with a well-kept courtyard. Two little girls, under five, ran to welcome him. He swept them up into his arms even before he pulled the cart through the gate. The scene tugged on my heart. Did Belen and Bemus miss me?

"Agatha and Iris, this is Eunice. She is my new helper."

The girls clung to his legs and peeked at me from behind. I smiled and stooped to their level. "I used to have a little sister just like you. She loved to play with her dolly. Do you play with dollies?"

First Agatha, the older girl, and then Iris, let go of their father and moved toward me. Iris ran and picked up her dolly. She held up a well-loved moppet for me to see. "This is Lole. She is mine." Agatha left to get hers but tumbled into her very pregnant mother.

Her father cautioned, "Careful, Agatha." He motioned to his wife. " Carisa, this is Eunice. She is my new helper until you are able to come back to the market."

His wife nodded. "Welcome to our home, Eunice. Do not let the girls wear you out. They love company."

I tried to curb my emotions. "Oh, I love children, especially little girls. Thank you for allowing me to be here with your family."

She smiled and headed for the house. "Supper will be ready, soon. Come, I will show you where you can sleep." She led me to a small alcove off the kitchen, large enough for a bed mat. "It is small, but you will be plenty warm. I will find some blankets after we eat."

My thoughts ran back to when Thera said nearly the same thing. I laid my small bag in a corner and joined the family in a simple meal of lamb stew with vegetables. It tasted wonderful after days of mostly bread and cheese. I helped her clean up after the meal and took the girls out into the courtyard. They were delighted and each vied for my full attention.

Carisa joined Ophelos outside. "That sheep owner who supplies our wool came by today."

"He did not come to the booth. Did he say what he wanted?"

"No, but he seemed anxious to talk to you. I wonder why he did not come into the city?"

I sensed a problem and decided to leave and go arrange the blankets Carisa had given me. "Please excuse me. I am very tired and want to be well rested to help in the booth tomorrow.'"

The girls were disappointed, but their parents nodded and said they understood.

I awoke in the night to a commotion that turned into loud cries. I thought I was in the middle of a dream, but soon realized it was the man's wife. Ophelos came to the opening where I lay.

"Eunice? Eunice, are you awake?"

I sat up. "Yes, can I be of help?"

"It is Carisa. Her time has come. Will you come be with her while I fetch the midwife?"

I jumped to my feet. "Of course. Give me a moment to dress. Are the girls awake?"

"Not yet, but probably will be soon."

"Do not worry, I will take care of them."

"Thank you. I am eager to go. My wife's babies come quickly."

I threw on my tunic and hurried to her side. I had no idea how to help. Sweat poured from under her hair and down her face. Her gown clung to the large mound that harbored her baby. I ran to the water barrel, wrung a cloth in the cool water and bathed her face.

I remembered how, without explanation, I was rudely escorted from the room when my mother was about to birth Chara. At only three, I had no idea what caused my mother to scream, nor did I know what to expect now. I only remembered how frightened I was.

Agatha and Iris arrived just as their mother let out a piercing scream. Terrified, they ran to her side. Each tugged at her arm and begged assurance she was helpless to provide. I was torn. I wanted to take them from the room and comfort them, but I did not dare leave their mother alone.

She shrieked and made the decision for me. "Help me! The baby is ready to come!"

I lifted her cover and gasped. A hairy, black ball emerged from her body. I reached out in time to catch the tiny bit of humanity that propelled from her womb like a rock off a slingshot.

Chapter Eight

I stood mesmerized by the bloody, new life that squirmed in my arms. Carisa cried out again. I startled, awakened from the miracle I had been privileged to witness. Her face pinched as she strained until her body expelled a pink, spongy substance. My heart raced. Was this normal?

A cord connected the infant to the tissue. Exhausted, the newly spent mother collapsed back on her bed and gasped for air. Blood still trickled from the opening that tore her flesh upon the baby's entrance into the world.

I forced myself to tune out the cries of Agatha and Eris and grabbed a nearby blanket to wrap the wailing baby.

I tried to hide my panic. "I have never witnessed a birth before, and I do not know what to do. Are you all right? "

She struggled to get the words out. "There, on the side table is some twine and scissors. Take the twine and tie it to the child's cord, close to its body, and cut it free. Then give the baby to me. What is it? Another girl?"

I did as she said then laid the baby on her chest. "No. It is a little boy and he...well, he is perfect." Tears ran down my cheeks. Would I ever know the joy of birthing a child?

"A boy! Ophelos will be so pleased."

The moment their mother's voice returned to normal, Agatha and Eris calmed and asked to see the baby.

I watched Carisa put the baby to her breast, awed at the contentment on her face. "What can I do for you? Shall I..."

Her husband rushed through the door. "We are here. How is she?" The midwife followed. She tossed her cloak to one side. Both stopped at a cry that came from under the blanket.

His wife said, "It is a boy! You finally have your boy."

The family took a few joyful moments to admire the baby before the midwife shooed us all out. "I must ask you to leave now. There is more to be done."

Ophelos' chest swelled as we left the woman to do her work. He looked at me, eyes wet and shiny. "You delivered my son. How can I thank you? Eunice, you are truly a blessing."

I helped get the girls back into their beds. Alone in my room, my heart nearly burst with wonder. I knew I had done little but stay with his wife like he had asked. She had brought forth his son. I merely caught the newly born and did as she directed. But he called me a blessing. I ran the words over my tongue. Was that not what Thera had said? Why was it so hard for me to believe? I wanted to stay with this family forever.

For the next few months, I went daily with Ophelos to help in his booth. The temperature dropped and few customers lingered over the goods. Most chose the heavier varieties of wool and quickly moved on. Occasionally, if Ophelos had not made the long trip to the farm, the man who replenished his stock brought fresh wool for his shelves.

Ophelos introduced us. "Eunice, this is our supplier."

I nodded at the thin, wiry man. He dipped his head at me. Deep black eyes twitched behind his hooded cover, and I wondered if my veil bothered him.

I busied myself while they talked. "Ophelos, as I told you before, last spring's shearing did not amount to what we normally collect. You would be wise to stock up before we sell out of the ones you, usually, order."

I waited on a customer, aware the man studied me. His comment reached my ears.

"She looks strong enough to manage your cart if you cannot get there yourself. "

He left and Ophelos explained their connection. "Shearing is done in spring, but this man's barns usually overflow past time to round up the sheep for the next year's bounty.

I never gave the man's evaluation of me another thought, until Ophelos' wife and girls came down with an illness that left them in bed with high fevers and vomiting.

Three days passed while one of us cleaned up and waited on his wife and girls, and the other attended the booth. Ophelos sighed. "Eunice, we have run very low on wool. I do not want to leave my family for a whole day. I need you to make the trip to our supplier's farm and bring back wool to refill the shelves. Do you think you could do it?"

I had pulled the cart from the booth back to the house a few times when needed, and it was heavy. This trip would take half a day to get there and another half to get back. It would not be easy. Could I do it? Ophelos had been so kind I decided not to mention my concerns.

"I can manage. I will leave at dawn and try to get back before dark. "

Ophelos was grateful. He instructed me on which road to take and assured me he had never had trouble with thieves or troublemakers. The next morning, I left well before dawn. He had readied the cart the night before and supplied me with food and water for the day.

"You do not have to worry about payment. I will take care of that the next time the owner comes to town."

The wooden cart was not light, but I kept it at a steady speed. Mentally, I marked off the landmarks Ophelos described, assured I was not lost.

The day was cloudy but there was no wind, for which I was grateful. I wore a long cloak Carisa lent me. It hung almost to my feet so I would not be cold. By late morning, I arrived. I congratulated myself. The sheep dogs barked a welcome. Their noisy herald brought out their owner to investigate.

"So, Ophelos decided to send you for some wool." The wiry man I had met in the booth commanded the dogs to retreat.

I told him what Ophelos needed, and he directed me to a barn a short way from his house.

"My assistant is there. Tell him what you want, and he will load your cart."

The young man opened the larger door so I could bring the cart inside. The plank that led through the door was steep, so he came out to help. He grabbed the handle closest to me and we pushed the vessel up inside.

He gestured at the door as he closed it, "Too cold to leave it open." He suggested I remove my cloak as I repeated Ophelos' order. He stood close and nodded at each item, but his glance never left my body.

I backed up until the cart stood between us. I had seen that look on my brother's face several times before he eventually raped me.

He handed me a bundle of wool. "We are a bit low on some of your master's needs. I will need to climb into the loft to find some. Can you catch what I throw down?"

My master? Did he think I was a slave? I nodded and waited until he climbed the ladder before I moved to the foot of it. He tossed several smaller bundles. I caught and stacked them into the cart.

He tossed a much larger bundle. "Watch out for this last one."

I thought I could catch it, but it hit me in the chest and knocked me to the floor. Before I could regroup, he was down the ladder beside me.

He pulled me up into his arms and said he was so sorry, but his smirk denied it. He ran his hands down my arms and onto my legs. I tried to pull myself out of his grip, but he tightened his hold.

"Do not be in such a hurry. You are such a pretty little thing, and you may be hurt."

I jerked away and got to my feet. He pulled me close and pushed his body against mine.

I yelled as loud as I could, "Let go!" Perhaps the owner was where he could hear me.

He grinned and backed me toward a pile of hay. I reached for a small, hand pitchfork that hung on the nearby wall, swung it, and hit him on the head.

He grabbed his ear. "You little..."

At the squeak of the barn door, panic covered his face. He gave me a quick push and stepped back toward the ladder.

The owner rushed in. "I thought I heard someone yell. Is everything all right?" He looked at me and then at his assistant. "What happened to your head? You are bleeding."

The assistant rubbed his ear. "I, ah, tripped over the ladder and hit my head on her cart."

"Well, go clean it up. I will finish so she can be on her way." He looked at me. "I am sorry for the delay. My assistant is new and tends to be a bit clumsy."

I tried to keep my voice steady. "Everything is fine." Should I tell him what really happened? Why would he believe me? My family would not have.

Chapter Nine

I was grateful for the time the journey took to get back to Ophelos' house. The cooler air helped clear my mind and gave me time to put the incident behind me. But I could not. My thoughts swirled and dipped like terebinth branches in a storm.

My garments were the same as most women wore, not that of a slave. I wanted to shout. Why did that assistant think I was one? And is that how slaves are treated?

My mother's words echoed."You will never amount to anything. You are not worthy of a decent life. You deserve every bad thing people do to you."

I stopped and put my hands over my ears, but I could not silence her brutal tongue. Tears flowed and when I reached to dry my cheeks, my finger caught my veil. It pulled from my face, and it landed on the ground.

I cried aloud, "Who cares?" and kicked it with a snarl.

It stared back, like the twisted face of an angry old woman. I sighed, reached down and retrieved it.

I quickened my pace. No amount of self pity would change anything. I vowed to be more careful, to never again be found alone with a stranger.

One of Ophelos' landmarks shadowed my path. It reminded me it was winter and sunset would be early. I plowed on. The cart wobbled on a rocky section. I needed to slow down to steady it. The wool did not add much weight, but if it spilled it would add hours to my journey. I was grateful the wind was at my back, but it blew the cloak I borrowed and tangled it with my feet when I did not hold it in place. Candles flickered in homes I passed. I wished I had a family of my own to return to.

Before darkness entirely ruled the sky, I reached the path to Ophelos' home.

He welcomed me back with a hot plate of stew and dumplings he had made himself. His wife and the girls were in bed, so he joined me at the table.

"How was the journey? Did you have any trouble finding the place? Did they have everything I needed?"

I told him about the day, but not the attack. "The man's assistant did confirm they were low on some of the things you normally buy."

He could not thank me enough and said I had done well. I excused myself and went to bed as soon as I felt I could. As tired as I was, my mind still reeled. I did not want to ever make that trip again, but how would I explain why?

The next morning Ophelos took the loaded cart to his booth, and I stayed with his family. It took most of the week for his wife to regain her strength, but the girls were up and at play in a few days. I was glad when I could go back with him to the market. It surprised me to find I dealt well with people and enjoyed it.

"So there!" I said to my mother's persistent taunts. "I am smart, and I am able, and I will amount to something."

By spring, Ophelos came to depend on me more and more. I often would be alone in the booth most of the day. Upon a return from a journey to replenish the wool in late fall, he was not himself. Nothing seemed to cheer him, not even the joyful steps of his baby boy. He often stared into space as if deep in thought.

A few nights later after dinner, Agatha and Eris clamored for his attention. He asked his wife to take them inside and motioned for me to follow him into the courtyard. He sat with his hands clenched.

I studied his face. What had I done wrong? I knew I worked hard in the booth, attended customers, straightened shelves, and tidied up each night.

Finally, he looked up. "Eunice, you have become a part of our family and a great help to me at the market. I am so sorry to have to tell you I will no longer be able to keep you with us."

My heart sank. No longer keep me? "I am so sorry if I did something wrong. I will work harder. I will—"

He looked miserable and shook his head. "No, no, you have done more than I ever expected of you. It is that, well, you are aware that the wool I buy has become sparse."

I had noticed some of the wool from the farm felt coarse. It was not the same quality as before.

"The farm you made the trip to has fallen on hard times. The man's herd has diminished greatly because of an infection that causes his ewes to abort a couple of weeks before lambing. Animals that survive stagger and refuse to eat. His wool output is now a fourth of what it was."

"Is there no other farm you can buy from?"

"Oh, there are some, but they are already committed to customers. I would be left with their less-than-top quality wool. I am going to have to travel much farther in search of a new supply. And winter always brings less people to the market so there is less income. My family will have to take care of the booth while I am gone...maybe for weeks at a time."

I groped for a reason to stay on. "You would not have to pay me, I will still — "

"No. That small amount I have given you will not make a difference. In fact, here," he handed me some coins tied in a cloth. "This is not much but maybe it will keep you until you find another family that needs help or a position at the market. If you like, I will ask among the vendors I know, and I will attest to your honesty and hard work."

I assured him I understood, but now what? It would soon be too cold to live out in the open or hide in someone's booth. I thought of my family but dismissed it just as quickly. I could never go back to their despicable treatment. Ophelos said I could finish out the week. The next few nights, I tossed in my bed but no answer came.

Ophelos was true to his word and the last day as I bid a tearful goodbye to Carisa and the girls, he asked me to come with him to the market. Before he unloaded, he took me to a man that owned a large stall that sold meat and produce.

I was familiar with the man as he sometimes spent time in Ophelos' booth. He often complained loudly about the Roman taxes or business in general. He never spoke to or acknowledged me, nor did his wife who came on occasion to purchase wool.

Ophelos called to him, "Crathis, this is Eunice, the girl I told you about. She is a very hard worker and can be depended upon to do whatever is asked of her."

The man looked at me and sneered. "You are not very big. Are you able to do housework and heavy chores?"

I swallowed my fears and nodded.

"Speak up, Girl. Do you want the position I am offering?"

Something inside me wanted to refuse, but where else could I go? "Yes sir, I am able to work hard and do whatever you need me to do."

He told me he would take me to his home as soon as his assistant arrived. An hour or so later I followed him into his house. It was much larger than Ophelos', with a second story and a large courtyard surrounded by storage buildings.

"This is Larna, my wife."

The woman's lips pulled to one side as she frowned and looked me over. "Why do you wear a veil? Is something wrong with your face?"

Heat rose up my throat and onto my cheeks. My head dipped as it always did at the question. I stammered and did not look up. "I was born with a purplish stain on my face."

"Hmm." she crossed her arms and cocked her head. "We have six children. The oldest is grown and the last is just two. There is a lot of laundry and meals to cook. You know how to bake and do all the rest?"

I assured her I did, aware she would scrutinize my every effort.

She muttered something about the failures of the last help she had fired. "Well, we will see." She took me into the house and showed me where things were.

I expected her to show me another small room off the kitchen, but she did not mention where I would sleep. I heard a cry and followed her upstairs to a nursery where a little boy awoke from a nap. "This is Gallus. You can begin by changing him." She tossed me a soft cloth folded into a triangle.

The child eyed me with suspicion while I took off his wet clothes and redressed him. I expected him to run for his mother when I finished, but she had gone downstairs. He did not seem upset that she had left, but toddled over to some blocks on the floor and sat among them. He ignored me and was soon engrossed in play.

Chapter Ten

I did not know if I should leave a two-year-old alone or take him to his mother. Larna's voice cut through my indecision. "I need you to come back downstairs, now."

She showed me around the kitchen. I was impressed that water could be pumped in from outside. After a tour of the house, I met four of the other children, which included three girls and Spiros, a son about my age.

She shooed the children off to themselves and bid me follow to the closest outer building. A young man approached from another structure. She stopped. "Wait, I want you to meet our oldest son." She explained that they butchered animals in the building he had come from. He wiped blood off his hands with a cloth and caught up with us. "Alistar, this is Eunice. She is my latest helper."

Her son shook his head. "Not another one, Mother. Why do you not just give up?"

I studied this handsome sibling. What did he mean by that? Sandy hair fell over grayish eyes as he picked up a heavy piece of equipment near the path, as if it were a child's toy.

He did not try to hide his disgust. "Mother, Spiros left this in the courtyard again."

She ignored the complaint. "Make sure you are on time for dinner. Your father said that large mutton order is not due for two days, so there is plenty of time."

Alistar gestured as if he had heard that a hundred times, nodded at me, and left.

Larna opened the door to the smaller building and took me inside. My senses balked at the heavy scent of animal food. Particles, that drifted in a shaft of sunlight, tickled my nose and made me sneeze. The fodder was piled in large woven sacks beside tools I assumed were for field work. She led me to a small room just off the entrance.

"This is where you will sleep and store your things. There is plenty of bedding, but it never gets very cold here. Come back to the kitchen after you get settled and we will begin preparations for dinner."

I took my time as I made up the bed mat, grateful the door closed out most of the obtrusive odor. The strange quirks I had observed in Larna made me squirm, but with a quick shrug, I determined to work hard. Fate left me little choice.

Dinner consisted of an abundance of meat and side dishes with salads, baked goods, fruit compotes and such, that I had never seen. All was for just one family. Larna worked beside me as I cleaned vegetables and sliced the bread. She talked her way through the main dishes as if she expected me to remember how to assemble them on my own... if I stayed.

She muttered something about the careless work of "some people," then told me to be sure to get all the dirt off the carrots and scrub the potatoes before I peeled them. Her continual frown indicated I probably would not measure up.

I ate in the kitchen after the family finished, grateful for time unobserved. She showed me where everything went and left me to clean up the dishes and counters. I worked hard and sensed she was not displeased.

Crathis approached me at the end of the week. "Larna tells me your work is acceptable, so I will pay you two obols a week. Agreed?"

I knew that was not much for all that was demanded of me, but at least I had food and shelter. Maybe in the spring I would find someone more pleasant to work for.

We did an enormous amount of wash. Gallus was still in diapers, except when he played naked outside. Line after line was filled with heavy white cloths that blew aimlessly in the wind, like wings of giant swans unable to lift from the ground. The chore took all day, and I was grateful Larna had planned a simple dinner. I left for my room as soon as clean up was finished. I opened the outer door of the building I slept in, surprised to hear someone inside.

A male voice came from behind a stack of feed bags. "Do not let me disturb you."

Part of me flinched, panicked at the danger of being alone with a stranger. I was about to pretend I had forgotten something and leave, when Alistar stepped from behind the pile.

"I am sorry, I did not think you would be here so soon. I will not be long, I need to count our stash of sheep food. Father needs to know whether we have enough to get us through the winter or if we will need to purchase more."

All thoughts of threat left as I gazed into his captivating, grey eyes. I had never seen eyes that color before. I could not think of anything to say, but Grandfather's diligence in being prepared came to mind.

"I understand. My grandfather raised horses, and he often told me how important it was to be prepared for their needs."

He turned from his tally and focused on me. "Really? I always wished we raised horses. Tell me about him. Where did he live?"

I told him all about my grandfather and how important he had been in my life. In turn, Alistar shared that his dream had been to have a horse ranch without cows, sheep, or pigs. Before I knew it, an hour had passed. Our conversation had been natural, unpretentious yet revealing.

He reached for his hat. "Well, good night. You must be tired. My mother is a taskmaster."

I smiled and told him I could manage. He left and a warm feeling snuggled me to sleep. Since Grandfather died, no one ever talked or listened to me as if they really cared about what I thought. I hoped it would happen again.

A week later, I was at work in the kitchen, when a scream pierced the walls. Crathis came on a run. I followed him up the stairs. Larna was on a rampage. Her former helper claimed she thoroughly cleaned the upstairs, but Larna had uncovered piles of smelly laundry shoved in a closet. Under the girls' beds, bits and pieces of leftover food with mouse droppings added to her rage. A covered pail of dirty diapers hidden behind Gallus' crib followed. She screamed so loudly, the girls ran and hid.

Her husband motioned for me to take them outside while he calmed his wife. I sensed this was not an isolated incident. The girls were four, seven, and eight. I asked them if they owned jackstones and they ran to get them. I played the game with them for over an hour with one eye on Gallus. Finally, Crathis came and told me Larna needed my help.

I worried about what I would find, but to my surprise, Larna sat in the receiving room, a tall glass of wine at her side. I asked her how I could help but she just looked at me with a blank stare.

"Would you like me to go and clean up the mess?" She managed a nod and I left. In the weeks to come, glasses of wine or ouzo were often needed to calm Larna on days things did not go her way. Gallus and the three girls sought me out when that happened.

By mid winter, much of Crathis and his older son's work consisted of slaughtering animals for his stall at the market.

Occasionally, Crathis would take me with him and leave me to sell his goods. Winter vegetables that could be stored were displayed with the meats, and customers were always plentiful.

One day, Crathis asked Alistar to drive me to the market to work in his booth. I was thrilled. Except for an occasional visit in the evenings, we had little time together. We were very busy, so Alistar stayed to help. We laughed over outrageous questions or demands customers made. A volley of accelerated gusts of wind threatened to pull down the booth's cover, but we worked hand to hand to restore it. The day went fast, and I found myself sorry when it was time to shut down. I could not remember a day where I enjoyed myself so much. I helped Alistar load the unsold meat and tie down the booth before we left for home.

"Does Father ever give you time off? Time for yourself?"

I was taken aback by his question. Should I have been given free time or asked for it? Before I could answer, another strong blast of wind rocked our wagon and blew off my veil. I gasped and quickly covered my blemish with my hands.

Already out of his seat, Alistar pulled the horse to a halt. "I will get it for you." He chased the veil several yards before the gust diminished and he was able to grab it. He came over and held it up to me. Embarrassed, I turned from him and tried to hide my face, but tears flowed as I took and reattached it.

He patted my arm. "Do not cry. It does not matter. You are beautiful with or without it."

I cried all the harder. His kind words and compassionate expression were something I had seldom observed from anyone other than Grandfather. Alistar waited until I composed myself before he climbed back and clucked the horses for home.

Neither of us spoke, but when he reached over and squeezed my hand, I felt my world spin into place.

Chapter Eleven

I awoke one morning to the sound of birds outside my window. Spring was not far off. The winter had flown. An occasional visit from Alistar was the highlight of my days. Sometimes he came to inventory the feed stocks, but just as often, he came for my company.

We talked for hours about everything. He detailed the necessity, though gruesome, of their humane slaughter of their animals. It made me shiver. I told him about my grandfather and showed him my tiny statue of his favorite foal. "It is all I have left to remember him by. The colt grew to be a prize stud that sired some of his best stock."

Alistar studied the replica like a piece of art. My heart warmed as he, tenderly, turned it in his hand. His genuine appreciation replaced the painful image of when my mother had wrenched the statue from my hands and viciously tossed it aside.

My days were full as I cleaned, did laundry, and cooked for a family of eight. Larna's attitude toward me softened, evidently convinced I handled things better than her former helpers. Still, I treaded lightly around her. I did not want to be the reason for one of her tirades.

The best days were when Alistar drove me to the market to work in their stall. It was a welcome relief from the endless housework. Sometimes, if the market was crowded and we were especially busy, he stayed and we worked alongside each other.

One day, a man charged up to our booth. He carried a package I had sold and wrapped, not an hour before. I was alone and I could see he was upset.

"Young Woman, you have cheated me." He spoke loud enough to turn heads of other customers. I calmly asked him to explain what he thought was wrong.

He tore open the package. "Look, I paid for five pounds of choice beef and there are not even three in here." He shoved the contents close to my face and went on with his rant, sure I had purposely cheated him. I said I was terribly sorry if I had made a mistake and offered to reweigh the package, but he seemed determined to embarrass me and cause a disturbance. Nothing I offered was good enough.

I was close to tears when Alistar showed up. He rushed over, pulled the man to one side, and listened to his complaint. With an additional two pounds, at no charge, he soothed the man, who glared at me and left.

I could not stop shaking. Alistar put his arms around me and held me for a moment. "Do not let that bully get to you. He has pulled a stunt like this before, once on my mother. He never tries it with me or Father."

I would have gone through it again to savor the comfort of Alistar's strong arms. He led me to a bench we kept in the booth. "You sit here and wait while I finish up and we will leave. It is nearly time and enough is enough." He finished with the customers and loaded the unsold goods back into the wagon, then took a different route home. Eventually, he turned onto a road that overlooked the sea. My insides echoed the clouds that spread a dark blanket over the water. My thoughts flashed to the day by the seat, when my brother had raped me.

Alistar secured the reins and turned to me. "How do you feel? Are you all right?" One look into his eyes assured me I was in no danger.

"I feel terrible. I do not know how I messed up that man's order. I would never—"

He put his arm around my shoulders and pulled me close. "Hush. Do not fret." We sat and watched the sun break through the clouds and disappear into the gulf. I hoped the day would never end.

Once home, he simply smiled and headed to the storage barn to unload. Before I could go to my room and change into work clothes, Larna rushed across the courtyard. "Where were you two? Dinner is only half done and look at the time."

The smell of wine wafted as she took hold of my arm. I backed away and told her I needed to change, and I would be right over. Her familiar complaints intruded on my desire to be alone and savor the last few hours undisturbed. I entered the kitchen and quickly discovered she had indulged in too much drink and, once again, our roles reversed. I took over the preparations and told her what needed to be done.

Each evening, I hoped Alistar would come by so we could talk. At night on my mat, I rehearsed the moments of our time by the sea and envisioned our relationship as something permanent. After two weeks, it became obvious. He was avoiding me. I felt like someone had pulled a plug and drained me of hope.

Now it was Crathis who drove me to the market on days he wanted me there. At days end, I hoped it would be Alistar who would come fetch me. That did not happen. He would not look at me when I served the family dinner or passed him in the courtyard.

One chilly wash day, I was fully absorbed in the huge amount of laundry that needed to be done. Spiros came into the courtyard where we washed and hung things to dry, his arms loaded with clothes that had been overlooked.

"Mother asked me to bring these to you. She is down with a headache." I was not quick enough to hide a grimace. "Can I be of any help? I know she usually works alongside you."

I smiled at him. Spiros seemed always to be in the background. Surprisingly, we were the same age, but hardly ever spoke. "Thank you, Spiros. That is very kind of you. Maybe...would you mind carrying this basket over to the lines so I can hang these shirts? Wet things are so heavy."

Spiros stayed all afternoon. He carried the wet clothes to the lines and even folded a pile of diapers that had dried. Unnoticed, when we had nearly finished, Alistar approached from the slaughter barn. Spiros stepped close and brought me some dry diapers. We laughed when he tripped, and some flew my way. Alistar stopped and scowled at us. Confusion crossed his face, then anger flared in his eyes. He spun on his heel and headed back to the barn. Spiros squinted at me and shrugged. I returned the gesture, and we took the load inside.

Larna had recovered enough that she managed to put together a simple meal for dinner. I helped her clean up and went into the courtyard to retrieve the rest of the dry laundry. On the way back, arms loaded so high I couldn't see in front of me, I ran straight into Alistar. Diapers went one way and towels flew in another.

Down on my knees, I gathered what I could reach and stammered, "I am so sorry, I did not see you. I—"

Alistar quipped, "Perhaps you should have asked Spiros for help." Without another word, he gathered the towels and took them into the house. His childish manner disgusted me. He sounded like my younger brother who often burned with jealousy over a privilege granted my older brother.

I was already tucked in for the night when I heard the door to the storage shed creak. I sat up and listened. My heart pounded. No one should be there at this time of night.

"Eunice? Eunice, are you awake?"

Alistar's voice sounded shaky, barely above a whisper. After the incident with the laundry, I was frightened and did not know what to expect. He called again and knocked softly on my bedroom door.

"I have retired for the night."

"I know. I know. I wanted to apologize for what I said to you. Could you come out and talk to me for a few minutes? Please?"

I rose, put on my heavy cover, and opened the door a crack. In the lantern's dim light, the face of a stranger stared at me. I had never seen him look so vulnerable.

Chapter Twelve

Alistar's chin rested on his chest. "Please come sit with me a moment. I need to know you hear me."

I hesitated, but he looked so troubled I stepped just outside the door. He tugged my hand and I followed him to the only bench in the room. I pulled my robe tight and sat on the far edge. He did not react when I removed my hand.

"Eunice, I... I don't know how to say this." He looked off and chewed his lower lip. "Ever since that day we sat and watched the sun set over the gulf, you have been constantly on my mind."

My heart leapt. He had not forgotten! But why ignore me? I hid my joy. I did not turn toward him or say anything. He was so near I could hear him breathe and smell the laundry soap that lingered in his clothes. Was he nervous? He had not hesitated to tell me things before.

Alistar drew a lazy pattern on some spilled grain with the toe of his boot, then turned toward me. "I know you wonder why I have...have not been around or talked to you." He expelled a lengthy sigh.

"It is because, well, I guess I was afraid. I have never been with a girl, and I began to think and feel things I did not know how to handle. I decided to put it all out of my mind, but when I saw you close to Spiros, how you enjoyed each other's company...well, it made me angry." He hung his head, "Jealous, I guess. I wanted it to be me, not Spiros, there with you, to talk and laugh like we did before."

My heart raced so hard, I was sure he could hear it. I was on his mind? He wanted to be with me? A thousand replies ran through my head but I didn't dare speak. What did it mean? Did he want a future with me? Could he really love a girl with a beard on her face? Was what I deeply longed for about to become a reality?

Alistar reached again for my hand. This time I did not pull away. "Eunice, I came here tonight to tell you I am sorry. I have treated you unkindly and I am asking you to forgive me. I would like to be friends again...like before."

Like an unexpected cold shower, his words drenched my dream. Friends? My heart sank. All he wanted was a friend? He searched my face. I stood, wrapped my hands around my arms, and gripped the sleeves. I wanted to tell him to leave and never come near me again. Instead, I smiled sweetly and forced the tremor from my voice.

"Alistar, there is nothing to forgive. You are very busy with your work, and I am too. Of course we can be friends, but I think you should go now. Tomorrow is a busy day, and it is late." With that, I stepped into my room and shut the door. He called out several times, but I did not answer.

I held my sobs until I was sure he had left the shed. If I was on his mind and he wanted to be with me, how could being nothing but friends satisfy? My mother's cruel words returned. No one will ever want a girl with a beard on her face. I cried myself to sleep.

I did not see Alistar for several days. Each time we passed, I nodded but made it obvious I was too busy to stop. When I would not come out of my room or talk to him, he finally gave up and did not come to the shed. I worked hard and saved my earnings, more determined than ever to find a different position.

The first time we worked together at the market was difficult. His gaze followed as I waited on customers or replenished shelves. I was pleasant but determined not to connect with those hungry, grey eyes... no matter how much I wanted to. He left around lunch time and I worked alone.

Just before the end of the day, another vendor approached me with an offer to work for him. Word had gotten around that I was a responsible person, that I worked hard. The man dealt in fine linens and silks, fabrics well-to-do women purchased.

He asked, "How much does Crathis pay you? I need a girl like yourself in my booth. Women prefer to talk with another woman about what is best for what they plan to make, and my wife does not want to do it any longer. I will double what he gives you."

I sighed. "It is not just the money. I live there and my food is included. I do my laundry and use whatever I need."

"I know, but I can give you all that and more. I have a large home with extra rooms since my two daughters married and moved on. My wife has a maid who cleans and cooks. You would not have to do anything but serve the customers in my booth."

His offer sounded good, less physical, and I enjoyed working at the market, but it would be the end of my dreams with Alistar.

"Let me think about it a few days." I was torn. Could I really let go of what once seemed possible? Would Alistar ever pursue a life with me, a future like I wanted to spend with him?.

"All right, but I would be glad to show you my house and you could meet my wife if that would help you decide."

We left it at that, and I went to a customer who fussed over the lamb we put out that morning. It was nearly time to pack up when Alistar arrived with the wagon to close the booth and take me home.

He loaded the leftover goods, and we left the market behind. Once again, he drove toward the road that led to the gulf. I grew uneasy. What was on his mind? I decided to tell him I had been offered a better job.

He listened without comment to what the owner of the fabric booth proposed. When we were at the end of the gulf road, he pulled up and turned to me. "Is that what you want, Eunice?"

Heat rose up my neck. Somehow, I did not blurt, "No, I hoped to marry you." "Well, it would be an easier job and you know I enjoy work at the market." "But what about us?"

I lifted my brows. "Us?"

It was Alistar' turn to squirm. "Eunice, you know how I feel about you, I—"

I could not stop the painful truth that snapped. "Yes, you want to be good friends."

"Yes...I mean no. You know it is more than that."

Knowledge that another position awaited me gave me courage. What did I have to lose? "More? Then tell me, Alistar. What is it?"

"I want us to be together, in more ways than friends."

"And where would that lead?" The pain I had bottled poured out. "Do you want me for someone to talk to occasionally, or are you ready to tell your father and mother that you want to marry a servant girl with a beard?"

Alistar's jaw dropped and I knew he had not even thought that through. "Please take me home. I need to tell your father of my decision."

His jaw clenched and I knew in my heart he was not up to such a challenge. So be it. I would no longer be subjected to the torture of everyday reminders. It was not to be.

When we arrived, Larna had managed to stay sober and had dinner ready. I told her I did not feel well and asked to be excused from the clean up. I did not care that she did not like it. My thoughts were so severed I decided to wait until morning to tell them I had taken a better offer.

That night, Alistar came again to the grain shed. He knocked and called my name several times, but I did not answer.

"Eunice, if you do not come out, I am going to break down this door."

I ignored his threat until I heard a loud thump. I sprang from my bed. "Alistar, are you crazy? Stop it!"

"I will if you come out and talk to me."

I heard another loud bang. "You are going to wake your parents. Stop that."

"Will you come out, then? "

I did not know what to do. I grabbed my robe and cracked open the door, determined to send him away. He clutched my arm and pulled me out of my room. All traces of the vulnerable, confused demeanor had left his face.

I tried to pull away and demanded he leave, but he gripped my shoulders and turned my face to his. "Eunice. Listen!"

His voice softened. "I am sorry. I handled this all wrong. I care deeply for you and when I realized I was about to lose you, I knew I did not care how my father would react. I am in love with you, Eunice." His hands slid down my upper arms. "I long to be with you, to hold you in my arms and..."

I did not hear the rest of his argument. He loved me? Did I hear him say he was in love with me? Did I dare to believe it was true? I looked up into those eyes I adored. "Alistar, I..."

He pulled me into his arms and silenced me with a kiss. It was nearly dawn before we tore ourselves from the longing that had billowed in each of us, and Alistar returned to the house.

Chapter Thirteen

My life held new meaning. I floated through the days and dreamed about the nights when I would be in Alistar's arms. For a time, we agreed to keep our relationship a secret from his family. On the days we worked at the market or no one was near, we spoke freely of our love.

Several weeks of refusal discouraged the man who owned the fabric booth and he finally accepted that I had refused his offer. Sadly, I did not get to work at the market very often. Larna had more and more days where she could not cope with even the most inconsequential events.

Things like when the girls built a clay statue in their room and left a grungy mess, or the time Gallus trailed diarrhea all over the upstairs, or when Spiros brought the wrong meat, and her dinner plans had to change-all were fodder for Larna's explosive temperament.

At each eruption, Crathis ran to her side. I followed and offered what help I could, but to reason with her was impossible.

I had no choice but to handle her myself on a morning Crathis left early for the market. I urged her into the room forbidden to the children and poured her some wine. " Sit and rest a while. I will clean up the mess. It was an accident. Spiros had no idea an oily sludge clung to the bottom of his boots. Listen, my mother taught me how to remove even that from a rug. You relax."

Larna slurred, "You do not know anything. That rug was woven from expensive Ephesian wool. You cannot just launder it."

I assured her it would be all right, as I could restore the rug to like new. I scoffed at my own, useless, effort to reason with her. She downed her wine and poured more before I lowered the curtains and encouraged her to lie down.

Spiros paced in the next room. "How is she? I never meant to—"

I hushed him. "No, no, you know her, ah, problem. Go on about your work. I will have the carpet cleaned, like new, in a few hours."

Relief swept his eyes, and he whistled a sigh. "Thanks, Eunice. I do not know what we would do, around here, without you."

I smiled as he left, confident he would easily accept me as a part of the family. The very thought brought a tingle as I walked to the supply cupboard. Cornmeal, vinegar, and a softer soap...was that not the formula my mother used? I dusted the spot with cornmeal and after it sat a while, scraped it with the blunt edge of a heavy spoon.

Down on my knees, for the first time I was grateful for all she had taught me. I mixed the vinegar and the gentle soap with water. Then with a clean, white cloth, I vigorously rubbed the surface before I tackled the rug's inner fibers and revived it completely. As I cleaned up, my thoughts flew to what I intended to ask Alistar that night.

I had no couch, so when he finally arrived, we sat on the edge of my bed mat while he told me about a deranged man who wandered the market and made threats at shoppers.

I shuddered, glad I had not been there. When he finished with how much he had sold that day, I asked, "Alistar, when do you plan to tell your parents about us?"

He shrugged, pulled me close, and covered me with kisses.

When I caught my breath, I lay my cheek against his. "Have you thought about it? I mean when might be the right time?"

"All I ever think about is you." Before long, it did not seem so important.

Later, as Alistar's snores rumbled in the dark room, I smiled at the everyday intimacy the sound conjured in my mind. I ran my hand over his tousled hair and snuggled close. Contentment filled my soul, and I covered my mouth to quiet the joy that threatened to spring forth in giggles. I belonged! The deepest desire of my heart lay beside me, and he loved and treasured me.

Spring brought a lot of busyness. Butchering increased, and often well into the night, someone had to tend the cows and sheep about to give birth. I spent days alone at the booth, and for nights in a row Alistar did not come to the shed. I missed him terribly. When he did come, he was too exhausted to discuss anything. Several mornings in a row I had to wake him to slip, unseen, back into the house before dawn.

I found it harder and harder to live the charade we had settled upon. To watch what I did and said, to cover our arrangement, became burdensome. Alistar seldom came to the shed after dinner anymore, only when the household was asleep. I missed the times we simply talked.

He brushed off my objections. "You know I must be careful, Eunice."

The voices, I had buried, began to return. You are not good enough. You are not worthy of a place in a real family. You are inadequate. You have deceived yourself...

It was well into summer when Crathis asked me to take a load of meat into the city to a Roman temple that had ordered it for a special festival.

"I cannot spare Alistar right now. We have too many orders to fill. Spiros can drive the wagon and help unload, but he is not experienced in dealing with customers."

A day away appealed to me and Spiros was good company. We left at dawn. I sensed Alistar was not pleased with the plan, but I assured him we would do fine. The wagon was fully loaded but we made good time. Neither I nor Spiros had been this far past the market, into the city.

When we reached the Lechaion Road, our eyes darted from statues of gods to temples and shops on both sides.

Slabs of rock hewn from the mountain paved the road, which was wide enough for carriages to pass, and walkways for pedestrians on each side. Cracks and uneven joints forced our wagon to sway, so Spiros pulled back on our horse. We stopped at the sacred fountain of Peirene to refill our water jugs and wished, in tandem, that we could explore the well-kept grounds.

"We cannot leave the wagon. Your father warned of a high crime rate in the city. Let us find the temple first and unload. Then, maybe we will have time to look around."

Spiros nodded and asked a man, who looked his father's age, for directions to the temple of Poseidon.

The man sneered. "Everyone knows where the temple of the ruler of the sea sits." He pointed further into the Isthmus. "Over there, not far from the arena of the Isthmian games. Our games are only second to the Olympics, you know." He looked pleased with himself.

Spiros thanked him and climbed back into the wagon. "I do remember that my father took me to the games years ago, but I was too young to know where it stood." As we drove, he described many of the events he had witnessed and the ceremonies where the victors received their crowns.

I thought a wilted piece of celery a strange crown for an athlete but did not say so. We found the temple and Spiros began to unpack our load for a rotund man. He was dressed in a costume with Poseidon's trident in one hand

and a silver crown on his head, designed with fish that swam in a circle. He looked like he could easily float well above the god's watery throne.

The man glanced at the sun and smiled. "Thank you. Thank you. We asked our god to have you arrive in time for us to prepare for the feast and he did!" He handed Spiros a pouch of money which Spiros passed to me. The man's smile faded. He squinted and looked at Spiros and back at me. I ignored his frown, counted the money as instructed, and climbed up beside Spiros. "We are glad for your business, Sir. Thank you and good day."

Spiros touched my arm. "I know his demeanor bothered you, Eunice, but you are very capable. You cannot let people hurt you...not even Alistar."

His eyes held only concern, and instantly I realized he was aware of my relationship with his brother. I sighed. Of course he had figured it out. They shared a bedroom, and he would certainly have seen Alister come and go in the night. My face colored, but a shake of his head said he understood.

We drove on and Spiros suggested we go back on the Lechaion Road and look around. Alistar had been to the city many times and told me about the things we would see and some of its history. My head swam at the sight of all the temples with their gigantic columns that gleamed in the sunlight. On the slopes of the Accu Corinth, the sanctuary of Demeter stood undamaged after seven centuries of earthquakes and the Roman demolition of the city years before.

At the very top, we could see a little of the ruins of the famous temple of Aphrodite, now ravaged by time, earthquakes, and wars. We had seen a few of her thousand, loyal prostitutes throughout the city, each in skimpy costumes that draped their bodies but covered little. Most came out at night when sailors from the gulf and the Aegean were in town, ready to spend their pay.

The sight of their veils sent my hand to my disfigured cheek. They looked close to my age and even younger. I thought about the difference in being raped by my brother and the love I experienced with Alistar and closed my eyes. What a terrible life, plying their trade for their idol in lofts above the city's thirty-three wine shops.

I knew I would choose death over that.

Chapter Fourteen

We drove back to the fountain and enjoyed the lunch I had packed. The day was hot, and we welcomed the mist that blew from the giant spray. Temples of Hermes, Isis, and many others stood among the shops, so we decided to see some up close. People hustled past most with hardly a glance at their beauty. "To all of the gods," was chiseled simply into the arch over one.

Their splendor faded before the famous shrine to Asklepios, the god of healing. We watched as a steady line of pilgrims waited patiently for entrance. Some joyfully carried goods or a replica of a body part, to leave in sacrifice for the help they had received. My heart went out to a woman who looked like she might not survive her turn at the altar.

We shaded our eyes to see up a hill that overlooked the main forum. There, surrounded by foliage, the 700-year-old temple of Apollo reigned like a revered regent.

Passed over in the Roman rampage, its presence gleamed, a continual reminder of Corinth's ancient splendor.

By mid-afternoon, I knew we should head home so I could help Larna with dinner. We reached the entrance of the agora. marveled afresh at just how far the market extended. Some vendors claimed it was the largest in all of Greece. I sighed at the memory of how I, frantically, had run the whole length many times as I looked for Little Sister, Chara.

When we approached the bema, we found ourselves in the middle of a ruckus. A bunch of people dressed in Jewish garb were intent on their effort to force a man up onto the judgment seat. At the same time, a crowd of Greeks swarmed and hurled threats and demanded the captive's release.

Spiros tried to weave our wagon around them, but the crowd increased and soon we were trapped. Cries of, "Make way for Gallio," sounded from behind.

A spokesman, the Jews referred to as Sosthenes, looked smug. "The proconsul of Achaia will settle this."

The Greeks countered, "You know this man only taught in a local synagogue, not on the street."

The Jewish leader shouted at Gallio. "The law condemns afflicting Romans with beliefs in other gods, and this fellow persuades men to worship a God contrary to Roman law."

Spiros turned to Eunice. "I suspect the finger-pointer doesn't think the proconsul will sort out the difference between Jewish and Greek gods."

Their prisoner, a Jew the Greeks esteemed, opened his mouth to defend himself, but Gallio exerted his authority and squelched every argument. "If it were a matter of wrongdoing or wicked crimes, O Jews, there would be reason why I should bear with you, but, if it is a question of words and names and your own law, look to it yourselves. I do not want to be a judge of such matters."

With that, he drove the Jews from the bema. Spiros and I sat mesmerized and somewhat alarmed when the Greek crowd took hold of Sosthenes, the synagogue ruler, and beat him in front of everyone. To our amazement, Gallio didn't stop them.

The Greeks gathered around the rescued man they referred to as Paul. They slapped him on the back and congratulated him on the outcome. When he lifted his hand, they quieted.

He encouraged them to not be afraid, that God had many people in this city. Then he admonished them to remember those Jewish men represented their heritage, and the Lord Jesus would have them love and pray for them.

My heart leapt when he added that there is no one God does not seek to save and bring into His kingdom. Could it be true, that there is a God who desires that all belong and receive His unfailing grace and forgiveness.? All? Even marked people, like me?

The way had cleared, and Spiros drove our wagon away from those who lingered and on past the market. I could not get the man's message out of my head. My family never worshiped the many gods our neighbors did. They said they were all a product of men's minds and could do us neither good nor harm.

Crathis was pleased with our report of the transaction, and I hoped for more chances to spend days away. Summer settled the rush of spring. On the rare occasions that Alistar and I both worked the market, we would take the drive down by the sea on the way home. How we treasured the privacy and the opportunity to be open about our love for each other.

"Alistar, I need to know—"

He held up his hand. "I know. I know. I just do not know how to approach Father. He can be very stubborn, and if something is not his plan or idea...he takes it as a threat."

"But you are a man, Alistar. Have you never disagreed with your father? Do you plan to let him run your life forever?" It felt like I had brought up an obvious rite of passage to a twelve-year-old.

His face reddened. He took my hand. "Let us walk down by the water."

We made our way down the bluff, careful not to slide on the sandy path, and climbed our way around the rocky edges. We held hands, took off our sandals and let the surf sweep our bare feet.

"Eunice, please be patient with me. I want you for my wife but what will I do if my father refuses to accept you into the family? I know he admires what a good worker you are...how you step up and handle my mother when he is not around and do whatever is asked of you. The thing is, how would I take care of you if we have to leave and go off on our own?"

That he had tried to figure it out comforted me. "Alistar, we would find a way if it came to that, but you have to decide for yourself what is important to you." Unexpected tears welled in my eyes. "I love you and will stand by you no matter what happens."

He squeezed my hand, and we made our way back to the wagon

I did not bring the subject up again. Near the end of summer, I awoke earlier than usual one morning. Alistar had left an hour before, and I had drifted back to sleep. I lay there and imagined what the day might bring. I hoped Larna would not go into another tirade while Crathis was at the market. How I hated to deal with her tempers by myself.

My mind drifted to what changes fall might bring. As I anticipated the season, my thoughts evolved to the realization that I had not evidenced my days of blood for a while. I sat up and sorted through the previous weeks. When had the last time been? It was midsummer, right after the trip into the city, six weeks ago. I was at least two weeks late.

I clutched my stomach. Could it be? A surge of warmth and love washed over me. A child. I could be pregnant with a child. Alistar's child! Oh, how I would love and cherish my very own baby! It would be so different than how I was treated. I needed to tell Alistar, but how?

Before a plan formed, I panicked. What if he was not happy about it? This would force him to talk to his parents about us. What if they refused to let him marry me? What would I do if he did not stand up to them?

"Do not get ahead of yourself." My whisper floated to the ceiling as I spoke caution to myself. My body might possibly have reacted to the heavy furniture I had lifted to please Larna, or the stress of dealing with her tantrums. I had heard women speak of being late or missing a menses, altogether.

A couple of weeks later, no doubt remained. By each mid-afternoon I experienced a weariness that was foreign to my makeup, and my stomach revolted at even the smell of certain foods. I brooded over how and when to speak to Alistar about it, but said nothing.

I came home with Crathis from the market one evening, tired after a long day on my feet. I hoped Larna had prepared dinner. I climbed from the wagon and headed for my room before he and the horse disappeared into the barn.

I was surprised to see Larna come from the shed. She clutched something under her arm and anger blazed from her eyes.

I sighed. Oh, not now. I am too tired to deal with another one of her fits.

She waved her findings before my face. "I went into your room to make sure you had enough bedding for these cooler nights. Would you like to explain how this came to be there?"

My heart sank. It was the outer tunic Alistar had worn the night before.

Chapter Fifteen

My face turned as red as the sliver of sun that had nearly disappeared behind Larna. How could Alistar have left his tunic?

She shrieked, "Have you seduced my son? We took you in when you had no place to go, gave you a place to sleep and fed you. Is this how you repay us?" Crathis came while she ranted. I ran to my room and locked the door. I could not stop shaking. What should I do?

I sobbed into my hands. "This was not how they were supposed to find out about Alistar and me!" Anger followed my disappointment. "He should have told them months ago."

The whole family heard Larna. They came on the run. Even before he understood the problem, Crathis sent the girls back to the house with Spiros. Everyone was used to Larna's outbursts, but I had noticed Crathis shielded the girls as much as possible from the worst of their mother's tantrums.

Alistar would be the last to arrive. Over time, he had frequently spoken of his disgust with his mother's temper, so it was easy to picture him in no hurry to hang up his work cover, clean his hands, and saunter over to the all-too-familiar scene.

Would he quicken his pace when his father roared his name?

I could not make out most of what Crathis said, but his voice raged. "Sneaky, deceitful," and other demeaning accusations spewed throughout his harangue. I cracked the door of the shed, so I could hear Alistar's defense, but it was too muffled. Larna's voice rose from time to time, until I heard Crathis order her back into the house.

The voices fell silent and I closed the door to my room, locked it, and sat down to wait. Had I seduced Alistar? Was this all my fault? Would his father come and punish me? I knew of servants who had been beaten for lesser offenses against their family.

An hour passed. I paced. Surely Alistar would come. What would he say? Had he pleaded his case, told them of our love? Would his parents accept me as their son's choice? My hope ran to despair and back again. Had his father given him an ultimatum: marry her and you both leave, or tell her it is over and she is to be gone by morning?

After another hour, my hopes plummeted like a waterfall that splashed on the rocks of my dreams, with no chance to reverse it. One way or the other, I knew I would have to leave. I dug out my small pouch and began to pack. With tender care, I wrapped grandfather's colt in my only spare tunic and added my night peplos.

Where would I go? I thought about the offer to work for the man who sold fabrics. No, I did not want to risk being where Alistar could find me.

My chin quivered at the thought. I snuffed my tears. If he were not man enough to defend our love to his parents, it was over. Nothing less than marriage would satisfy me. To meet on occasion or sneak moments alone were not my ideas of love and commitment.

But what about our baby? The thought wobbled my knees, and I sank to my mat. I clutched my stomach and whispered to my barely rounded middle. "He does not even know you exist, Little One."

I pulled myself together and rehearsed, afresh, my grandfather's advice. "It is something you never intended to let happen, Eunice. Choose to put it behind you. Be strong and rise above it. Do not let guilt destroy you. Resist it and survive."

I had almost stepped out to leave when I heard footsteps outside my door. My heart raced. Was it Alistar or had his father come for me? I could not move.

"Eunice?" Relief flooded every part of me at the sound of Alistar's voice. But would that change to grief when I faced what unfolded? A family of my own, or...or what? I did not want to know.

He tried the door. "Eunice, let me in. We need to talk."

I knew I had to hear what he had to say... his plans, good or bad. I pulled myself together and opened the door. He stood there and looked at me, his face wreathed in uncertain hope. I sat back on my bed mat and heard him close the door.

He sat beside me and took my hand. "I cannot tell you how sorry I am for letting things happen the way they did."

I nodded and held my breath. I could not risk even a glimpse at his face. "I know, I—"

"No, let me...let me explain. My father has held onto his grandiose plan of how life is to work out. He has preached it to me and Spiros for as long as I can remember...how we would build his business into a large enterprise with several outshoots, each managed by one of us. Nothing could alter what he intended to make happen, that included wives he would choose for each of us from the city's elite families. So silly... we would never measure up to their standards."

I tried to follow his logic, but none of this made sense to me. "Alistar, I heard—"

"I am sure you heard him spout off at what mother found, but that is nothing compared to his fury that I would upset his schemes for power and wealth. His greatest concern, even more than my mother's drinking problem, is how it might affect his status."

I had heard all I needed to know about Crathis' plans. I needed to know what Alistar had decided about us.

"Alistar, I heard your father's angry reaction, but not what you told him." I looked him in the eye. "What did you tell him about us? What are we going to do?"

He lowered his head and stared at his boots. "Well, marriage is out of the question for now. There is no way he will approve our being together permanently." He sounded apologetic.

Panic climbed my throat, but I choked out a reply. "What does that mean?"

"Well, he does not want to lose your help with the family and at the market, so he said he would tolerate our relationship as it is.

Months ago, I uncovered that he has a mistress he visits in the city from time to time. The solution is not foreign to him."

His eyes pled like a lost puppy as he looked up at me. "What I hope for is that the idea of us married will grow on him, and eventually we will make it permanent"

He wiggled his brows and donned a crooked smile. "Meanwhile, we will not have to sneak around to be together."

His antics made me sick. I wanted to slap the expression from his face. To have me as his mistress, obviously, would be all right with him. When I did not say anything, he reached over and lifted my chin. "You know how much I love you and want to be with you, do you not?"

I nodded and murmured something about how difficult a day it had been, that I needed to sleep, and we could talk more tomorrow. He sighed and gave my shoulders a brief hug. He looked relieved, like the time he dropped a huge sack of animal feed and it did not split.

"You are right. This has been tough on both of us. We will go together, first thing tomorrow, and tell him we will wait and see how things work out." He kissed my cheek.

"Sleep well, and do not give up on us. All right?"

His footsteps echoed before the latch on the shed door clicked a finality to my dreams.

Chapter Sixteen

I waited until all the lamps were extinguished in the main house and no movement or sounds were evident. I dried my tears over what would never be. Not far from the house, I glanced back and thought a shadow moved. Perhaps it was Spiros. I would miss his friendship almost as much as Alistar. I wondered what he thought of it all and remembered his caution that I not let Alistar hurt me. I would probably never know. Maybe what I longed for was more than a husband. Maybe, it was a family. Perhaps, the unconditional love and acceptance of a man would never fully satisfy what my soul longed for.

I was familiar with the road to the market, so I set out in that direction. The moon was nearly full and my eyes quickly adjusted to the night.

The whole world seemed asleep, not even a dog barked. Occasionally, some animal rustled the bushes or tree leaves as I passed, but hid or scampered before I reached it. The trip to the market had seemed quick in the wagon but after I had walked an hour or so, I realized it was farther than I thought. I pulled my cloak close as the cold night air settled in earnest.

I shivered and walked faster. Winter, not spring, would soon be here. When I reached the stalls, it was dark. The quiet hovered like an expectant owl that watched the every move of its prey. I sat on a bench and had rested but a few moments before I heard distant voices. They sounded like young men engaged in taunts laced with slurred challenges.

My heart began to race. I needed to hide before they saw me and decided to use me for sport. I ran into the stoa and found a stall with three sides that reached almost to the ground. I hunched in the furthest corner and hoped they would not come my way.

The voices grew louder. I heard what sounded like booths being toppled amidst bouts of drunken laughter. The closer they came, the more frightened I became. I did not dare run. They would see me.

They had begun to tear apart the stall across from where I hid, when horses' hooves sounded, followed by, "Stop where you are!"

The young men were too drunk to escape. I peeked through a crack and saw the Roman soldiers round them up and bind their hands to one other. That same voice commanded. "All right, move."

A different soldier said, "I think I see another one hidden in that stall."

I panicked. They had spotted me. Two soldiers entered the booth I cowered in. One called to his superior, "It is a girl."

"Bring her out. Maybe she was their lookout." The soldier pulled me to my feet and propelled me onto the stoa.

His superior looked at me with contempt. "Well, Young Woman, are you part of that gang of troublemakers?"

I shook my head, too terrified to speak.

He poked the closest captive. "Is she with you?"

The unruly young man turned his bloodshot eyes on me and sneered. "Her? No. Never saw her before."

The soldier, in charge, walked over and looked at me. "What are you doing out here in the night, and what is in your bag?"

My voice shook. "My clothes. It is all I own."

"And where are you headed?"

"I...I do not know. I lost my position with a family I worked for and need to find a new one."

"Well, you are not safe out here in the dark." He gestured at the younger soldier. "Put her on your horse, and let us take these rebels to the lock up."

We started for the city. One soldier led my horse and another herded the captives along with his spear. I clung to the horse's mane and wondered what they would do with me.

When we reached the city, the soldier in charge pointed out a row of inns. "If you knock long enough, someone will probably let you in."

I thanked him and decided to spend some of the little money I had on a safe night's lodging.

At the third door, a sleepy innkeeper finally answered my knock. I almost laughed at his unusual headgear. The nightcap stood up on one side of his head and rested on the opposite cheek. It looked like it protected or hid him from everything, maybe even intruders like me.

I tried to sound respectable. "I am sorry to wake you, but I need a place to sleep. Do you have a vacant room?"

He grunted and motioned me inside. "There are empty beds in the women's quarters." He gestured toward the stairs. "Up to the top and to the right. Breakfast is shortly after the cock crows."

I paid and thanked him, then made my way to the room, relieved to find I was alone. Until I pulled the blanket over me, I did not realize how tired I was. I blew out the lamp he gave me and relived the last moments with Alistar. Disappointment, regrets, and anger ran rampant. How could I have let myself be deceived and think he truly loved and cared for me?

Maybe it was my fault too. We were young, caught up in first love, and I so wanted someone to belong to. I caressed my stomach and fell asleep. I never heard the cock crow.

I awoke to a portly, older woman in a long apron, who shook my foot. I shot up and stared. Where was I?

"We do not allow guests to sleep past mid-morning. You have already missed breakfast."

The events of yesterday crashed and overwhelmed my senses. I had found courage to leave Alistar and escaped the likely outcome, had the young men found me. That and being believed by and brought into the city by the soldiers left me dizzy. I jumped from the bed. "I am so sorry."

The next thing I remembered was waking on the floor with the woman above me. She called for her husband and fanned me with a large towel. The innkeeper, who had let me in, soon joined her.

She sounded worried. "I do not know what is wrong. One moment she stood up and the next, she collapsed."

"Young Woman, can you hear me?" His voice was firm but gentle.

I opened my eyes and stared. What had happened? Who were these people? Within seconds my mind cleared.

The woman put her arm under my shoulders and sat me up. "Come on Dearie. Let me help you."

I was mortified. "I am so sorry. I have never fainted before. I—"

"Do not worry. Do you think you can stand?"

I nodded and let her help me to my feet. She stood close, arms extended. I tottered a bit, but she steadied me. "Here, sit back on the bed until you are sure you are all right." She gave her husband a sidelong look. "You go on, Teris. I will take care of her."

She straightened the bottom of my nightshirt. "My name is Phobie. My husband

and I own this inn. How long since you have eaten?"

"Oh, not long. Yesterday noon, I guess."

"Well, lots of things can make you dizzy. Hunger, if you stand up too quickly, or is it possible you are expecting?"

My jaw dropped. I swallowed every answer that came to mind. No one knew about my baby.

She patted my arm. "It is all right, Dearie. Whatever or whoever you have run from is not worth it. Do you feel better? Think you could get dressed?"

I nodded.

"Good, then come down to the kitchen and I will fix you something light to eat. That little one needs nourishment."

She was gone before I thought to ask why she was being so kind to a stranger.

Chapter Seventeen

When I reached the kitchen, I noticed Phobie had removed her long apron. She motioned at a small stool next to the counter and brought me a plate of lightly scrambled eggs and a thick slice of barley bread.

"I cannot thank you enough for your kindness. I never meant to — "

She held up her hand, "Nonsense, you need to eat to keep strong for...for whatever you plan to do."

I ate what she had prepared, surprised how hungry I was. She brought me a steaming mug of tea, returned with one for herself, and sat down beside me.

After a few sips, she looked at me and raised her brows. "You never told me your name."

"I... it's Eunice."

"Well, Eunice. I suspect you need some help, and as a matter of fact, so do I." I could not imagine what she had in mind, but it must have been obvious that I needed to find work.

"What kind of help do you need? Is there something I can do to repay your kindness?"

"I expect a large number of people when the carriages arrive from the docks later this afternoon, and I need to go to the market and stock up on meat and produce. My flour vats and oil drums are full, but I do not have time to shop and do all that needs to be done here to be ready. Do you have any experience or know how to prepare food?"

My spirits lifted. Maybe her needs were the answer to mine, at least for now. "Yes. Yes, I have cooked and baked all my life, first at home and then for various families. What would you like me to do?"

"Come, I will show you." She led me to her storage closet where she kept everything needed to bake bread. "And here are black beans, chickpeas, and lentils that need to be cooked and mashed for the pork dish I plan to have ready. Can you do that?"

I assured her I could and was more than happy to help. She showed me where her vessels and cutlery were kept and donned her cape.

"You are a blessing, Eunice. Teris will be around if you have any questions. I should not be gone more than a few hours.

A blessing? How was it others saw me as a blessing? I felt like I battled a curse.

I plunged into the tasks and when she returned, proudly showed her eight loaves of bread I had set to cool, alongside a kettleful of mashed vegetables. I could see she was pleased.

She smiled. "Someone taught you well. Would you be able to help me with the rest of the preparations?" I agreed and she added, "By the time everyone eats and the cleanup is done, it will be late, so plan another night with us. Your help will more than pay for your lodging."

I was happy and relieved to put off my quest for an additional night. By mid afternoon, travelers began to arrive. We worked, nonstop, to prepare beds and feed everyone. The inn was full and Teris had to turn away the last few inquirers. Before dawn, I rose and dressed as quietly as possible, so I did not disturb the snoring women who had shared my room.

Phobie already bustled about the kitchen. "I thought you might like some help,"

She looked up and sighed. "Oh, Eunice, I sure could. Would you place these dishes and silverware on the tables?" She chuckled.

"Some guests want to eat and be on their way before the cock even opens his eyes. The ham is fried, and the eggs are boiled and ready. I just need to watch that this bread warms and does not burn. I, also, must bring out the cheese and legume casseroles."

In light of what she had served for dinner, I should not have been surprised at the enormous amount of food laid out for breakfast. I hurried to do what was needed and replenished the table as groups left and others replaced them. When the last guest had finished, Teris joined us, and we sat down and ate.

He patted his full stomach. "Well, Young Woman, I thank you for helping my missus. She does a grand job, but when the ships bring a full house, it can be a bit much for her."

I loved the way he gazed at her. "Does that happen every day?"

"No. Most ships do a turnaround in a week or so, but all make port on a nearly predictable schedule...unless there are storms. We have gotten so we can anticipate most of their arrivals."

Phobie nodded her agreement. "Eunice, we would love to have you stay here and work for us. Your room and board would be provided and we would give you a small salary.

You are great help in the kitchen, but it would include cleaning and help with laundry and bedding."

I blinked at grateful tears. Who looked out for me that I should end up at this particular inn with these kind people who needed help?

"Phobie, Teris, I would love to stay and work for you. Thank you for your kind offer."

Phobie's face lit up with relief. "No, thank you, Eunice. You are a hard worker and God surely sent you in answer to our prayers."

I wondered which god she referred to. I hoped it was the God the man at the market spoke of.

Life settled into a routine. Twice a week or so, we scrambled to prepare for the onset of visitors from the docks. Other days were more peaceful, with time to clean or rest in the garden behind the inn. Occasionally I explored the city. On days void of the rush of travelers, Phobie and Teris attended evening meetings in the city. I was happily left with instructions on how to accommodate anyone who needed a place to sleep.

A month at the inn had passed when I first noticed my stomach had expanded. I agonized to think I would soon bring a child into the world with no father or a real home.

As the reality mounted, more guilt pummeled my heart. What could I do? I would not be able to provide properly for a baby. I could barely provide for myself.

Days, I was mostly too busy to think about the future. But at night, in the dark, I wrestled with what to do. It was not right nor did it seem fair to deprive a child of a normal family life. At times, I thought I might drop the baby off to Alistar with a note, *This is your child. I cannot take care of it. Please take responsibility and raise it with love. Regretfully, Eunice.*

I knew, though, I would not do that. The thought of Larna raising my child made my stomach churn. The pain I had experienced with a mother and father who did not want me, haunted me. In time, I convinced myself that rather than be deprived of the love and nurture of a normal family, the baby would be better off to have never been born.

On a day we did not expect a crowd, I asked Phobie if she minded my being gone for a day or two. I made up a story of a visit to relatives in the city. She was happy to let me go. I took the money I had earned and headed into the city. I knew there were midwives who knew how to relieve a woman of an unwanted pregnancy but had no idea how to find one.

I sat by the fountain across from the beama and tried to figure it out. I thought about the woman who came to deliver the wool merchant's baby, but could not bring myself to seek him out and inquire about her. Who could I ask? When a young woman who looked like she might deliver any day passed, it occurred to me she surely would know of a midwife. Before she disappeared, I hurried over and touched her arm.

"Please excuse me, but I see you expect a baby soon and I am in need of a midwife. Would you please tell me of the one you use and how to find her?"

The woman's eyes went to my stomach. Suspicion furrowed her brows, and her thoughts probably ran to why a young woman's family would not have an established midwife.

I quickly blurted, "I am new to the city and have no family here." The lie did not concern me. I was desperate.

"Yes, of course." She told me her midwife's name and where to find her. I thanked her and went back to the fountain. Could I go through with it?

It was already noon by the time I found enough courage to find the address. It was a small cottage on the gulf side of the city. I knocked, surprised when a woman in her twenties answered the door.

My heart pounded so hard I could hardly speak. When I only stared, the woman cocked her head. "Can I be of help to you?"

I gulped the cool, winter air and asked, "Yes. Are you the midwife?"

Her head shook and I suspected she sensed what I was there for. I felt ashamed and had to restrain my feet from running off.

"No, my mother is the midwife. Please, come in and I will get her for you."

The home was bright and cheerful, not the den of darkness I imagined a woman who dealt with terminating life would have. I was directed to a chair and asked to wait. What was I doing here? I decided to leave, but an older woman pushed aside a curtained doorway and entered the room.

Chapter Eighteen

The woman looked no older than my mother, but not nearly as old as the wool seller's midwife. Would she know what to do? My heart raced as she pulled a chair close and looked into my eyes. Her voice was gentle.

"What is your name, Dear?"

I stammered like one who was not sure how to answer. "Eunice."

"Well Eunice, I am Reah. What can I do for you?"

I swallowed the lump in my throat and opened my mouth. Nothing came out. She reached over and touched my arm. "Do not be afraid. My daughter said you were looking for a midwife. How long since your last blood flow?"

Her serene demeanor soothed my fears. "I... I am not sure... two, maybe even three months now."

"I assume this is your first. Is your husband pleased to become a father?"

My chin began to quiver. "There is no... the father is not..." I burst into tears.

"Oh, Eunice. I am so sorry. Do you have family that can help you care for your baby?" The pain of rejection I had known from birth, soared. I hesitated, but soon the whole sordid story poured forth. She did not interrupt but, occasionally, patted my hand.

"And where do you live? Do you have a place to stay?"

I told her about the kind innkeepers. "But it is not permanent. I cannot live there with a baby. It would not be fair to them. I cannot give the baby a proper home, so I need to — "

"Have you thought about the possibility of giving birth and releasing the child to a woman who has been unable to conceive? I know of one right now who would love to raise your child."

I gasped at the thought. "I could not! Once I saw my baby, I would never be able to give it away. For the child's sake, I must..." Tears streamed down my cheeks. "I must let it go."

"Eunice, no one can make this decision for you, but know you will likely carry the pain forever if you do not let your child live. I have seen it many times. Are you sure that is what you want to do?"

My head swam with arguments I had wrestled for a month. To bring a child into a world without a family to love and care for seemed cruel, much worse than any pain I would endure.

With a deep breath, I swallowed my dread and fears. "I have given it a lot of thought. I am sure."

Her voice dropped. "All right. I do not participate in the process, but I will take you to a woman who does."

She left the room, and I heard her order her carriage be brought around. The driver helped us up the steps, climbed into his position and urged the horses on. We drove north of the city in muted consent. About half an hour later, the driver turned onto a windy road.

Reah's silence hung like a blanket of condemnation. Society considered women simply a vessel for a child to grow in. A child was not a person until it was born. Could I sever my heart from this part of me? Most pregnant women kept to their homes. Some of the temples even banned them until after the child arrived. I had no home, no safe place to harbor.

Whispered tales spoke of men, and even women, who had no qualms about leaving an unwanted or imperfect baby out somewhere beyond the city. There, at the mercy of the elements, death or an uncertain fate awaited them. Laws against that or the use of a drug or device to end the life of a viable infant had not ended the practice. Was that not worse than to prevent all the heartache my child would never know? I had not, yet, felt movement... my baby had no awareness of a life to come.

We passed a long bog, but few houses. The driver pulled the horse to a stop at the end of the road in front of a small cottage in bad need of repair.

Reah touched my arm. "Still sure about this Eunice?" I turned from her sad smile and nodded. "Then you go on in and I will come back tomorrow, at this same time, and bring you back to the city. The woman's name is Aello. She is a bit gruff but she is an expert in... these matters."

I fought the urge to leave with her. "You are so kind. I do not have much money and I—"

"No. Do not worry about that. I want to help, and I will pray for your safety."

I thanked her. Could prayer change things? Did not gods live in temples where people went and gave offerings? How could they hear when the person was not in their presence? And did they really answer cries for help? Phobie and Teris seemed to think their god did.

The driver turned the carriage around and they disappeared around the bend. I looked at the rundown house. Dread, like bile, rose in my mouth. I assured myself it was for the best and knocked on the door.

When no one came, I knocked again and listened for movement. At last, the door rattled and an elderly woman opened it a crack. She wore an apron with evidence of spilled food and stains I could not identify. Her greasy, gray hair was wound into a matted bun with tendrils that hung, haphazardly, over her face and ears.

"Are you Aello?" I hoped she was not.

She sounded irritated at the interruption. "Yes. Do you have business here?" "Reah, the midwife sent me. I—"

"All right, all right. Come in before this cold gluts the house." She turned and I followed her into a room cluttered with debris and dust on every surface.

She told me to remove my cloak, looked me over and frowned, "You do not show much. How many months are you?" "Two, maybe three."

She put her hands on my stomach and pressed in several places. I held my breath as I followed her dirty hands. Nausea revived as the smell of an unwashed body and the heavy scent of feces and urine drifted from somewhere.

"Feels like not much more than two. Have you gone through this before?"

I balked. "No. No!" Did I look like someone who slept around?

"Well, you know a baby is not real until it moves in the womb. So since you are early, we will try the simplest method and see if the seed will disperse on its own."

The seed? Fall out on its own? My brows met. What could that mean?

"I want you to go back out onto my porch. This old house cannot take much shaking." Before I could ask what she meant, she continued.

"I need you to try the Lacedaemonian method."

My jaw dropped but she did not waste a moment. "

"It started in Sparta and can be very effective. Now, go outside and jump into the air, and while you are up, kick yourself as hard as you can in your buttocks. And I do not mean once or twice. Do it over and over until you can jump no more, and then come in and we will see if it happens."

I could only stare. Had age or a life of solitude in this forsaken place affected her mind?

She put her hands on her hips and glared, then cocked her head and motioned at the door. Reah's words returned. "She is an expert in these things..."

I grabbed my cloak and went out on the porch. What did I have to lose? The air was chilly, but the task soon left me overheated. I jumped and kicked myself over and over until exhaustion sent me to my knees. I pulled myself to my feet, staggered through the door, and headed for the closest bench.

Aello yelled, "No. Do not sit down! You need to remain upright so the seed can escape."

Her instructions grated on my ears but could not drown the gasps from my lungs. For what seemed like forever, I leaned against a door frame, but nothing happened.

She frowned, "Well, I guess I need to prepare my potion.

I collapsed onto the bench. What else was I in for?

Chapter Nineteen

Aello did not say another word, but went into the cluttered kitchen and gathered things onto a table that tipped with each addition. A heavy pot lay on top of a stove. She threw a few sticks of wood and some kindling into its belly where coals festered and soon ignited the fuel. She carried the pot to the table and began to add things.

I recognized the pennyroyal. Everyone knew more than five grams of that were toxic. Others, labeled wild colocynth, resin, quinine, and opium were not familiar to me. She pulled out a cloth bag and began to add its contents to the pot. Nothing was measured, simply spooned out with a rounded vessel that she shook to level.

I shuddered. "What is that?"

Surprise covered her face, followed by a grimace. Had she forgotten I was there? "This is ground worm fern root, with crushed and dried queen Anne lace, dried crows' eggs, flowers, and other plants. You can go back in there and sit down. This will take a while to brew."

Her tone suggested I leave and bank my questions. Faded light through windows, scrummed with years of neglect, confirmed near darkness. To have to spend the night there horrified me, but I had made my choice and could not turn back. I sat in the only chair not covered with soiled clothing or things I did not recognize. The odor of what she brewed wafted into the room. It smelled awful, earthy, and rotten.

Aello hobbled back into the room. "Well, your mixture is set to cool...should be ready before long."

Fear wound tentacles around my stomach. "What...I mean... exactly, what will happen if I drink it?"

She snapped at my question. "If you drink it? I have not gone to all this trouble for nothing. You will drink it!"

Panic bounced between my ribs and up my throat.

"I will give you a half a cup every little while until you begin to cramp. It may take most of the night."

Much later, with no sign that anything had happened, Aello told me to lie on a couch, she had cleared, and wait. I did as she said and hoped I would not vomit the vile liquid she brought me. I could not sleep. Eventually, I crept into the kitchen to ask where I could relieve myself. On the burner, a pot of onions boiled, and on the table heaped before her lay a vile concoction.

She startled when I cleared my throat. "I need to relieve myself." I pointed at the table. "What...what is that for?"

"It is what we will need if the brew fails." "What is it?'

"It is my last resort...if all else fails. Mouse dung, crushed ants, more dried crows' eggs and hairs from a deer–I mix it with camel's dung I send away for. She added a few more pellets of the mouse dung, Egyptian salt, and honey.

My hand shot to my lips. Surely, she did not expect me to eat that.

She pointed toward a small room with a crude pail. "It is not a good idea to use the outhouse in the dark."

I uncovered the pail. A foul odor, akin to a badly decayed animal, rose to greet me. I nearly passed out. No wonder the house smelled so badly. I finished as quickly as I could and left to lie down again.

She lifted her hand. "Yours is a stubborn one. Take off everything below your waist and sit over this pail of freshly steamed onions. It may move things along."

I did as she said and squatted over the onions until they no longer steamed. She looked at me with disgust, and insisted I drink more of her brew. My stomach rebelled and I retched the vile liquid directly into the pail of onions. I stood and took hold of the table to keep upright. Anger fired from her eyes as she glared and covered the pail.

"Well, those are ruined. Go and lie down until your stomach settles."

I gathered my clothes and crept back to the couch. Had she intended to eat those onions? I managed to keep the next dose of her brew down, but after a few more she finally gave up.

"Go to sleep. I will try something else in the morning." She wheeled about, anxious to leave. "If you start to cramp or anything happens, call me. I will be in that next room."

I lay there and began to doubt my decision to rid my body of this child. After all, it had been conceived in love...at least I thought I was in love. Maybe my desire to have someone who wanted to have a life with me had colored my judgment. Hours passed with no sign the brew worked as she promised. Could it be because I had made a poor decision? Was a plan about to unfold where I could love and care for my baby in a safe place? I caressed my stomach. "I do not know Little One. I just do not know."

A fitful night, with only an extremely upset stomach, validated what I had gone through. I awoke to the reality of my situation. A sound, as if something forceful had fallen and landed on the floor, made me jump. I peeked into the kitchen and watched as Aello lifted a meat cleaver and vigorously pounded the mixture she had spread on the table the previous night.

She did not hear me approach. "I believe I will use the outhouse."

She glanced at me and shrugged. "Suit yourself."

When I returned, she pointed at her creation. "This has never failed me." Pride diminished the negative expression she had worn, till now. "Things always begin in a few hours."

I tried to keep the horror from my voice. "How...does it work?"

"You will pack the mixture up inside of you and —" I visibly jerked back from the table. "Are you serious? That is full of things that would cause sickness and a raging fever."

She pursed her lips and looked at me with disgust. "Well, not always. Depends on how long it takes to bring out the substance you want to dispose of."

Dispose of? The words clattered like stones on a marble path. Dispose of...like something you toss into a garbage heap. Is that what I wanted to do? To destroy this precious child that depended on me for life and safety? As if a curtain had been pulled, I clearly saw that I considered to end the life my baby, a kinder option than to allow the child to live and face whatever hardships life brought to a fatherless child.

I backed from the room. "I am sorry. I cannot do this. I cannot kill my baby no matter what consequences I face." I laid all the money I had on the table, grabbed my cloak, and headed for the door. Aello came out on the porch and screamed curses until I was well down the road. I did not look back. Reah would not come to pick me up for hours, so I walked until I reached the main road.

A man with a load of hay invited me to ride on the back of his wagon. Before he turned off at the market, I jumped down and thanked him. On my way to the inn, I practiced the phony tale of my visit to relatives that I would tell Phobie.

She welcomed me back. "You look a little tired, Eunice. Rest until dinner. The crowds will not arrive until tomorrow, so tonight should be easy to handle."

I thanked her and crawled into bed. It took all my willpower to keep the miserable trip I had made from thoughts. But I was thankful that I had not gone through with it. I would find a way and my baby would know it was loved. I slept but woke to violent cramps in my stomach and up into my back.

Chapter Twenty

I went to find Phobie, sure she could help or advise me. She met me at the bottom of the stairs. "Eunice? What is wrong? Are you sick?"

I staggered under the pain. "Something is not right... terrible cramps in my stomach."

Concern etched lines across her forehead as she helped me into a chair and brought me some water. "It may be your baby. Let us get you back in bed and I will make a warm compress to hold against your middle."

As we reached the stairs, a warm liquid seeped into my underclothes. She led me to a cot they kept in a small storage room behind the kitchen. I lay still and the cramps lessened. Soon after, the bleeding stopped.

She hovered over me. "Stay right here where I can keep an eye on you while I start my bread. Sometimes, it is just an interruption in the baby's development and it will pass."

I lay with heated towels across my middle, terrified at the likelihood Aello's potion had taken hold. Now and again the cramps raged, but each time they subsided. Phobie brought me some broth and I sat up and drank it. Hours later, when it seemed things were back to normal, I told her I thought I should return to bed and try to sleep.

Phobie helped me up the stairs and into bed. I fell asleep but woke throughout the night as cramps escalated then slackened, built, and dwindled. There were no guests at the inn, for which I was grateful. Phobie checked on me at first light. I stood to my feet, appalled at the watery blood that had soaked my bedding.

She helped me clean up and supported me down the stairs. The smell of barley porridge brought waves of nausea. Dry heaves followed.

She was close by when a knife-like, brutal cramp sent me to my knees. I cried out at the pain that cut across my middle and up into my back. Phobie kneeled beside me and put her arm around my shoulders. I heard her mutter something that sounded like the prayer I had heard Chrisa utter before her baby came.

I drenched the fresh tunic Phobie lent me as sweat poured from beneath my hair and oozed out of every part of my body. I shook violently, but desperate to protect my baby from my folly, I wrapped my arms in a deadlock across my stomach.

I cried, rocked front to back, and whispered, "Forgive me, Little One. Forgive me." I pulled myself to my feet and as if a dam had broken, blood and liquid soaked me and everything beneath me. The room began to spin. I grabbed the back of a chair, vaguely aware clumps passed with the liquid.

Hours later, I awoke in bed. Phobie sat in a rocker beside me. She rinsed cloths in cold water and laid them on my forehead. I tried to sit up, but she put her hand on my shoulder and pushed me back.

"Do not try to get up, Dear. Your body has had a shock and you need to rest." She put a cup to my lips. "Try to drink. It will help ward off a fever."

Desperate to deny what I knew had happened, tears choked my sorrow. "My baby, my baby..."

Phobie bathed my forehead. "I am so sorry, Eunice. I wish there were something we could have done, but sometimes nature has its own way. After we carried you upstairs, Teris put the remains in a tiny box and buried it in the garden."

I turned my face and sobbed. My faulty wisdom and futile effort to change the outcome proved too little and too late.

She patted my shoulder. "I will bring you a tray with some soup. Do not try to get up."

When she returned, I raised up onto my elbows and choked out what I needed to know. "Phobie, did you see it? Did you see my baby? Was it a boy or a little girl? Could you tell?"

Strain wrenched her face. "Oh, Eunice, I only had a brief glimpse before Teris wrapped the remains in a cloth. I am afraid it was too soon to tell."

She left the tray, and I was glad to be alone. I could not stop my tears. I had killed my baby. In time, for her sake, I ate a little soup, then spent the night in and out of sleep. A nightmare, where I served our guests the dung mixture along with Phobie's casserole, woke me with a start.

A constant weight dragged my heart as I reentered the inn's routine. Phobie tried to comfort me, but she did not know what caused my pregnancy to fail. For several weeks, she would not allow me to carry anything heavy, and insisted I nap on days that were not busy. I was glad to comply. Only with my legs elevated, could I pacify the ache in my thighs and hips. I had little energy.

I did not want to close my eyes. Faces of newborns haunted me. Was this how my baby might have looked? Was it a little girl with auburn hair like mine? Or could it have been a feisty little boy with Alistar' cleft chin? I chose to believe it was a girl. Day after day, Reah's warning returned. "You may forever carry the pain of not bearing your child...not bearing your child..."

I welcomed times when ships embarked, and we were busy. We fell into a routine, on those days, as we prepared and precooked many things right after breakfast. On quieter days, we cleaned and washed bedding. I marveled at Phobie's ability to make sure everything was done when needed, and was glad to have someone direct my days. Couples and singles arrived from the Port of Cenchrea. Some even brought children who, by dinner time, were tired and cross.

By the time the trees budded and flowers bloomed, I found there were fewer nights when I cried myself to sleep. The tiny garden, behind the inn, was my oasis. I often stood by the flower bed where Teris showed me he had buried my baby. Sometimes, I talked to her. I told her about my day or how much I loved her and wished we were together. On especially long days, like today, after guests bedded for the night, I simply enjoyed the solitude.

A young man broke the quiet. "Mind if I enjoy this peaceful place with you?" He pushed back the thick hair that fell over his eyes. It was close to dark, but I recalled that he had registered late for the last available bed in the men's section.

"Yes...of course." His gentle demeanor and warm smile disarmed me. He sat opposite me at the small outdoor table, where Phobie and Teris shared morning coffee after the guests were fed. Most people were exhausted from their voyages and went straight to bed after dinner and left right after breakfast. If they had business in the city, sometimes they stayed a day or two, but few interacted with me or the owners.

He leaned back in his chair and drew a noisy breath. "I smell hyacinths. Or is that something else?"

When he turned and searched the garden, I could not help but notice his broad shoulders and muscular arms. "No, it is hyacinths. Phoebe, the owner, loves them and has pink and purple and white ones planted in several places."

"I thought so. My name is Pavlos. Have you been in Corinth long?"

I was taken aback by his inquiry. Did he recognize me from somewhere? Why would he want to know? I told him my name but nothing more.

"Well, it is my first time in Corinth. I have heard so much about it. I cannot wait to finish my business and explore the city. Is it difficult to find your way around?"

He was so unassuming, I relaxed. "Actually, I have only been past the market and into the city a few times. It is filled with beautiful temples, statues, and monuments. They were, mostly, built by Romans. Be sure you see the fountain. It is lovely. Take the path up to the Accu Corinth and enjoy the view. I have heard you can see both the Aegean and the Gulf of Corinth from up there."

"Really? That would be worth the climb. We saw some of the mountains on the Sardonic side, shortly before we docked."

Darkness fell and the night air chilled my arms, still we talked. He said he came from the southern part of the Peloponnese and he found this somewhat cooler temperature a relief. He worked on his father's sheep ranch and had come to Corinth to buy two pairs of young sheepdogs, because theirs had become inbred.

Before I left, I told him about the sheep farm where the family I once stayed with bought their wool, and how to get there.

I picked up my cup and stood. "I must be going in. At the time I was at that farm, puppies ran all over the place. Have a great time in the city, tomorrow."

He bid me goodnight but did not seem in a hurry to leave.

I did not see Pavlos until dinner time, the next day. After we cleaned up, I headed straight for the garden. A family with a baby girl had checked in and I could not take my eyes off her. She was tiny, about the age my baby would have been. She would sleep with her mother in the women's quarters where I slept. I did not want to hear her cries nor hear her mother comfort her.

I was not surprised when Pavlos joined me, but I would have preferred to be alone. He began to tell me about his day in the city. As he spoke, I remembered the talks Alistar and I shared before our relationship turned intimate. A warning flashed. I jumped from my seat and said I was sorry, but I needed to go in.

Disappointment clouded his face, but I did not look back. When I reached the stairs, the cries of the baby drew me to a halt. Now what? There was no place to go but the sitting room, but a few guests lingered there. I would have to interact with them, and I was in no mood for meaningless chatter.

It would not be dark for nearly an hour, so I decided to go for a walk. At the end of our road was a small park dedicated to the goddess Athena. I stopped and sat on the only bench and released the tears I had held. I had to get a hold of myself. I could not fall apart every time I saw a baby.

"Eunice? Is that you?"

I looked up, surprised to hear someone call my name. I blew my nose, cleared my throat, and tried to sound normal.

"Pavlos, I... I was not..., did not expect anyone."

He sat down beside me. "I am sorry to bother you. I decided to take a walk and saw you there. You are crying. Can I be of any help?"

He sounded so kind and genuinely concerned, but what could I say?

"I am sorry. My thoughts returned to a loss I went through a few months ago. It was someone I cared deeply for, and grief overwhelmed me. I did not mean to be rude to you."

He shook his head. "Oh, no. You were not, and I did not expect to find you here. Compared to my house, which sprawls in three directions, the inn closes in on me."

We stayed a while and he talked more of home. I told him about my grandfather's ranch, and he wanted to know where it was and what kind of horses he raised. Darkness fell and I said I needed to get back. He walked with me and stopped me before we went into the inn.

"Eunice, I did not get to go up on the Accu Corinth yesterday. I want to see it tomorrow, before I get the dogs and return home. Is there any chance you could go with me? It could be fun, and maybe a day away will brighten things for you."

I liked the idea of getting away, if only for a few hours, and I really wanted to climb the mountain. "I will have to check with Phobie. I do not think any ships dock tomorrow. If not, I am certain she will be happy for me to go. If she is up, I will ask. If not, I will see you at breakfast."

Chapter Twenty-One

When I reached the inn, Phobie was still in the kitchen going over her plans for the next day. She smiled and showed me what she intended to make for dinner. I told her about being invited to go see the Accu Corinth.

"Of course you can take time, Eunice. You are right, we do not expect any ships to dock tomorrow, and I am more than happy to see you do something for yourself, something fun. You work hard and it will be good for you. You have not been away since..."

She looked embarrassed. I hugged her shoulders. "It is all right, Phobie. Even though I do not talk about it, the loss of my baby will always be with me."

Phobie's eyes filled. She hugged me back and I told her I planned to help serve the morning meal before I left.

Pavlos seemed pleased when I told him I could go after I helped Phobie with breakfast. I lay awake second guessing my desire to accompany him. When had I torn down the protective shield I had raised to isolate myself? I finally drifted off, but startled when the young woman's baby began to fuss. The mother tried to soothe the infant, but its cries grew until the faint sound of sucking followed.

I pulled the pillow over my ears, but my heart still heard. Once again, the baby began to wail heart-wrenching cries. The noise went on for a long time and women, in the other beds, began to complain.

One woman whined, "Can you not feed that baby or something? We need to get some sleep."

Another broke in, "Have a little compassion. You know how babies are when their routines are upset or their tummies hurt."

The infant would not be comforted. More grumbling followed. I felt sorry for the mother. She looked no older than I and did all she knew to quiet her child. When walking the floor did not help, she stopped by my bed. "Miss, you work here, do you not?"

I pulled back my blanket and lit a candle. She looked desperate. "Yes, what can I do for you?"

"I need to find my husband. I do not know what to do. I do not want my baby to disturb everyone. She is my first and I cannot seem to quiet her. Could you hold her for a few minutes?" She thrust the infant into my arms before I could think to refuse.

I swallowed hard and held the distraught child out away from my body. Despite my will, my eyes were drawn to her tiny face, painfully aware my little girl's cries would never be heard. Seconds later, pity snuggled the baby to my chest. It felt so right... so natural. Truth stabbed with a harsh awareness: If I had let another woman raise the child I destroyed, even though she had not carried her beneath her heart for nine months, my baby would have been equally loved.

I sang a soft lullaby as I paced, my head against the baby's, my tears upon her cheek. In minutes, the cries muffled and she slept. I hoped her mother would not hurry back, but she soon found me.

"Oh, thank you. You are a blessing." With reluctance, I relinquished the infant. "My husband said we must finish out the night, but I am so relieved to have her asleep. You must have a special touch."

Her comment ripped my heart. What would she think if she knew I caused my own child to die? I followed her back into the room, and we crept into our beds.

A blessing...she called me a blessing. Had not Thera, mother of the twins I had cared for, called me a great blessing shortly before she died. And Ophelos the wool dealer... was that not what he said after I helped deliver his son? I had failed my baby and my little sister, Chara, but maybe to help others empowers ones heart to release its own loss. I ran my hand over the warm place on my chest where I had held the baby. It had cooled, but I would pack that memory with those of Rose and cherish it forever.

In the morning, Pavlos waited patiently for breakfast to be over. Phobie insisted I get going. "I can do the cleanup and if need be, I will get Teris to help."

He backed her up. "I used to do it all the time before you came along, Eunice. Now get out of here before I change my mind." His smile matched hers.

Pavlos brushed his unwieldy hair back in place and held the door for me. "We can get a carriage if you like."

I inhaled the fresh morning air. "I would really rather walk if that is all right with you."'

His nod affirmed I had pleased him. He spoke of his fascination with the marble-paved roads, and we stopped often to look at the more elaborate temples. As we passed the Isthmian stadium, I thought of my brothers, so disappointed I had ruined their chance to see the games because of Chara's disappearance.

Pavlos gawked at the huge buildings. "We do not have anything like this in the Peloponnese, except a grand theater. It must have taken a lot of years and manpower to construct all this."

"Teris says that Corinth is one of the largest, most important cities in all of Greece. Supposedly, the Romans made it the provincial capital after they rebuilt what they had destroyed and allowed construction of the temples. That was almost 100 years ago. He says that over 7,500 people live here- Romans, Greeks, Jews, and a multitude of others." I pointed at an especially beautiful structure. "That one is the city's theater."

Pavlos shook his head, "So beautiful! Let us get something to eat before we climb the mountain." I waited by the many facets of the Peirene fountain while he went off to buy something.

I tried not to think of the last time I had been there, but every detail of the dreadful day whirled like a child's carousel.

"Eunice? Is something wrong?"

I had not noticed Pavlos' return until he touched my shoulder. I jumped as if Aello stood before me with her threats.

His brows flinched. "I am sorry. Are you all right?"

"Oh...Pavlos. Yes. I am sorry. I just..."

His brows twitched but he let it drop. "Come, let us sit over there in the shade. I hope you like a lamb and vegetable mix wrapped in grape leaves."

I nodded and followed him to a bench. My stomach was in turmoil, and I could not even look at the food he had brought. While he ate, I wrapped mine in a cloth from the bag I carried and assured him I would eat it later. I fought desperately to purge the ugly memories and not ruin the day.

He asked directions, filled our water jugs, and led me to the path up the Accu Corinth. The breeze increased the higher we climbed, and the view became more and more magnificent. The bad memories, the fountain revived, faded and I enjoyed the moment. The wind caught my veil, as it once had with Alistar, and flipped it back over my forehead. Pavlos saw it, but no disgust registered on his face. I quickly retied it. What did he think about a girl with a beard on her face?

Soon, he was several steps ahead, almost childlike in his joy of discovery in everything we saw. Near the top, we gazed in awe upon the harbors.

"Look at that view," he shouted above the wind that grew even stronger at this height. We sat in silence on some large rocks and took in the scene. He pointed out a ship sailing on the Aegean and my heart skipped a beat. Once again, I had to squelch the memory of how my older brother used that distraction before he attacked me.

We walked over to the temple of Aphrodite and gazed at its enormous, fallen marble columns. "Teris says she is still known as the goddess of beauty and love. They claim she was born from the foam of the sea."

Pavlos stared. "It must have been a beautiful structure."

"The Romans called her Venus, but Aphrodite is the patron goddess of Corinth."

"Is that why hers is the only temple up here on the mountain?"

"I suppose so. The people revere her. She has 1000 temple priestesses and some male prostitutes who dwell in the new structure in the city and serve her. "What is their purpose?"

I squirmed. "Well, their main function is to fund the deity by coming out each night to entice men to buy sexual favors. These are usually carried out in brothels in the city.

"Why would they devote their lives to such a demeaning practice?"

"It is their offering to the goddess."

Pavlos shook his head and wove away from the site. I knew very little else about the lives of these women or men. Most of what I had learned of the city, or any of the temples, I had gleaned from Teris or visitors at the inn. I glanced at Pavlos and wondered why my explanation seemed to bother him.

He scanned the path away from the sea. "Maybe we should head back."

I nodded and followed him down the mountain. Something tugged at my soul and drove me to turn and survey where we had been. Nothing other than what we had seen stood out. I shrugged, but without fanfare, a knowing seeped into my heart. This temple would someday take part in my life.

Chapter Twenty-Two

The next morning, Pavlos told us he needed to leave early for the sheep farm. He hoped to buy puppies sired by their trained dogs. From there, he would board a ship for home. I walked him to the door.

He thanked Phobie for her good food and smiled at me. "I really enjoyed the time we spent together yesterday. Perhaps, I will see you next time my father sends me to Corinth."

An unexpected sadness rose as I waved him off. I would miss his company in the garden and the easy camaraderie we had shared. I could not admit, even to myself, that I had hoped our relationship might grow into something more.

As Pavlos walked out of my life, No one will ever want a girl with a beard on her face, echoed in my mother's harsh voice. I silenced her likely prediction and went to help Phobie with the breakfast cleanup. A ship was expected to dock by noon. I welcomed the predictable demands it would bring. To keep busy and work hard was my only escape from the sorrow of what would never be.

By midsummer, Phobie leaned more heavily on me for help. I had taken over trips to the market to buy food for our guests. Occasionally, I saw the man called Paul, the one Spiros and I saw being rescued from some angry Jews. Today, he was up on the Beama where he repeated his message of the love of a God who would forgive all one had ever done.

I turned away. He did not know of the evil, I nor any other, could ever overlook.

The days turned into weeks, then months. Soon, fall hinted at the certainty of winter. Except for some mums, the garden's flowers had faded. The trees and bushes lost their leaves and left naked branches that pointed to the dreary season to come. I had no way to keep track, but thoughts of my little girl often made me wonder if this day marked a year since her death.

Because of dangerously strong winds, almost no ships sailed this time of year. Summer storms could be harsh, but they were no match for the fierce blasts that accompanied winter's fury. With so few guests, I began to worry whether I might be a burden to the inn's upkeep.

Phobie groaned. "Goodness, no. I do not know what I would do without you. Put that out of your head, right now."

Time hung like dreary clouds, over the Accu Corinth, as if helpless to flee the bare tree branches. When the weather was not fierce, I walked to the park where Pavlos had found me lost in grief for my daughter. I avoided the market except for the inn's needs. To run into Alistar or someone from my family was a possibility I did not want to face.

Signs of spring had sprouted on the morning I heard a loud wail from Phobie. I rushed down the stairs and found her on her knees, sobbing hysterically.

"Phobie? Phobie, what is it?"

She looked up, her face a picture of despair. "It is Teris! It is Teris. He is gone!" "Gone? What do you mean?" The truth struck before she could answer: Teris was dead. I gasped. "Are you certain? Come, show me. Maybe he has just passed out."

She pointed to their bedroom. I hurried and found him, in his nightshirt, in the bed they shared. I put my hand on his. It felt cold. I leaned close but no breath rose from his lips. An involuntary groan rose in my chest. There was no doubt. His arms had already stiffened.

I returned to my broken-hearted friend. "Oh, Phobie, I am so sorry. Come, let me help you up. I will make us some tea."

She sat, arms clutched. Like a cracked cup, tears leaked slowly down her cheeks. I gave her a mug of hot tea and encouraged her to drink it.

Her body weaved with grief. "Teris! Oh, Teris, please do not leave me."

I put my arms around her and held her until her tears were spent.

"He was such a good man, Eunice. How can I go on without him?"

Before she sank deeper into grief, I encouraged her to talk about him. "How long were you married, Phobie? How did you and Teris meet?

Behind the pain, her eyes brightened slightly. "Oh, Eunice, I was but a girl of thirteen when Teris started to work on my father's farm. He was so handsome. I did not think he even noticed me until one day when I was at work in our vegetable garden, he stopped and began to hoe the tomato plants." Her chin quivered. "We worked together for hours that day and talked about everything and nothing."

As if the scene replayed before her, she sighed and continued. "It was not long before he asked my father's permission to marry me. My ever-cautious father said Teris would have to be more established. So, it took another year before we could marry.

Eventually, we bought this inn and together worked hard to make a go of it. That was forty years ago."

I hung the No Rooms Available sign and made us a light breakfast. After Phobie arranged for Teris' funeral, I heated water for her to wash and prepare his body. As she preferred, I left her alone to perform that final feat for her beloved.

The word of Teris' death spread and soon friends stopped with words of sympathy and trays of food. I stayed, mostly in the kitchen, and replenished plates and utensils for the visitors.

Over and over, I heard friends say things like: "What a comfort it must be to know where he is. "Rejoice, one day you will see him again."

I wondered what they meant, but the comments consoled her and I did not ask.

A week later, when gifts of food and condolence visits dwindled, I asked if she wanted to open the inn.

"Let us wait another week, Eunice. I have enough money set aside, and I am not ready to face people with all their demands."

I busied myself, cleaned, washed all the guest's bedding, and gave the kitchen a deep going over. All we had hoped to accomplish, but had been too swamped with the new season's traffic, was finished.

Two weeks passed before Phobie, with slumped shoulders and vacant eyes, announced her decision. "All right, Eunice, take down the sign. My neighbor said a large ship docks tomorrow. She hesitated. "Teris always kept track of that sort of thing. How will I ever keep up?"

I assured her we would manage. "Make out your list. I will go to the market and buy what we need."

It felt good to get out of the house. The cool spring air filled my lungs, and I delighted in the smell of daffodils and the sight of colorful crocuses. I was reminded to check and see if the hyacinths had blossomed.

To plan and prepare food quickened Phobie's purpose. We worked hard and when the guests arrived the next day, we were tired but ready. Phobie greeted each new arrival and made sure they had what they needed. I checked people in and showed them to their rooms. Some, I helped with their chests, wearily aware Teris had handled that chore, also.

We began the clean up after the last guest had eaten dinner. We, often, had to pause to answer questions about when breakfast would be served or how to find certain places in the city. The constant queries were another responsibility, the more knowledgeable, Teris had handled.

I suggested going out into the garden to relax a while. "The hyacinths are in full bloom." Phobie's breath caught. Her eyes brimmed before she shook her head and turned away.

I went out alone.

The smell of the flowers, Pavlos had especially admired, brought thoughts of our times there together. Did the puppies he bought work out? Did he ever think about the day we spent on the Accu Corinth?

I walked over to the flower beds. Without Teris' care, weeds crowded the plants and leaves cluttered the gardens. Much work would be needed to care for them as he had. I did not mention it to Phobie. She had enough to deal with. Maybe I could do some gardening when we were busy with guests.

By midsummer, Phobie showed serious signs of being worn out. I took over more of the work, but some nights I went to bed too exhausted to sleep. I returned from the market on an especially hot day and found Phobie deep in conversation with a man I had never seen. I busied myself in the kitchen, put things away, and tidied the counter until I heard her call me.

"Eunice, this is Aegeus. He owns the inn down the road from us. He has offered to buy the inn, and we have agreed on a price. I have made arrangements to live with my sister in Athens. She is a widow, too. It will be good...we will have each other. I need time to pack and arrange passage, so it will not be for a week."

My jaw fell and my heart sank. She had never mentioned plans to sell the inn. The man stood and appeared to study me. He was tall and thin, with a flat nose that seemed too big for his face.

"Greetings. Phobie has told me you are a hard worker and what a great help you have been to her. My wife and I intend to run both inns, but we would be pleased if you agreed to stay on and work for us."

I nodded, too shocked to say anything. He left and Phobie touched my arm. "I am sorry I did not tell you beforehand, Eunice. I have thought about it since Teris died, and my sister wrote she would be delighted to have me. The opportunity came, and I decided it was the right time. Aegeus seems like a nice man. To work for him should be the same as with us. I have never met his wife, but I am sure it will all work out. By the way, I told him I paid you twice what I do, and he seemed fine with the amount.".

A week! Once again, changes I was ill prepared for threatened to undo me.

Chapter Twenty-Three

We closed again, this time to allow Phobie time to prepare for her move. Aegeus came, often, to check on supplies and note changes he intended to make. More than once, I found Phobie in tears over something she could not take with her. She handed me a carved pelican that had stood in the entryway. It was nearly two feet tall.

"Here, Eunice. Teris bought this, years ago, on a trip. He loved to watch them dive for fish." She sniffed. "It is too big to..." She wiped her eyes. "I would love knowing it is being cared for."

"Thank you, Phobie. It will remind me of the love you and Teris shared." I took the statue upstairs and put it in my little alcove in the women's section.

The time passed quickly. Around midweek, we hailed a carriage, and I took her to book passage to Athens. Her eyes grew wide as we entered the port that lay between the Saronic Gulf and the Gulf of Corinth. Teris had seen to any business that required a trip to the ports, and Phoebie had never gone with him.

I had seen the ports only from the Accu Corinth and a brief glimpse on my trip from the Peloponnese. It had been late when I returned that night, and the docks and booths had been deserted. At midday, I too found the rush of crowds, merchants, sailors and vendors to be overwhelming. I asked the driver of our carriage to direct us to the Cenchrean Port. We found the place and booked Phobie's passage.

Her voice rose as she looked around. "Eunice, how will I know where to go? It is so...so big and so crowded."

"Do not worry, Phobie. I will come with you and see you off. And see, right there on the paper he gave you, is the name of the ship and the time it sails." That reassured her and she relaxed.

The smell of roasted lamb drifted from a vendor. She took hold of my arm, "Let us buy some lunch from that booth and watch the ships come and go. I never knew they were so big!"

Like a child on an adventure, she pointed out all she saw. We sat on a bench and enjoyed our food. People dressed in clothing, foreign to us, hurried past to hail carriages or lined up to board ships.

A familiar looking figure approached from across the walkway just as Phobie jumped up.

"Eunice. Did you see that pelican that flew over us? It looked exactly like the statue Teris gave me."

I assured her I had, but my focus remained on the man. He stopped, stared, then sprinted in our direction. I squinted and hoped I was wrong.

I was not.

Dread swooped like her pelican and landed on my chest.

There was no doubt. It was my father! I lowered my head. Where could I hide? What was he doing here? I did not remember him going to the port when I lived at home. It was too late. He saw me and quickened his steps.

"Eunice, I thought that was you." He sneered as if knew I wanted to hide. "What are you doing here?" His tone accused. "We never heard from you after you left the orchard where we sent you to work." He put his fists on his hips. "The owner stopped sending your earnings and later informed us you had left. Your mother has worried about you."

I did not respond to his lie. I knew my mother. She only missed having someone to use or abuse.

Neither did I cower, amazed that I could keep my voice steady. "This is Phobie. I am her caregiver, and we leave for Athens at the end of the week."

Phobie was quick to sense that I did not want this man to know where I would be. "Yes, Eunice is sailing with me. I could not manage without her. We will be gone for several months."

My father looked confused, then angry. "Well, you owe us a lot of money for your care and what should have been sent from the orchard. You are to bring it to us as soon as you return. Understand?" He stepped close, and I feared he might grab hold of me.

"In fact, you need to resign this position. The minute you finish this plush position, you are to move home." He snorted. "Caregiver, indeed! Your mother needs your help." He looked at Phobie. "I do not know what you pay her, but it belongs to me. Now, where is your place?"

Phobie gave him directions to an area far from her inn. My father glared at me and made note of it. "We will expect you as soon as you arrive back from this venture."

I could not stop shaking. "Phobie, let us get out of here." She agreed and I hailed a carriage, after I made sure he left the area and would not follow us. The time we traveled six miles up the Isthmus and to the inn flew as I shared with her the misery of my childhood. Over and over, I thanked her for backing me up.

Phobie listened. Her eyes glistened as I shared about losing Chara. I had never told her about my past, and tears flowed with the memories, as painful now as then.

She took my hand. "Eunice, you are a wonderful person and have been a blessing to me. There is not a thread of evil in you, only kindness and caring. Do not let the words of people who are twisted in their opinions bring you down, no matter who they are. Do not let what they say or think affect you. Choose to rise above them.

My Grandfather's sentiments revived in her words. We arrived at the inn, and the next day, I offered to help Phobie pack. All the things she hoped to take were laid out in the entry room.

When it became obvious, she could not take it all, I suggested, "Let us bring your trunks in here and see what will fit." She nodded and soon realized she needed to purge more. We divided her things into two piles, one of absolute needs and the other things that depended on available space. It was painful for her, but at last the trunks were closed.

On the day of her voyage, we arrived an hour before she was to sail. The captain, himself, checked passengers in at the gangplank. I handed him her voucher and he motioned for a sailor to take her trunks.

Phobie took my hand. "I will never forget you, Eunice. You became the daughter Teris and I wished for. I am not very good at expressing my faith but I want you to take this." She handed me a piece of paper with a name written on it.

"This woman hosts a speaker who has the words of life. I hope you will go find her and let her tell you about the God who loves you, dearly. His name is Jesus, and He became everything to Teris and me. He will get you through everything life throws your way."

With that, tears mingled at our last embrace. She walked up onto the ship and out of my life. A lump rose in my throat. The loss was as physical as the door that shut her from my sight.

I waited until the captain was not busy. "Please watch over the elderly woman that just boarded. This is all new to her and she may need help to know where to go and what she is to do."

His brief "humph" made me wonder if he would remember my request beyond the minutes that followed. I found a carriage ready to leave and joined the people already aboard.

The inn seemed eerily quiet. Aegeus would not take over until the next day, so I fixed myself some dinner and took it into the garden to enjoy the serenity of the evening. I thought about Phobie. Would she be all right? Would she find her sister in Athens? The paper she gave me rustled in the fold in my tunic. I took it out and smiled at her shaky handwriting. She and Teris often went in the evening to some kind of meetings, but they never spoke of a god.

Right after I had sat down to breakfast, Aegeus walked into the dining hall. "There you are, Eunice. When you finish, I would like you to go through the inn with me, and I will point out what needs to be done. Day after tomorrow, we are expecting two ships to dock, one on each port. I want to be ready for guests."

I assured him I would only be a few minutes, and he left to inspect the garden and landscaping around the inn. I had finished my breakfast dishes when he returned. He did not look pleased.

"It is summer, yet the outside of this inn has been sorely neglected. People want to stay in a place that presents a nice appearance. Why did Phobie not hire someone to keep things up outside?"

I did not like his criticism of my friend, but I tried not to be defensive. "She still grieved her husband's death. He took care of the garden and outside work, and all that needed to be done overwhelmed her. She tried..." His attention had already turned to a window that refused to open.

As he requested, I climbed to the third floor, the men's quarters, with him right behind. His proximity made me uncomfortable. The room was not much more than an attic, but it held several beds. Some were wide enough for men to sleep with one or more others they had never met.

I inspected the bedding while he watched, a strange expression on his face. I wondered if I did not measure up to what he expected, but dismissed the thought when he began to instruct me on what he wanted done.

Chapter Twenty-Four

Aegeus pointed at the beds. "This is what I want you to work on, today. Start here in the men's room, then go down into the women's section. Clean them top to bottom. Air the bedding and launder what can be washed. Clean the receiving room next. It is the guests' first impression of the inn. If you run out of time, start there first thing tomorrow."

I worked hard, throughout the day, but only finished the guests' quarters. Aegeus worked on foliage that surrounded the front steps and down the sides of the inn. He left around dinner time, calling out he would return. I fixed and ate a quick meal. Shortly after, I started on the receiving room. It was getting dark when I decided to leave the rest until morning.

As I entered the dining area, I startled. Aegeus sat at the table. He shot to his feet. "I am sorry. I did not mean to scare you."

I had not heard him come in. What was he was doing here? We still had tomorrow to get ready for guests. I wondered if he had come to tell me he expected me to buy and prepare the food we would need for a full house. It had taken both Phobie and I to keep on top of that. He stayed and asked me about my home and family, then made meaningless small talk. I was relieved when he finally left.

Aegeus came early, the following morning, but I was up and ready to work. I finished the receiving room and asked him what he wanted me to do next.

"Clean the dining area and then the kitchen. My wife will bring over the food this afternoon, and she will come early tomorrow to prepare it. She insists on a spotless kitchen and will expect you to help with the preparations."

I cleaned the dining area, then dug into the kitchen. Phobie and I always kept it clean, but I wanted the owner's wife to be happy with what she saw. She arrived, a tiny, thin woman with her hair tied up in a scarf. A young girl accompanied her. Both carried baskets loaded with food. They laid them out in the kitchen, after which the woman turned to the girl and jerked her head toward the door. Relief flashed on the helper's face, and she was quick to leave.

The woman's name, I learned later, was Cyanea. She stared at me and frowned. "Why do you wear a veil over your face? Have you been scarred?"

Jolted by her question, my hand flew to my face. I...I was born with an unsightly blemish. I keep it covered so as not to offend people."

She grunted, and I knew she did not believe me. She made no introduction. She simply turned to the food, and began to tell me what I was to do. We worked until dinnertime, with no conversation outside of her orders.

"I will be here early tomorrow. Be up and ready. There is still much to do."

She left and I understood why the girl, who had accompanied her, was eager to escape her presence. This innkeeper was no Phobie.

The rooms filled early, the next day. I found I liked having people around again. Phobie and Teris had lived on site, but it was lonely when we had no guests. Cyanea was well organized. She kept me and the servant girl hopping. But under Cyanea's curt demands, my satisfaction in a job done well changed to an unappreciated obligation.

Weeks passed and I came to value the times when there were no guests, and I could enjoy a quiet dinner in the garden that overlooked the flowers. One evening, as in many others, I knelt before the rose bush that protected my baby's grave. I had decided to call her Rose, in honor of Teris and his tender nurturing of the roses he grew. With gentle strokes, I brushed the leaves and debris from the area, but in my heart, my fingers caressed my little one. It was a poor substitute for the affection my bad decision denied me.

On days when no ships docked, Aegeus came by with instructions for me. I was, usually, busy with the cleanup from the last group of visitors. I knew he was aware he did not have to oversee my progress, but he often hung around and watched me work. Sometimes, he pointed out something I had missed and, occasionally, commended me for a job well done. His presence made me uncomfortable, but I could not have said why.

One day, Cyanea came with him. She went from room to room, seemingly on the lookout for things not done right. When she came into the kitchen where I worked on the extra dishes, she pointed at a large kettle. "You need to scrub the black stains off the bottom of that."

Phobie and I used that kettle over an open fire for hours and it was impossible to keep the bottom shiny. "I will try, but that is our soup kettle, and those stains are burned deep into its bottom."

She gave me the huff, I had come to hate, and turned to her husband. "All seems to be in order. What is it that bothers you...keeps you continually checking on things?"

Aegeus squirmed and avoided eye contact with both of us. "I just want to make sure everything is done right." He gestured at the door. "I need to spend some time on the gate. That broken hinge needs to be repaired. You ready to leave?"

Cyanea looked at him and then at me. Suspicion wrinkled her face. She glared at me and stomped out the door.

Aegeus gave a quick nod and followed. I was glad to see them leave. What was on her mind? Surely, she did not see me as a threat to her marriage.

I saw a lot less of Aegeus, after that. Several times a week, guests came and left a flurry of work that needed be done before the next ship docked. One morning, Cyanea sent her servant girl over early to help me with breakfast.

"The mistress is overwhelmed with a full house at the other inn this morning and cannot leave. She told me to come help you while she and the master take care of guests over there. What would you like me to start on?"

I directed her to break eggs in a large bowl. "What is your name?"

"It is Agatha. And you are Eunice? Right?"

We chatted the whole time we worked. Agatha was a great help. She saw what needed to be done before I thought to ask. We served the last guest and she and I began the cleanup.

"Agatha, you need not stay and help me. I will have all day to finish up here."

"Oh, I would rather..." she stopped and covered her mouth.

I was not sure how to respond. "Well, sometimes it is fun to work on something different. If you do not think Cyanea will mind, I would love to have your help."

"She told me to stay as long as needed. She knows how messy some guests can be."

An impish grin split her lips. "I will tell her there was a lot to do."

As if we had worked together for years, we finished the kitchen and headed for the men's quarters. We chatted about our work, families, and whatever came to mind. I learned she was one of nine children. When her mother birthed another set of twins, her father decided to place Agatha and a few other older siblings for hire. She said she had not minded.

"Our house was small and crowded. We girls slept three to a bed and the boys slept on the floor. To cook for that many was an all-day challenge. My oldest sister stayed with the family and became a second mother to the ones too young to leave home."

I told her I, too, had been hired out to work at an orchard but said little about my home life. We finished the men's area and joked about who had to dump and clean the spittoon. When we entered the women's section, she asked me where I slept.

I pointed to the small alcove at the end of the room. "Over there."

She looked pensive. "I wish mine had a door I could lock."

I had never heard of anyone having a lock on an inside door and thought it a strange thing to say. "Is your room like mine, with the women?"

She paused, her response noticeably suppressed. "No. I have a small area off the kitchen that is open to anyone."

"Well, I suppose it is mostly the owners that walk in. Is it not?"

A grimace twisted her lips. "Yes, that is the trouble. I have no privacy when I dress or bathe. Either of them can march right through...and both have."

The last phrase was barely a whisper, and I almost missed it.

Chapter Twenty-Five

After Agatha left, I could not stop thinking about what she had said... and what she did not say. I could understand her frustration with lack of privacy, but something about her wish for a door she could lock, made me wonder. Cyanea sent her, often, after that first day. Agatha was pleasant to be around, and I appreciated her willing attitude.

Once again, Aegeus frequently came by. I found myself more and more wary of his presence. He never did anything, but he would slip into a room unannounced. He would laugh off my shock and I wondered how long his eyes had followed my every move.

A few weeks after Agatha had helped me, on a regular basis, she showed up with a dark bruise on her cheek.

"Agatha, what happened? Did you fall?"

Her head dipped, and she covered the side of her face with her hand. Something was not right. I put my arm around her, and she burst into tears.

"What is it? Did someone deliberatcly hurt you?'

She snuffed her tears, "It was Cyanea. She caught Aegeus trying to kiss me outside the kitchen and blamed it on me." She gave in to sobs. "I cannot get away from him, Eunice. He follows me around when she has gone to market or is not where she can see us. Cyanea came out to dump some water and saw him with his arms locked around me. She screamed at me and hit me with the pail she carried. Oh, Eunice, what can I do? Aegeus says if I say anything to my father, he will deny it and tell him I did not work hard enough...that I have made it all up so he can justify sending me home."

"Agatha, I am so sorry. How long has this been going on? Has he done this to that other girl that works for them?"

"No, she is his niece and her father would kill him. Aegeus and Cyanea do not get along. They fight all the time and do not even sleep together."

"She must be aware he does this kind of thing."

"I think she is well aware of it. Maybe she blamed me and struck me to save face. It does not matter. I need to find a way to leave that does not cause trouble for my family. Aegeus gets bolder all the time. He finds excuses to wander into my room, unannounced. I am afraid of what he will do next."

A week later, Cyanea informed me that Agatha no longer worked for them. I was told I would have to manage breakfast and everything, myself, until they found more help. My unease around Aegeus grew. If I heard a sound in the night when the inn was empty, I imagined him coming up the stairs and into my bedroom.

I had no way to contact Agatha. I hoped Aegeus had not forced himself upon her. In the weeks that followed, he would find reasons to brush up against me when I cleaned a room or mopped, and then made a joke to cover it. Sometimes, he would mention inappropriate things, like the size of a lady's backside or breasts and watch for my reaction.

I was tending Rose's burial spot, one day, when he stopped and he asked me what I was doing. I did not want to talk to him about her, so I briefly explained she was a baby I had lost early in a pregnancy.

He quickly lowered himself beside me. "Tell me about the baby's father. Do you still see him...love him? Were you married? Did he know you expected a child?"

His eagerness to hear intimate details made me uncomfortable. Why did he want to know?

I told him as little as possible and excused myself on the pretense of much work to do.

He followed me into the kitchen and placed his hands on my shoulders. "I am so sorry about your loss." His fingers moved in a circular motion. "It must be lonely for you here without any family."

I jerked out of reach and grabbed a skillet. His jaw dropped. He looked at the heavy pan and then at me, backed slowly toward the door and muttered, "Well, I will leave you to your work."

I was careful after that to never work in the upper quarters or any isolated rooms when he was around. Cyanea had yet to find a replacement for Agatha. I worked from dawn till after dark when the inn was full and just as hard after the guests left.

Aegeus was busy signing in guests on an occasion when two ships docked, on the same day. Every inn was crammed and both of his were close to full. "You are in luck," he said to a late arrival. "I have one bed left in the men's quarters and one in the women's. Sign right here."

Cyanea brought over food for me to cook for dinner, so I was too busy to notice the latest arrivals. Vegetables to clean and meat to chop consumed my attention until I heard someone call my name. I assumed it was Aegeus and did not look up from the dough I was kneading.

"Too busy to greet an old friend?"

My head jerked in that direction, and I almost screamed, "Pavlos! Welcome back. I am so glad to see you. How long do you plan to stay? Are you after more puppies?"

I knew I rambled, but could not say what really raced through my mind: Do you remember the day we went to the Accu Corinth? Did you ever think of me...miss me? Did you hope you would see me here again?

He laughed. "No, no more puppies. This trip is pure pleasure. Maybe, we can talk in the garden after dinner...like we did before."

I brushed the flour from my hands. "Oh, I would love that."

He laughed and pointed at my face "Do not miss the spot on your nose. See you then."

Cyanea came to help me serve dinner. I saw Pavlos at the long table, seated next to a young woman. Both were engrossed in animated conversation with an older couple, but I thought nothing of it. When the cleanup was finished, I hurried upstairs to freshen myself before I headed for the garden.

As we passed in the hall, a smile lit the face of that same attractive woman "You must be Eunice. I am Frona. Pavlos told me so much about you and the day you two went up the Accu Corinth. I hope we can make that trip, tomorrow."

We? She was with Pavlos? Why would she...? Truth struck like a knife, sharp and unyielding. His pleasure trip was with this vivacious, newly acquired wife.

I swallowed the lump in my throat and nodded. "Yes, I am sure you will love it. How long have you been married?"

For a second, the question twisted her brows. A gusty laugh followed, and she swept aside her long dark hair that fell and covered her face. "No, no we are not married! Pavlos is my brother. He told me all about his former visit to your city. I begged our father, and he finally permitted Pavlos to bring me to Corinth. One last fling before I am betrothed to the son of a family friend. Do you think you could accompany us up the mountain, again?"

I hardly heard her invitation, shaken to my knees by the gnawing despair that had miraculously turned to relief.

Pavlos was already at the little table, off the garden, when I arrived. "It is just as I remembered, but the hyacinths are not in bloom."

"No. That season passed, but the mums are pretty."

I told him the grounds were never the same after Teris died. He asked about Phobie and looked genuinely saddened that she felt a need to sell the inn. "So, how do you like the new owner?"

My hesitation raised his brow. "Not so good, hmm?"

I explained the man and his wife owned this and another inn, were short handed, and left it at that. I asked him how the puppies worked out.

"Those little rascals wormed their way into everyone's heart, but they became great sheepdogs. I am so glad you directed me to them."

Pavlos had registered for four days. While I worked, he took his sister into the city and showed her the temples and marketplace. They returned with Frona loaded with clothes and linens, things she said were hard to find in the Peloponnese. Most guests had left, so the workload was light. Each night, I could not wait to meet Pavlos in the garden.

One night, we walked to the little park, where he had found me grieving for Rose. A light breeze blossomed into a hefty wind, and I shivered. "Cold is nearly upon us. Ships will soon need to winter."

Pavlos pulled my shawl around my shoulders but did not remove his arm. "Yes, and I promised Father I would get Frona safely back before the storms start."

We sat on the lone bench. "Eunice, I have enjoyed being here with you. I regret that we have to leave, day after tomorrow. You have told me almost nothing about yourself. Did you grow up here? Do you have a family?"

I tried to sound casual as I told him my childhood home was a good distance away, and we seldom connected. Superficial information about my father's kilns, of two older brothers who worked with him, and of the loss of a little sister filled in the gaps. My far from normal home life sounded surprisingly ordinary if the ugly details were omitted.

I knew much more could be told, but I could not bring myself to speak of Alistar or Rose and what I had done. Instead, I asked him about his sister.

"Oh, she can convince you of anything. I could hardly believe my father let her come with me, but she has a way with him. By the way, she wants you to go up to the Accu Corinth with us tomorrow. Think you could?"

I stood to go. "Yes, I would relish a day away with you." Color flared on my cheeks. "I mean with both of you. I will ask the owner for a day off."

Pavlos smiled. "I am so glad to see you again, Eunice. I have thought, often, of the day we spent in Corinth and our talks in the garden."

I wished the evening could go on. I floated into the inn and found Aegeus in the front room. A sour expression rose when I told him I wanted to take the next day off.

"You know there will be a lot to do when the guests leave after breakfast."

"I am sorry, but an old friend stayed with us last night, and I want to spend time with him and his sister."

"You mean the one from the Peloponnese? Keep your guard up. Those southerners live a different lifestyle than we are used to."

I hid my disgust and did not ask what he meant. The next day, the three of us left after I finished the breakfast cleanup.

Chapter Twenty-Six

Frona was a delight. She ooed and awed over everything she saw. Once again, we had lunch by the fountain before we headed for the Accu Corinth. Pavlos managed to sit as close to me as possible. I was in a much better place this time and quickly dismissed the ugly memories that threatened to ruin the day.

It was sunny and warm for late Fall, but the breeze grew stronger as we climbed. I held my veil in place, sure Frona had noticed it and wondered about my face. We found that same flat rock, as last time, and the three of us sat and admired the view. When Frona's attention was elsewhere, Pavlos reached over and squeezed my hand.

I wanted to stay there forever.

After a while, Frona asked to go see the ruins of Aphrodite's temple.

I jumped to my feet. "Sure, it is a short walk from here."

Pavlos shrugged. "You two go...I will wait here."

His sister teased, "Oh, come on...too worn out for a little jaunt?"

He gazed back at the ports. "I have seen it. You go."

Something in his tone must have struck and his sister quit teasing. The two of us began the trek. All the way, Frona peppered me with questions about the temple. I filled her in with all I knew. She was, especially, fascinated by the belief that the goddess was born from the foam of the sea. Like nearly everyone who first sees what was left of the structure, she stood in awe and quietly admired it. A short distance from the fallen pillars and remaining facade, we saw a group of young women enjoying the grassy slopes.

She pointed at them. "Look Eunice, who do you think they are?"

It was not hard to decipher as they were dressed in temple garb. "Those are the temple's priestesses. They live in the city's new temple and serve the goddess from there." I was hoping to avoid a conversation about their duties. Frona was young, and I had no idea how much she knew or could understand about something so depraved. But the girl was not satisfied until she heard the sordid reason for their existence.

It became obvious facts about prostitution were not new to her. I tried to explain how the priestesses deemed it as their religious obligation. But, when I mentioned that it happened in brothels down in the city with sailors, or any man willing to pay for their favors, even Roman officials, her hand flew to her mouth.

"Oh...now I understand."

I had no idea what she referred to. "Understand what?"

"It is my brother. I know why he did not want to come up here."

Before I could ask, she touched my arm. "Eunice, I can see Pavlos cares for you. I probably should not tell you this, but he has little tolerance for women who resort to this kind of lifestyle."

"But, but I—"

"I know, it does not make sense, but Pavlos was once betrothed to a young woman who...well, she resorted to prostitution to keep her family from losing their estate. I am not even sure prostitution fits her situation. It happened when the Roman who held the debt on her father's property convinced her that if she slept with him one time, he would cancel the debt and the family would keep their home.

"Her mother was occupied with several younger children and her father was not well enough to do manual labor, so she saw no other way out. When Pavlos found out about it he was furious...first at her, then at the Roman who coerced her into the agreement. The sad thing was, after Pavlos' betrothed gave herself to the man, he reneged on the promise and she was helpless to prove his deceit."

"Oh, Frona. That is terrible. The poor girl... poor Pavlos."

"Yes, he was torn between disgust and feelings that lingered for her, but my father found out and refused to let Pavlos marry her. And that is not the worst of it. The girl's father died, and shortly after, she took her own life. I do not know what happened to the mother and other children... probably, sold into slavery."

I shuddered as I remembered Pavlos' strange reaction when I answered his questions about the priestesses. His mood had changed and suddenly he wanted to leave the mountain he had so enjoyed moments before.

Frona and I joined him on the rock before we started for the city. My mind whirled with what his sister had shared. It did not take long before my thoughts ran to what his father's reaction would be to my past. Unmarried, but living with Alistar as though we were, rejected as a wife, pregnant, and then my deceptive decision that caused my baby's death... no, there was no way I would be accepted.

As my dream of a future with Pavlos diminished, I tried to keep things light. But my hopes had crashed like an avalanche of mud that smothered every possible escape and left nothing to salvage.

Frona and Pavlos were the inn's only remaining guests, so I quickly fixed them a light supper and excused myself, with an explanation that I had much to catch up on.

I thought I had avoided a painful encounter, but Pavlos searched till he found me about to empty the garbage. He asked me to meet him when I finished. I could not think of a believable excuse to put him off but vowed to keep it brief.

"You have been quiet since we left the mountain, Eunice. Is something wrong?"

My insides shook and I fought to keep my tears in check. Such a gentle person did not deserve another betrayal. How I wished Frona had not told me what she did, but I knew it was for the best. To have my past come out after we had invested more of our hopes in one another, would make it worse.

I began to ramble about all I needed to do, when Pavlos took my hand and looked into my eyes. "Eunice, I do not know what it is that has bothered you, but every memory I treasured of you while back home has been confirmed in these last few days. I have come to care deeply for you and would like you to come with me tomorrow, to my home, to meet my family."

The depth of hunger in his voice nearly broke my resolve. How I had longed to hear those words. But now... I took a deep breath. I needed to leave before the fervor in my own heart overtook my better judgment. It would be such a comfort to convince myself that I could go with him and hide my past from everyone. After all, the Peloponnese was a long way from here and who would know?

I forced my voice not to quiver. "Pavlos, I am fond of you too, but we hardly know each other. Perhaps if you come back when ships sail in the spring, you could stay longer, and we can see if this is right for each of us."

Disappointment engulfed his face, but I could not build a life on a lie. It was better to end it now than to destroy his future with the revelation he had fallen for another tainted woman.

Chapter Twenty-Seven

The next morning, I waved Pavlos and Frona off with a heavy heart and a phony smile. I called out, "I will see you in the spring." I did not yet know how I would manage to renege on that promise, but I had to find a way. The ship disappeared and tears, I had denied all night, flowed in abandon.

I was grateful no arrivals were expected. By midmorning, I pulled myself together and began to clean things I had postponed to spend the day with Pavlos. In the women's quarters, I found a note on Frona's bed.

Dear Eunice, I have tried to understand why you refused to come with us and meet our family. Surely, you know how much Pavlos loves you. I want to assure you that he is more than ready to move on, so please do not let what I told you on the mountain deter you. He confided in me how much he wants you for his wife, and I want you for a sister. Please wait for him. He plans to be on the first vessel that sails in the spring. With love, Frona.

I wanted to run all the way to the port and beg them to take me with them. Instead, I spent another hour in tears. That afternoon, Aegeus stopped in to check on my progress.

"Looks like you are doing fine, Eunice. Cyanea has found a replacement for Agatha. A large ship is docking tomorrow, and we expect to be full, probably for the last time this year. She will be over tomorrow to help you prepare dinner.

I was surprised they hired someone so close to the end of the season. Aegeus hung around and tried to make small talk. "How was your outing yesterday?"

"It was good."

"You said that man was an old friend...how long since you have seen him?" "Probably a year." I wished Aegeus would leave. I was in no mood for his meaningless chatter.

"And that was his sister with him? How did —"

"I really need to work on the receiving room. Please excuse me." I left the kitchen and threw myself into a superficial effort to appear busy in the already spotless room. He followed me but my sparse answers finally discouraged him. He mumbled his disgust and left.

We only had a few guests, once a week, as the sailing season wound down. I spent some of the empty hours in the garden, surprised at how much I enjoyed tidying up the flowerbeds for winter. It was impossible to keep my mind off

Pavlos. Maybe I had been hasty. Maybe I should have... I shook it off. I had done the right thing.

The new girl, hired to help me, was a disappointment. Unlike Agatha, I had to continually tell her or show her what to do. It did not matter, as she quit after two weeks. I wondered if Aegeus had invaded her privacy, too.

To my surprise, Cyanea showed up one morning. I rarely saw her, which was fine with me. She inspected the kitchen and dining area, then complimented me on their condition. I did not know what to think. It was so unlike her. Why was she here?

Our small talk soon faltered and left an awkward lull. She forced a smile. "You have done a good job over here, Eunice. Is there anything that we need to go over...discuss?" She stood close to the hearth and worked her hands as if they needed to be warmed.

I had no idea what she had in mind, so I mentioned some minor needs. "I think most things are in good shape. Perhaps, you could replace the broom. It is pretty worn and the handle on the oven needs to be fixed. It comes loose and could be dangerous. Is there something you want me to know?"

She squirmed, her answer almost an apology. "No, no. I... we just want to take care of things."

I did not know what to say and was relieved when she headed for the door. "All right. I will replace the broom and tell Aegeus about the oven handle." Before I could respond, she was out onto the porch and down the path that connected the inns. I stared after her. What was that about? The more I rehearsed our conversation, the more I knew she never really arrived at the reason for her visit.

Aegeus came to work on the oven door the next day. Most days, he continued to find reasons to hang around. Once sailing halted for the winter, he announced his plans to do a deep cleaning of the men's section. My suspicions rose like fog over the Gulf's warm waters. I had cleaned it thoroughly after our final group, and he knew it.

Winter was nearly upon us, and already I had grown weary of his unnecessary visits. That room was small, and the thought of being in close quarters with him left me uneasy. "Why do you not look and see if I missed anything."

"I know you cleaned up there, but all the bedding must be washed or aired so it will be ready for the spring rush. Come up with me and I will help carry it to the washroom."

I grimaced but followed him up the stairs. He began to pull the bedding loose and pile it on the floor. I had bent over to take hold of some sheets when I felt his hand slide from my waist down my thigh. I shot up and glared at him. "I do not appreciate your touching me. I work for you, but I am not your property. If this ever happens again, I will inform your wife and resign my position immediately."

He faked a shocked expression. "Oh, I did not touch you on purpose. I must have brushed up against you when I reached for those quilts."

My insides shook as I stormed from the room, the bedding left where it lay. I knew he did not want to lose me. I worked hard and practically ran the inn. He brought several loads of sheets and blankets down before the back door closed.

To my relief, after that, he stayed away. The winter dragged on and I longed for spring. Without Phobie to talk to, it was lonely. Plans for how to avoid an encounter with

Pavlos ran nonstop through my mind. Mostly, I hoped he would find someone else and not return, or that the long separation would bring him a change of heart. I knew I did not mean it, but reality said I needed a plan. I could not desert the inn when the busy season was upon us.

One night, I awoke to find Aegeus standing beside my bed. I screamed and drew the blankets to my chest.

He held a small lamp and a blanket. "Shhh, Eunice. It is only me. The temperature has dropped and it is quite cold. I came to see if you had enough blankets."

I was terrified. How could I defend myself if he...

He sat on the side of my bed and touched the bedding that covered my leg.

"We are all a family here and need to look out for each other. I really like you, Eunice. You are such a good worker and so pretty, I—"

I sat straight up and pulled a deep breath. "I want you to leave, right now." With all the force I could muster, I added. "You do not belong in my bedchamber. It is... inappropriate." I hoped I sounded like I knew what was right and proper.

"Oh, do not be upset. We could be good friends and I—"

"Leave now, or I will tell Cyanea that you came here like this."

He stood to his feet. "Now you know I meant no harm. I just wanted to check to make sure—"

I shrieked, not caring if anyone heard me. "Get out of here!"

He backed up and sneered. "Who would want a woman with hair on her face anyway?" He stopped by the door. "I would not mention this to anyone. No one would believe someone who looks like you. Your face is proof of evil."

I listened for his footsteps to reach the first floor and for the sound of the door shutting. I could not stop shaking, so afraid he might return.

His words tore at my heart, an echo of those spoken by my older brother. I tried to dismiss them, still the remark tortured. Pavlos had not thought I was evil. He wanted me for his wife. Why would a man, I could never have, be the only one who saw me as a woman worthy of his love?

In time, I rose and lit a candle. It did not take long to pack. I glanced at Phobie's pelican. "I am sorry, My Friend. I, too, have to desert your prize possession. Maybe some kind soul will find it and treasure it like you did."

I went downstairs and gathered some food for the road. The first strains of dawn found me out in the garden saying goodbye to Rose. I looked back at the inn that had been a safe harbor for three years, swallowed the lump in my throat, and headed for the city.

Once again, I belonged nowhere and to no one.

Chapter Twenty-Eight

Braced against the cold, I entered the market. Thankfully, I remembered to fetch my heaviest shawl. I found a bench near a booth that buffeted the wind and waited, for what, I did not know. Gratitude flowed for having escaped Aegeus' clutches. I wondered how he would explain my leaving to Cyanea.

The market came to life as shop owners and daily vendors began their set ups. Nearly two years ago, I had once helped Alistar or his father, lay out and display the meat we had brought to sell for the day. I determined to be grateful for what I learned that year about how to sell merchandise and refused to dwell on how it ended.

Back then, a merchant of fine fabrics had offered me a job with very good prospects. I toyed with the idea of finding him, but quickly dismissed it. His stand was too close to Alistar's father's booth. I found someone who sold hot tea and let it warm me while I ate the bread and cheese I had brought. For more times than I could count, I second guessed my decision not to go with Pavlos. It did not help. I always ended with the assurance I had done the right thing.

I wandered among the booths, along the stoa, and examined things upon which I dared not squander money. I hoped to find a merchant who needed to hire someone, and more urgently, a safe, warm niche where I could sleep. Spring hinted at its arrival, but was still weeks away. A couple of hours later, I gave up on a place to find work and concentrated on the approaching night.

A temple I had seen, when Pavlos and I spent a day in the city, came to mind. It was a shrine to Asklepios, a god of healing. Maybe I could go in before dark and find a nook to hide in till dawn.

The sun was still bright and the walk into the city warmed me. By late afternoon, I found the temple. It bore a beautiful marble façade, but the aura depressed me. People came and went, some with obvious needs. One lady carried a replica of the arm I assumed she wanted the god to heal, and another limped in with what appeared to be a knee joint carved from olive wood. Behind them, an elderly person on a slate mat was laboriously dragged through the door by a younger man who bore a strong resemblance. None stayed very long.

While it was still light, I ventured in to see what it was like. Perhaps, I could find a place to shelter where I would not be discovered. I passed through the entrance and was confronted by a grey-haired woman whose haggard face made me suspect she, too, needed the healing line.

Her loud, expectant tone startled me. "And what malady do you wish our god to heal?"

I had not anticipated that. My hand rose to the hidden disfigurement on my face, and for a moment I could only stare.

Her face softened. "It is all right. Your need will be kept in confidence."

Could this god heal my unsightly blemish? It had never occurred to me to seek healing. But, what if... At the possibility, my insides lurched. I clutched my stomach, speechless. I had yet to rally enough courage to ask when the woman gave a sympathetic nod.

"Oh, female problems. Do not be embarrassed. We see a lot of young women who suffer with that. Take the aisle to your right and it will lead you to someone who will guide you to the source of help you seek."

The moment had passed. I felt foolish and deceitful. I should have left the building, but the lobby was crowded with people plagued with legitimate needs. The woman gestured for me to move on, so I swallowed my disappointment and obliged. The enormity of the place was impressive. On the outer walls were several little inlets that would serve my purpose... if I could ignore the pile of fake body parts left behind by grateful or desperate people.

At the end of the aisle, a group of young women stood before an altar. Carved upon it stood the figure of a lovely woman in a flowery gown. She lifted her hands in a surrender-like pose, her countenance a picture of peace.

Each candidate bowed before it, lifted her arms in a like manner and chanted something I could not understand. Behind the altar, a man with a crown of leaves wreathed around his bald head waited. He wore a white tunic that criss-crossed his chest. In his hand, he held a golden rod. Undeniable authority poured from his expression. As each girl finished her petition, he touched the scepter to the top of her head.

I searched for a way to avoid the ritual, but the man motioned me forward. My face flushed but I complied. Would his god tell him I was a phony? Like those before me, I bowed and lifted my arms. I did not know how to chant, so I made up some words and repeated them over and over. The attendant looked at me somewhat strangely, but finally crowned me as he had the others. With forced restraint, I resisted the urge to run and walked slowly to the exit.

At twilight, all the attendants left. No one locked the entrance nor posted a guard. I waited another hour then approached the door. It opened without a sound. I stepped in and quickly pulled it shut. It was dark, but a few oil lamps and candles lit the hall. As I followed the route I had taken earlier, my eyes adjusted. At the first cove I came upon, I crept in as deeply as possible.

My heavy shawl blanketed the marble floor with enough fabric to cover most of me. Thankfully, the temperature had not dipped like it had a few days past. My mind wrestled to remember the name of the woman Phobie gave me before she boarded her ship to Athens. I had not thought about it since that day. What was it she said? That the woman would help me with whatever problems came into my life? I pondered the possibility as I fell asleep, but her name escaped me and I had no idea what I had done with the slip of paper upon which Phobie wrote it.

The night seemed long. I awoke several times and wondered where I was. An hour or so before dawn, footsteps sent me deeper into the cove. I tried not to breathe and hoped the darkness hid me. A man with a hunched back passed. I thought he had not seen me, but he backed up and aimed his lamp at me.

He glared at me and his tone was laced with anger as he spoke. "What are you doing in there? You were hired to sweep the place, not sleep. Get up and get to work before the early seekers arrive." Hands on hips, he sat the light on the floor and thrust a broom at me.

I forced my insides to quiet and decided to play along. "I am sorry. I decided to rest a bit until it was time. I am new and no one told me when to begin the work."

He harrumphed and muttered about lazy help as he made his way down the next hall. I rose and started to sweep with one eye on him and the other on the door. He looked back a few times and seemed satisfied with my progress. When he was out of sight, I grabbed my shawl and parcel and hurried through the dark to the exit.

My stomach growled. I had finished the food from the inn, and dawn was still a good way off. I aimed to target the first vendor with bread and cheese. I waited on a bench in front of Apollo's temple. A young woman, dressed in the Aphrodite's priestess' garb, came out of a tavern across the way.

She wandered over and sat beside me. "Hello. We do not see many young women here, alone, at this hour of the morning. Are you all right?" Her smile was warm, and I was touched that she cared to inquire about my welfare.

"I ah...I am between jobs and hope something will open up when the merchants arrive."

"Oh, you should join us at the temple. Aphrodite always has room for a young girl like yourself. How old are you?"

"Fifteen, but I do not think..."

"Oh you would be perfect. You are slim and pretty. The sailors would love you."

Her enthusiasm for such a scornful profession amazed me. I tried to hide my horror, stood to my feet, and backed away. "Thank you for your interest, I do not think I would make a good candidate. But I wish you well. Goodbye."

I turned and walked swiftly toward the market. In my haste, I ran headlong into a Roman soldier.

He looked beyond me. "So, what is your hurry? Is someone after you?"

"No. No, I was..." I could not think of anything that sounded believable.

"It will not be light for a while. Are you a temple priestess?"

Was he looking for a prostitute? Stories about abuse at the hand of these soldiers terrified me, so my answer was emphatic.

"No, absolutely not."

"Well then, what brings you out at such an hour? It can be dangerous on these streets in the dark."

I told him the truth. "I have left my position at one of the inns and I wanted to be here when the market opens. I hope to find someone who needs help."

He twisted his lips as if deep in thought. "Can you clean, cook, and wash clothes?" Caution swelled in my chest. Why would he ask? "Yes, I..."

"Yesterday, my captain said he needed to find new household help. Come meet him.

It is just a few blocks from here."

Should I trust him? My instincts said I could. Anyway, it would not hurt to look into it.

Chapter Twenty-Nine

I had to scurry to keep up with the soldier. He did not look back, but moved as if he were on a mission. No lamps burned in the curtained windows of the homes we passed. He turned down an alley and I began to wonder if I had made a mistake. Before I had time to decide, he grabbed a gate at the back of one of the houses and gestured for me to follow.

I swallowed my apprehension and stepped through the entrance. He knocked on the door and in seconds a small, raged-dressed young man pushed it open a crack.

The soldier barked. "Tell the captain I may have found the help he hoped to find."

Fear leapt from the youth's face. He nodded, but did not invite us in. When he returned, he pointed at a patio just outside the back door and mumbled, "The captain said you should wait there. He just woke up and will be out, in time."

I sat on a bench, but the soldier paced. I wondered what kept him on edge. At last, he stopped, eyed the sky, and crossed his arms. "My shift is about up. I have men to dismiss and properties I need to secure. Tell the captain that his first officer brought you here and the reason."

Dawn had yet to lighten the sky. I looked around and hugged my upper arms. How would I protect myself if...?

He noticed. "You will be fine. No one would dare accost you anywhere near the captain's house." He picked up the sword and shield, he had leaned against the fence, and left.

I sat there and tried not to shiver. Why was it always coldest moments before sunrise? In time, the smell of bacon wafted from the house. Minutes later, the odor changed to burnt biscuits.

A man's voice blared from inside. "Can you not do anything right? I want breakfast, not burnt offerings! Be gone with you, and do not come back."

As if the house itself had caught fire, the young man who told us where to wait, scrambled out the door. Behind him, a stocky man dressed in a nightshirt with rumpled hair, followed. "And do not expect to be paid for your incompetent service. "

He was about to shut the door when he saw me. He squinted then snarled, "Well, what are you doing here? You with him?"

I gulped to retrieve my voice. "No, I ah...I came... I mean your first officer brought me here."

"Why? You under arrest? What did you do?" He looked ready to pounce.

I shook and inhaled a quick breath. "No, no, nothing. I hoped to find work in the market, and while I waited for it to open, he suggested I talk to you. He said you needed household help."

The man's face softened. "Can you cook?"

I nodded.

"Then get in there and show me. I need breakfast and I am due to meet with my men in less than an hour."

I followed and he pointed at an open area. "There is the kitchen." Before I thought to ask anything, he disappeared behind a curtained doorway.

I stepped in and surveyed a filthy mess. The floor was sticky with what was hard to decipher. Dirty towels hung on chairs and unwashed dishes piled near the water pump. I cleared a spot to set aside the burned pan of food. There were plenty of eggs, so I scrambled them with feta cheese and tomatoes. Dried food on the table turned my stomach. I scrubbed it clean and set a place with some sliced olive bread to add to the main dish.

The captain brushed aside the curtain and looked at the food. He wore the complete uniform of a Roman soldier. With a sweep of his hand, he brushed his red cape to one side and sat down to eat. "This is more like it." With his mouth stuffed with eggs, he reached for the bread and asked, "What is your name? You say my officer found you near the market? Not a safe place for a woman after dark."

"My name is Eunice. I left the inn where I worked and hoped to find a merchant who needed help."

"Well, if you can clean and wash uniforms as well as you cook, you can stay and work for me. I will pay you a drachma a week and, of course, your room and board."

He rose, grabbed his helmet, and gestured behind him. "Over there is a storage room with a small alcove where you can sleep. Most of the time, I am gone all day but will expect a warm dinner each evening. The people in the market know me. Tell them whatever you need, and they will hand it over and charge it to me."

He left and I sat in silence. What had I gotten myself into? He seemed to be a decent man. Maybe this would work for both of us. I fixed myself some food and tackled the kitchen.

It was early afternoon before I could get to the market. There would be plenty of time to prepare dinner, so I bought some small hens. At a produce stand, when I told the woman to charge my selections to the captain, her brows rose.

"So, he finally found a cook, huh?" She looked me over and muttered something I barely heard. "Yeah, he likes them young."

I wondered why she said "cook" with that tone, and "he likes them young." An uneasy feeling crept up my chest. I had escaped one lecherous man and was not about to take on another. I marched my parcels back to the captain's house determined to set the record straight.

At sundown, dinner waited over banked coals on his wood burning stove. Over and over, I rehearsed what I planned to say to him. "I am here to clean and cook and will not put up with any advances you might have in mind."

He charged through the door before dark and tossed his gear on the receiving room floor. "Whatever that is smells wonderful." He stopped at a wash stand, headed straight for the table, and looked expectantly at me.

My bravado sank. Maybe it would be better to feed him first. I hurried to the stove and filled a shallow bowl with a large portion of the stewed hens and vegetables. He finished that in a hurry and asked for more.

I dished up another, large serving and added some bread left over from the morning. "I am sorry I did not have time to bake. There was so much to clean and —"

"This is fine. I see you scoured the place. The boy, you replaced, could neither cook nor clean. I would have tossed him out the first day if he..."

The captain bit off a huge hunk of bread and did not finish. I wondered what the "if" was. It struck me that his last cook was not a young girl but a boy. Could that woman at the market have been mistaken about him? While he ate, I watched him closely. He never glanced my way or showed any interest in me. I decided to give it a few days before I said anything.

He left the house an hour later. For the first time, I inspected the storage room and saw where he meant for me to sleep. There was no door on the small alcove. My thoughts ran to Agatha and how she would have hated the lack of privacy. The blankets smelled like they had not been washed in a long time. I sighed and laid my shawl over tomorrow's first priority.

I had blown out my candle but was still awake when I heard the captain return. I listened carefully to where he walked, relieved his footsteps stayed in the opposite side of the house.

After I heard nothing for a good while, I relaxed and fell asleep.

Chapter Thirty

I never knew what the captain's mood might be. Often, seemed preoccupied with things he never spoke of. Under his breath, he would grumble, as if I should sympathize with whatever ills his day brought. I'd noted what he liked best for dinner and varied it with hopes a welcomed choice would cheer him up.

One evening, I spread skewers of pork and vegetables before him. I added a generous portion of fried potatoes and set a small pitcher with lemon sauce beside his plate. "Here's the souvlaki you are so fond of, Captain."

All I heard was "hmmm," but he attacked the food like a jackal over a lion's kill. In minutes, as if he feared the beast might return to reclaim its rightful prey, he devoured all before him. I wondered who the "beasts" in his life were? The emperor? His superior? The head magistrate of Corinth?

It wasn't unusual for soldiers in his unit to stop by at dawn or after sunset to update him on uprisings, arrests, or disturbances. Early on, he made sure I understood he was responsible to keep the peace and oversee everything that occurred in his district, night, or day. He never told me where he would be, and I hated to answer the door after dark when he wasn't there. His orders: I should refer any soldier who came for him to take their requests to his first officer.

Late one evening, I was surprised to find, not a soldier, but the heavy-set young woman who lived next door. We'd chatted casually near our gate a few times and I knew her name.

"Eleni, I am so surprised to see you... is something wrong?"

She pushed back the dark shawl that covered her copper-colored hair and peered around me. "Is the captain home?"

"No, he's out. Is there a problem? Can I help?"

She seemed relieved to find me alone and I motioned her into the sitting room. Until the lamplight shone on her face, I didn't see the bruises or notice her torn tunic.

"Eleni, what happened? You're hurt."

She collapsed onto a couch and held her head in her hands. Blustery sobs poured in such a torrent they shook the excess flesh that hung from her upper arms. "It's Stelios. He lost his position at the docks and drank himself into a stupor. He says it's my fault. If I weren't so heavy, he might be able to secure a better position. I've grown so tired of his tendency to blame me for his failures. I screamed back that if he were a better worker and didn't drink so much... that's when he hit me."

I knew Stelios was her husband. I'd caught a glimpse of him a few times. A surly-faced man who always seemed focused on the ground.

Eleni touched her cheek and winced. "I tried to run from him, but he grabbed my tunic and wouldn't let go. I thought he intended to kill me, so I reached for a nearby statue of Aphrodite and hit him on his head. Eunice, I'm scared. He fell and hasn't moved." Her tone increased to panic. What if I killed him? What should I do?"

I tried to process what I'd heard, but my head just wagged. I swallowed the shock and found my voice. "Eleni, we have to go over and see how he is. No matter what, he may need help."

She pulled herself together and the two of us headed for her door. I dreaded what we might find. She went in first. I could see furniture upturned and trinkets and dishes smashed on the floor.

She called his name, her tone hopeful. "Stelios, are you here?" There was no answer. The lamps had burned out, but she found an undamaged and lit the wick.

I saw him first. He lay on the floor, doubled up, as if he had sunk slowly into the position and never moved. Eleni heard my gasp.

"Oh, Stelios!" She dropped beside him. "Stelios, wake up, it's me, Eleni."

My heart hammered. Was he dead? "Eleni, put your hand there on his neck. Do you feel any pulse?"

She did as I demonstrated. In seconds her voice rose. "I can't find anything. Eunice, please, will you try?"

I bent down and turned him on his back. A large lump bulged on the side of his forehead. There was no pulse, no breath, no sign of life. "Eleni, I'm afraid he's gone.

"No, no! I didn't mean to kill him. I never wanted him dead, I just wanted him to stop hurting me." She fell back on her knees, overtaken by hysterics.

I had no idea what to do. Should we notify the authorities and tell them what happened? What if they didn't believe her... arrested her?

Through the window I caught a glimpse of the captain headed home for the night.

"Eleni, the captain is home. He'll know what to do. I'll be right back."

She rose to her knees, eyes wide with fear. "No, you can't tell him, he'll..."

I didn't wait for her to finish. I ran outside and called, "Captain, Captain, wait."

He stopped in front of the door. A frown twisted his face as I approached. Perturbed, I suspected that I wasn't where he expected me to be. In broken gasps, I poured out what happened. With one fist on his hip, he listened, then grimaced.

"You get inside." His gesture left no options.

"But Eleni may need me, she's..."

"No. I've known these people for a long time, and this is no surprise. You stay here. Is that clear?"

I nodded and went in. One window faced Eleni's house, but for a long while I saw and heard nothing. At some point, the captain came out into the yard and flagged down a passerby. I saw him point and give instructions before the man took off in a run.

Not long after, four men dressed in Roman togas arrived in a carriage. They hurried into the house. Soon, two of them carried out Stelios' shrouded body. They laid it in the cargo area, didn't return to the house, but simply waited.

It grew late, but I knew I wouldn't sleep until I found out what would happen to our neighbor. And what did the captain mean when he said this was no surprise? Out of the dark, I heard a scream. Seconds later, the other two men forced Eleni to walk between them toward their carriage. Hands tied behind her back, she stumbled.

Her cry carried through the night, "No! No! You don't understand. It was an accident. He beat me. I had to defend myself or die. "

The officials didn't pause. One said something I couldn't hear, then shoved her into the carriage and they took off.

I jumped away from the window before the captain opened the door. He looked right at me and scowled.

I tried to keep tremors from my voice. "What happened?"

He scoffed. "Civilians!" She killed him, and they've taken her to prison."

"But... but he hit her. She was afraid for her life."

He looked at me as if I were an imbecile. "Listen, Eunice, after years of squabbling the man's wife found a legitimate reason to be rid of him and acted on it. It's over." He started for his room, then turned back. "Women need to learn their place, and it would be better if you stuck to the house and didn't involve yourself in people's affairs."

With that, he disappeared into his room. I stood there for a long time trying to process all I'd seen and what the captain thought about his neighbors. I struggled to reconcile what happened to Eleni and her fate. So what if they fought in the past and even hit each other? Wasn't she entitled to defend herself if her life was in danger?

And what did the captain mean by "women need to learn their place?" Was a woman to suffer at a man's whim if he decided to abuse her? My heart ached for Eleni. Maybe she was less than a perfect wife, but she didn't deserve to be punished because she defended herself. What if she were the one found dead? Would they have justified her husband's actions?

How could I stay and work for a man who took such a position? Did I have a choice? Besides my grandfather and Pavlos, my opinion of men dropped even lower. I'd met few men I could vouch for. Why did I expect him to be different? Maybe being alone isn't such a bad way to live. At least I would be somewhat distanced from a world that sees women as lesser persons.

Chapter Thirty-One

The captain never mentioned the incident after that night... not that he ever really talked to me about anything. I thought of Eleni often and wondered what became of her. Anger, I did not know where to place, grew into resentment of men in general.

People cleaned out Eleni's house and, soon, new neighbors moved in. I heeded the captain's advice and kept my distance. But I was lonely. I missed having someone like Phobie to share my day with.

When the cleaning and washing were caught up, I often wandered into the city or went to the market. It became second nature to scan crowds for those I wanted to avoid. I never forgot that my father or Alistar, or even the owners of the inn I had left, could appear at any venue.

The evenings dragged. The captain went out most nights. If he had a tough day, he went to bed shortly after dinner. Sometimes after I tidied the kitchen and it was still light, I walked to a small park, similar to the one where Pavlos and I had sat and talked. Most nights, an elderly man shuffled over and lowered his bent body beside me on the park's only bench. His white hair caught the glow of the setting sun, coloring his thick tresses pink or orange.

He reminded me of my Grandfather. For several evenings, he simply nodded. One night, he said hello and asked me my name. At first, I was cautious. Men did not normally talk to women. He said his name was Kyros, and I sensed he was lonely too. Our conversations soon leapt from how hot or cold it was, to our lives. He asked where I was from, and I shared briefly about my family. In turn, he told me of his son, his only living child.

Once he asked, "Tell me, Eunice, how is it you always come here alone? Does not your husband care to come along?"

I felt my face flush. "I do not have a husband. I work for a Roman captain who lives a couple of blocks from here." He asked about my responsibilities and what I did when I had time off. One conversation led to another and soon we knew a lot about each other.

His wife had died after a long illness, years ago, and he lived with his son and daughter-in-law. Sifting through what he did not say, I sensed his son's wife was not pleased with the arrangement.

He walked with a cane, so I asked, " Do you live very far from here?"

"No, about the same as you, but in the other direction. It is a short distance." His head drooped and he cleared his throat. "It can be good to get out and leave the young people to themselves sometimes."

A light breeze permeated the silence that followed. Neither of us felt a need to cover it with meaningless chatter.

He shifted his body with a slight groan and looked directly at me. "Tell me more about the grandfather you mentioned. Is he still alive?"

I told him about my grandfather's estate in the Peloponnese where he bred horses, and of the joy his visits brought to my childhood. I added that he died before I left home. My eyes filled, and unexpected tears spilled down my cheeks as I spoke.

Kyros reached over and patted my hand. "I see you are a woman who loves much, Eunice. That is a great blessing. Do not let the things you see and hear in this life change you. Forgive and continue to give and love people. It will be a mainstay when the tough times come."

I walked back with a lighter step. How I relished Kyros' words. Surely, as his name implied, he had been sunshine to me. My spirits lifted the way they had after a visit from my grandfather. For the first time in years, I thought about the advice he gave me after I lost my little sister, Chara, at the market.

It was an accident...not your fault...do not carry the guilt or let the incident destroy you.

And now here was Kyros, telling me it is a blessing to be a woman who loves. I thought about my reaction to Eleni's unfair treatment. In some mysterious way, Kyros' counsel helped me release the animosity that had mounted in my heart towards men.

I was asleep when the captain returned, but later I thought I heard voices, even a muffled cry. I leaned up on one elbow to listen, then adjusted my pillow. It must have been a dream.

He finished his breakfast the next morning, but stopped before he rushed out the door. As if something important struck him, he jerked back toward me. "Oh, I brought ah....a guest home with me last night. He is still asleep, but I told him you would give him something to eat when he wakes."

He left no time for questions. I thought about peeking into his room to see where the other man slept. The house had only one bedroom and no other beds. It was well past midmorning when I heard movements. I began to fry some bacon and soon the curtain parted. To my surprise, a boy about twelve or thirteen stepped into the room. I tried to hide my shock, grateful he did not seem to notice.

He smoothed his hair with his hands, walked over to the table, and sat down. "Captain said you would fix me some breakfast, Missus."

I nodded and turned to the stove, but not before I noticed he wore Aphrodite's gold trimmed, white tunic. Most prostitutes who wore the identifying colors were young women. I had never seen a youth in these garments until Phobie once pointed one out at the market. I felt sick as I imagined what went on only a room away from where I had slept. He looked so young.

Like my brothers, without a word, he wolfed down the food. I tried not to stare at the angry red blotches that stood out amidst the pimples on his face and neck... whisker burns, I assumed.

His voice squeaked when he spoke. "Do you think the captain would mind if I bathed before I leave?"

I was astounded but managed to close my jaw and keep my voice even. "Well...I, I guess it would be all right." The captain bathed in a tub in his room, so I told him to wait while I heated some water.

"You do not have to do that. We are not allowed to heat water at the temple, so I am used to cold water baths."

I pointed at the back door. "The pump is outside and a bucket is next to it. Feel free to get as much water as you need and put it in the captain's room. I will lay out a towel for you."

For the first time he smiled. It was the grin of a little boy, comfortable in his mother's care. I cleaned up the dishes, while he bathed. Where had he come from? How did he end up being a male prostitute? Where was his family?

I cringed at the memories my thoughts unearthed. Where were my loved ones when I was that age? Perhaps he too had to escape a home where he was not wanted, or worse, where no one valued him. My vision blurred as pictures of the rejection I had endured resurfaced. I wiped my eyes and chastised myself. Why dig up what I thought I had buried years ago?

He brought the towel to me, neatly folded, and carried his bath water outside. My heart wept for the life he led. I wished I could have washed his tunic or done something for him... anything.

Before he left, he ducked his head inside the door. "Thank you for your kindness, Missus, and for the breakfast. Reminded me of my mother before she, before..." His voice broke and he turned his face to one side. "Thanks again. Cannot be late... temple's harsh on rule breakers."

With a quick wave, he jogged to the gate. I knew I would never see him again, but his likeness would forever be imprinted on my soul.

I sighed. The commitment of Aphrodite's prostitutes was known to be unbending, but I had never witnessed the humanity of one up close. I thought about the day Pavlos and I visited the temple ruins and the haunting within, that forewarned it one day would affect my life. Was this it? To require those who chose to honor a deity and enhance her treasury by servicing decadent men seemed wrong. I sighed, grateful to have been given an opportunity to do good to one of Aphrodite's lost souls.

All day, I pondered the sorrowful reality of his life, and what he did not say about his mother.

The urge, to tell the captain what I thought of his using an innocent youth for his lustful pleasure, arose inside me. But, by dinner time, reason overflowed my judgmental, black water well. Even if it felt wrong to me, who was I to admonish the captain for what was wholly acceptable in our society? What would I have said to one who confronted me about living apart from marriage with Alistar, or destroying my baby? What was it Kyros said? Forgive and love people.

As expected, the captain did not mention the boy that stayed with him last night. He ate in silence, remained home that evening, and went to bed early. I thought about the many nights he went into the city. How many young boys had he preyed upon, there?

I hurried to the park, eager to pour out my frustration and hear Kyros' thoughts on the matter. For the first time since we met, he was not there.

Chapter Thirty-Two

For a couple of weeks, I hoped Kyros' absence was due to illness and that he would show up once again. I wrestled with the idea to try to find his son's house. I so wanted to see him and to encourage him. Had he told his son of our meetings? Fear his family might consider a servant a less than proper friend doused my good intentions. When a month passed, I accepted that Kyros had likely died.

I did not want it to be true. I missed my elderly friend and wished I had told him how much his comfort and support meant to me. The loss gushed like a waterspout in my soul. In its wake, regrets and guilt over losing Rose revived and created waves that left me sinking in despair. Alone, with no one to share my sorrow, I grieved afresh and mourned Kyros as I had my grandfather.

I tried to keep busy, but to cook and clean for just one person did not fill my time. I thought of Pavlos. Would there ever be another special person like him in my life, one who truly loved me and wanted love in return?

No one will ever want a girl with hair on her face.

To shut out my father's nagging prediction, I went outside and began to pull weeds. The day was sunny, but I soon grew weary of tending to the area that surrounded the house. Too much quiet often led me to rehash things that could never change. The captain had not asked me to clean up the yard, but I usually enjoyed the respite from housework.

Today, I did not. I decided to go into the city for no other reason but to while away the long hours. I sat near the fountain and watched people go in and out of the many temples. I studied them and wondered if I had been too quick to dismiss the idea of a god's capability to give guidance. I had no idea how gods worked, but I knew people sought them out in difficult times. Could they show me how to cope with losses that weighed like a dishonest butcher's scale on my heart?

Despite my disdain for Aphrodite's policies, on a whim, I decided to enter a temple and see what I might be missing. The temple to Poseidon loomed above the others. A huge statue of a powerful-looking, bearded man, naked to his loins, stood at its entry. He held a trident, and at the base, waves swirled with dangerous sea creatures. His expression and the enormity of his temple made me shudder.

A beautiful limestone building caught my eye. Chiseled across its opening were the words, *Temple of Apollo*. I decided to follow the people who stopped before they entered to rinse their hands in a marble laver near its door. I cleansed mine, as they had, and walked in behind them. It was very dim inside. I waited while my eyes slowly adjusted.

I had never seen such beauty. Gilded gold statues of the god, posed with a lyre or a bow, were everywhere. The main sculpture stood in the center of a large room. It was almost as high as the ceiling. The triumphant god glared and pointed a sword at a writhing serpent near his feet. The walls were painted in lush reds and golds, and candles burned in ivory stands on every wall and on the altar.

What I assumed were temple priests walked up to each visitor and bowed from the waist. Each spoke in hushed tones, then he led them to a station on the altar. I could not see what they did, but each patron bowed and left shortly after.

A priest in a flowing red robe swept across the highly polished floor toward me. The movements of his cape created an illusion that he floated above the surface. He stopped in front of me. I had no idea what to do or say, so when he gestured toward a station, I followed.

"And what sacrifice did you bring to entreat our great god to grant your inquiry, Daughter of Apollo?"

Sacrifice? I was speechless. I began to back toward the door. "I... I am not a member. I mean I have never been here before. Perhaps, I should leave."

"No, no. We welcome you. Apollo is a god of light and power and he wants to help you. All he asks is that you declare him to be your god and..."

Within, I recoiled. I had no idea what it meant to declare him my god, and I was not about to commit to something I did not understand. A promise to think it over spewed from my lips, and I left before he could object.

Out in the fresh, spring air, I tried to figure out what purpose it all held. The priest had asked me for a sacrifice. Is that how gods worked? You give money or something of value and if you declare him to be your god, he will consider your request? Maybe my father was right. Gods take from you and grant only empty promises.

But then, I recalled the peace Phobie had in the god she served. I wished I had asked her about it. I gazed at several nearby temples and decided I probably would not find answers there either.

Home alone that night, someone knocked on the door. I waited. If it were a soldier with a message for the captain, he would leave as they often left when he did not respond right away. The knock grew louder. I opened the door, surprised to see a soldier from his regiment.

"The captain has been injured in an uprising. He has been taken to the healing temple for treatment. He asked that I inform you he will not be back until he is well enough to recover at home."

I merely nodded and tried to take it in. The young man left before I thought to ask which temple or how serious were the captain's wounds. I paced a few minutes, then stopped short. The soldier said the healing temple. Of course. That had to be the eerie one where I had spent that first night. It was late, so I decided to wait and go in the morning.

I awoke early. Was I doing the right thing? I was not family. I did not know if the captain had any or if they lived in the area. I prepared to go. If he did not want to see me nor receive the fresh clothing I planned to take, I would just go home and wait for his return or more word on his condition.

This time, I walked right up to the person in charge at the Asklepios temple. "I am here to visit the Roman captain who was injured last night. I am his housekeeper and I want to see how he is and if he needs anything from home."

It was the same sickly-looking woman I had talked to the last time. She checked a tally board in front of her, then looked up. "Oh yes. The captain. Wait here while I check on his condition. If he is ready, you may take him home."

That surprised me. Perhaps his injuries were not that serious.

The woman returned and pointed at a door. "Go through there and take the stairs to the underground passage. At the end of the tunnel, someone will direct you to his room."

The tunnel ended in a large space. In the center stood a life-sized statue with a banner that read, *Asklepios, god of healing*. He wore a serious, but approachable expression. Across his burley body, a cloak draped from one shoulder to the floor. Long, curly hair hung from below his ears to his bare, hairless breast.

I stepped close enough to read the plaque positioned beside him and stared. Was he really able to heal people? I touched my cheek. Could he remove the hairy blemish on my face and make it normal? Would he?

A worker stepped beside me. "Did you come for healing?"

Lost in thought and the list of the god's credentials, I jumped, too uncertain to ask about my ever-present blemish. "No. I was directed here to see the Roman captain who was brought in yesterday. I do not know how serious his injuries are. "

She nodded at me. "Well, if he slept here, our esteemed god has listened to and divined the dreams your captain had last night. Out of what he hears, our brilliant god is able to discern whether spiritual, physical, or emotional disorders are the cause of one's problem."

"Dreams tell... I mean, they tell your god how to treat the injury?"

She looked impatient. "Asklepios is a god of medicine and healing. He discerns the root cause of one's illness or injury by their dreams and determines from that what course to take. But sometimes, he is able to simply heal with the herbs and medicines he created." She beckoned over her shoulder. "Come, while I check my list."

I waited while she paged through something bulky on her desk. "Ah, here we are." She picked up some keys and motioned for me to follow. "Did you know Asklepios was sired by Apollo's union with a mortal woman?"

Before I could answer she added, "But Zeus, Apollo's father, in a fit of jealousy killed our god with a thunderbolt. Imagine, being concerned that Asklepios would render all men immortal...how foolish!"

The god was dead? I did not dare ask how he could hear dreams or heal if he were no longer alive.

We arrived at a wall with a large, floor to ceiling door. The workers unlocked it and gestured for me to enter. They whispered loud enough for me to hear that the lock was for the patients' safety. We passed cubicles with people on beds close to the floor. I tried not to look but could not shut out the pitiful moans that came from several.

She pointed to a curtained room at the end and told me not to stay long. She was gone before I could ask what to do when ready to leave. I looked for attendants but saw none.

Ever so carefully, I moved toward the cubicle. There was no way to knock, so I stepped inside. Nothing could have prepared me for what I saw.

Chapter Thirty-Three

Jaw ajar, I stared at the captain. His eyes were closed and for that I was grateful. A multi-layered bandage bound his stomach. The edges were dried and dark, but oozed bright red near the center. From beneath, drips trickled to the sheets and left them stained with his life blood. I recognized the astringent tannin. Its vinegary, herb and bark mixture could not hide the odor of rotted flesh and human waste. The smell nearly overpowered me.

When he moaned, my stomach lurched. "Water...please, water." His voice was hoarse, the words slurred.

I glanced back down the hall but saw no one. A carafe sat on a nearby table. I picked it up and sniffed. It was water. When I held it to his lips, he raised himself slightly and slurped the liquid like a camel newly escaped from the desert. The effort must have disturbed his wound because the flow of blood strengthened enough to puddle on the floor.

Panic reduced my voice to a bare whisper as I backed toward the doorway. "I...I will try to find you some help."

He opened one eye and groaned. "Eunice? That you?"

"Yes. Please do not move. You are bleeding. I am going to find help."

He murmured something I could not understand, so I left to try to find somebody. Only patients filled the area. I ran to the door I had entered and found it locked. No one answered my knock. I tried again, louder, then put my ear to the door. Nothing. I took off my sandal and pounded as hard as I could, but no one came.

I searched the hall and rooms for another entrance, but there was none. My stomach churned and my heart raced. The captain could die, and I was trapped, unable to rouse help.

"Misses?"

I spun around but saw no one.

Barely audible, "Misses?" came again.

I followed the sound to the cubicle across from the door and pushed the curtained doorway aside. A man lay, uncovered, on a cot. Bandages hid all of his body and head, except for one eye and his lips. He did not move or turn toward me but motioned with his one free hand. I took a few steps, not knowing if I should.

I strained to hear him. "I heard you pounding on the door." He took a slow breath and let it out. "No one will come because they lock it to stop people who try to leave before they should." The effort appeared to exhaust him. "You will have to wait...until they do the next rounds." With great effort, he tipped his head toward the small window in the ceiling. "I would say the routine will start soon."

Soon? I clutched my chest and gasped. "Soon? A man down at the end is bleeding badly. Surely, there is a way to notify them of an emergency."

The man gave his head a brief shake. "The great Asklepios is with him. Try not to worry."

I retreated into the hallway and paced. At one point, I peeked in on the captain. He looked pale but his wound no longer seeped. I had just decided to go pound on the door again when something slid across my foot. Before I could stifle a scream, the shock raced up my throat and out my lips. In horror, I watched as a snake slithered its way into the captain's room and up onto his bed. Its tongue flickered as it nosed around his bandage and settled on the dampest spot.

I ran from the room, unable to believe what I had seen. I reached the entry door just as it opened.

The woman who led me in earlier arrived, accompanied by a small man in a long grey tunic. He nodded at me and started for the first cubicle.

I grabbed his sleeve. "Wait! There is a snake in that last alcove. It climbed up on the patient's bed and he is bleeding badly. I tried to get help but found myself locked in, and no one answered my knocks. Please attend to him. I am afraid he could die."

The man gave the woman an accusing glance. She lowered her eyes and turned from me. As he hustled down the hall, the man called back over his shoulder, "The snakes are harmless. They are a symbol of restoration, ordered to roam freely by our great Asklepios." I started to follow, but the woman held up her hand. "Visitors are not allowed while Asklepios' workers examine patients. Please leave and wait in the main room if you plan to stay or come back later."

I left, more than relieved to be out of there. Neither the woman nor the attendant came out after a while, so I decided to go out into the agora and find something to eat. When I returned, a different woman greeted me. I told her about the morning visit and asked if there was news on the captain's condition. She seemed perplexed about my inability to rouse anyone. "I am sorry about that mix-up. It should not have happened."

A few excuses were offered, but none made sense. She gestured toward a bench, "Wait here and I will see what I can find out."

She returned sooner than I expected. "The attendant assigned to watch over the captain says they have stopped his bleeding but advise that he rest and not have visitors until tomorrow."

I trudged home and wondered, again, if the captain had family in the area. In the morning, they led me through that same door and assured me they would hear me knock when I was ready to leave. I made my way to the captain's small room with an eye out for snakes. His stomach looked newly wrapped, but areas rippled pink where blood and fluids spotted the bandage.

An untouched bowl of broth sat on the table by his water. Though I had tiptoed in, his eyes opened a slit. "Eunice?" The effort to speak seemed to exhaust him.

I forced a smile. "How do you feel today? Are you—"

"You should not have come. I will be home soon."

I shrank at his tone. "It is no trouble. Is there anything you want me to bring you?"

"No... need rest. Listen, you have proved trustworthy... done well. If you need money, there is a small box in the back of my dresser. Take what you need and...and..." His voice trailed to silence.

I waited but deep, labored breaths assured me he had fallen asleep. I went to the door and knocked. The woman who greeted me appeared almost instantly.

I left. He had not looked any better to me. Had they told me the truth? I shuddered as I pictured him, blood seeping from his wound and possibly another snake curled upon his stomach. With the captain's favorites in mind, I stopped at the market and bought some meat and vegetables.

The lady in the produce stand handed me my purchase and said she had heard the captain had been injured. "How bad is it?" I told her it was a stomach wound but the attendant said they had stopped the bleeding.

She looked skeptical. "Well, that could prove fatal. Until I know he will live and be around to make good on your charges, I will need you to pay for your purchases."

Her disparaging attitude shocked me, but as I walked, I realized she needed to look out for herself. Maybe I needed to prepare too, but for what? For the first time since I had heard of his injury, I thought about where I would be if, indeed, he did die.

I went back to the temple, first thing, the next morning. I was told the captain was undergoing a purification process and could not be seen. I asked for an update on his condition but was told that information would have to come from the man assigned to him, who would not be available until the next day. I arrived early that next morning, determined to get some answers. Once again, I was put off with excuses and began to suspect something was not right.

I waited an hour and then confronted the woman on duty. "I insist on seeing the captain. I have been given no word on his condition for two days now. I need to see him for myself." She looked uneasy. "Please wait here and I will see what I can do for you."

I watched her leave. She returned shortly.

"The captain has requested no visitors. He appears to be resting comfortably." She turned and busied herself with something on her desk.

I considered charging down into the section where he lay, but knew the door was locked and they were not about to open it. A helpless foreboding covered my thoughts and remained as I wandered aimlessly down the agora. What was the true condition of this man I worked for but hardly knew?

With hopes he would get better, I decided to skip a day. That night, the same young soldier knocked on our door. "I have been asked to inform you that the captain has died. His superior has taken care of his remains and asks that, if possible, please notify his family."

Chapter Thirty-Four

I could not sleep that night. The upheaval, of the last few days, ran like water through a sieve and flooded my mind. The locked door, no way to get help, the attendant's frown when he heard about it, the woman's guilty response, and her replacement's lame excuses–nothing made sense. Did the captain really say he wanted no visitors or was that their pretext to be rid of me? And what is a purification process? Did it follow a dream the god discerned? Could it have led to the captain's death?

I could not shake the likelihood that something was amiss. Had they tried to hide how badly he had been injured. Why would they? Did his death reflect, negatively, on the god's ability to heal?

I wanted to find the captain's family. It was the least I could do. I asked some of the closer neighbors, but none had ever seen anyone drop by or visit him. I wandered into the city and asked some soldiers. All knew the captain, but none knew of any family. One, who had come to the house with messages, said the captain had spoken of relatives back in Rome, but never mentioned a wife or children. I thanked him and it struck me that if the captain's desire was for young boys, there probably was no immediate family.

I gave up the search and kept to the house. When my food supply grew low, I remembered the captain's instructions about funds and opened his dresser. As he said, a small chest in the top drawer contained a pouch with coins. I emptied it and counted the contents. There was enough for my wages and food for about two weeks. I stashed some in my room and headed for the market.

On the way, I decided to return to the healing temple and see if I could find some answers. The same, tired-looking woman directed me back through the tunnel into the reception area. To my relief, the person who had locked me in was not on duty.

Another woman, a surly one I had encountered before, was focused on a scroll she carried. "May I help you?"

When I did not reply right away, she looked up. Her cheerful expression instantly faded, and her lips twisted.

"Oh... it is you. Were you not informed the captain died?"

I ignored her crude reply and drew a quiet breath. Disgusted, and more determined not to leave without an answer, I pulled myself to full stature and glared at her.

"Yes, I was informed, but I have a lot of questions. I would like to talk to someone who was with him at the end."

She sighed. "Well, I can see if his attendant is finished with his routine checks. You may have a long wait."

I plopped down on a bench, cocked my head, and folded my arms. "Yes, well, I am not about to leave."

She chewed her lower lip and nodded.

Time dragged, and I was about to give up when the same small man who had attended the captain came into the room. He walked over and sat beside me. "I understand you have questions about the Roman soldier who was here. What is it you want to know?"

I gathered myself, looked him straight in the eye, and spoke boldly. "Sir, I felt like I was being put off with excuses when I tried to see him. No one would tell me how he was, and then he was gone. Why was I not allowed to see him before he passed?"

The man slowly shook his head. He looked defeated and I had to strain to hear him. "It was a very touchy situation." He closed his eyes and sighed, "Two nights before the captain died, he had a disturbing dream. It was as if he had lost touch with reality. Over and over, he shrieked for help. None of the night attendants knew what to do.

"They were unable to wake him, and in the morning reported that his account, of the dream, portrayed him clinging to a flimsy rope upon which he swayed over an active volcano. One said he screamed in pain and insisted that flames spurted on all sides and had reached his feet. In his mind, he was in desperate need of rescue. The whole ward held their breath and trembled as he screeched in terror that the rope had begun to unravel. None could convince him he was not about to drop into the scorching abyss. They gave him something to calm him, and it helped some. But despite orders, after they left, he refused to sleep. He would get out of bed and pace. The activity fatally reopened his wound and he died."

As I contemplated the horror the captain experienced, blatantly real to him, all my objections vanished and left me drained and speechless. I grappled to regain some composure.

"Could not someone have watched over or restrained him?"

The attendant's voice grew confident. "Asklepios told me the captain's dream foretold he was in mortal danger and agony because of the way he had lived his life. We tried to counsel him and to purify him, but he refused to listen. Nothing we said comforted or consoled him. We found his body on the floor that next morning, his face painfully contorted." The man stood to his feet. "I am sorry for your loss, but it was impossible to let anyone near him."

I mumbled a thanks for his time and hurried from the place. My brief encounters with gods left me cold. I vowed never again to step into any temple, for any reason. My insides churned too much to think of food, so I hurried home and fixed a cup of tea. The sweet smell of orange peel and cinnamon soothed my senses, and later some toasted hearth bread became all the dinner I could swallow.

I tried to make sense of all the captain's attendant said but came to no reasonable conclusions. My relationship with the man, whose home I lived in, had been strictly housekeeper and employer. We knew next to nothing about one another, but I felt sincere sorrow for what he had suffered. I pondered, those I had watched, gratefully present molded body parts at the temple. Would the captain have lived if he had been able to acquire a clay replica of his stomach?

Several days later, I answered a knock on the door. A man with slicked back hair and a scar on his right cheek announced, "I am here to collect the rent."

I had assumed the captain owned the house, but then, he had never said so. "I am sorry to have to inform you, but the captain passed away about a week ago."

The man looked surprised. "Really? Are you his wife?"

"No. I was his housekeeper."

He grimaced. "Well, is it your intention to stay and rent the place?"

I was taken aback by his question. "No. No, I have lost my income now. I cannot afford to stay here."

"Well then, I am sorry, but I will have to ask you to leave by the day after tomorrow. I will need to find new renters immediately."

I nodded and shut the door. Now what? Once again, I had no place to go.

Chapter Thirty-Five

The next day, I wandered through the house in a daze. I packed my few belongings, which included Grandfather's statue and the money I had found. It would not keep me going for long. Since the captain had no heirs, I looked in each room to see if there was anything I could sell and add to my small stash. A beautiful bronze statue of Aphrodite had promise, if for nothing else but the price of the metal. I held up the replica of the nearly naked goddess. Why did she have such a powerful influence in Corinth? I shrugged and packed it, and all the food that would keep for a few days.

In the morning, I cooked a hearty breakfast of eggs and sliced ham. I added some biscuits, I had made the day before, to my parcel and left after I cleaned the kitchen. I wanted to be gone long before the man who owned it returned. What would he do with the captain's things and spare uniforms? Maybe I should have taken one to sell...but no, Rome probably provided them for their soldiers.

I wandered into the agora and sat on a bench that faced the Bema. People scurried about, caught up in their busy lives. Would I ever have a family to hurry home to or a meaningful purpose in life? My thoughts returned to the day Spiros and I saw a man forced up onto the platform, by men from a Jewish synagogue, who hoped he would be put on trial. The words the man spoke to the crowd, after he had been rescued, returned as if it had been yesterday.

He said, *There is a God who loves you so much He gave up his life that you could become one with the Father, God. Do not be afraid. I have many believers in this city. There is not anyone that He is not seeking to save and bring into His kingdom. His desire is for all to receive God's grace and forgiveness.*

I chewed my lower lip. Was that not what he said? What was grace? It did not matter. I was in no mood to explore the promises of another god. And why would he love or want me? I had nothing to offer anyone.

In the stretch of the fifty booths, where I inquired, none had need of help. Most shops displayed their goods at street level, but the family lived in the upper story where they worked their trade.

The last owner I spoke to, gestured at the piles of animal skins, awls, needles, and oil for preparing leather. "Have you ever worked with leather or made tents?"

I admitted I had no experience and had never worked with leather but could learn.

The man shook his head and called to his wife. "Priscilla, do you know of any merchant who needs help?"

His wife came down and introduced herself while her husband began to close shop for the night. I explained that the man I had worked for had passed away and I needed a new position.

"My Dear, it is late. We would be delighted if you came up and had supper with us and stayed the night."

I was touched by her generosity, but could not bring myself to accept her offer. "Thank you, but I think I will ask at a few more shops down the market."

She insisted that if I found nothing, I should return and stay with them. I was touched at her kindness to a stranger, especially one of such low status. It had not taken me long, after leaving the Peloponnese, to grasp that, in Corinth, your value depended on who you were or your wealth.

The market closed for the day, and I wrestled with where to spend the night. There was no way I would sneak into the Asklepios temple, again, in hopes I could sleep there. Perhaps, I should have taken up the tent maker's offer. I reviewed my funds and decided to spend a little to sleep in an inn.

I found some at the opposite end of the market, far from the one Phobie had owned. A portly man answered my knock and informed me his beds were full. He pointed to the north, "Try that third one down. He does not fill up so fast, and frankly, I suspect it is because word gets around that the food and accommodations are not the best. But his prices are low."

I left and tried to decide whether I should go there. The sun had already set, and to be out in the city after dark could be dangerous.

The woman who answered the door eyed me with suspicion. Her sharp nose and beady eyes honed in on my simple clothing and small parcel. "Where are your travel bags? You know you must pay before we give you a bed."

I was shocked to be greeted so rudely and debated whether to walk away. But it was late. "I have the money. It will only be for one night."

She looked like she doubted my word, but opened the door and gestured for me to come in. It did not take long before I wished I had not paid for the night's lodging. I followed her up the dusty stairs to the women's quarters. The stale smell of unwashed bodies and bedding tweaked my nose the minute she opened the door. The room was small and the two beds, each, had three pillows set up for the guests. She led me to the second one and pointed, "That pillow will be yours."

I looked at the crumpled bedding and silently vowed that pillow would never touch my head. The dressing table was covered with stains and spider webs hung from the lamps. She descended the stairs and called over her shoulder, "Dinner will be in a half hour."

I sat on the edge of the bed and covered my lips, grateful not to have to share the bed with a stranger. The filth sent a shiver of disgust down my back. I squeezed myself and tried to shake off a mounting revulsion. "Oh, Phobie, you would be appalled at the condition of this place."

Dinner was not as bad as I expected. Roasted fowl had been baked with potatoes, carrots, and rutabaga. It was a bit greasy, but edible. A young woman, in clothing that bore weeks of spilled food, brought out the dishes. At least the bread was fresh and there was plenty of watered wine to wash it down. The only other guests were two men, who mostly talked to each other. I excused myself as soon as I felt I could and climbed the narrow stairs.

I could not persuade myself to get into the dirty sheets, so I pulled a blanket over the bedding and my assigned pillow. I, then, laid on top with my heavier shawl as a cover. About midnight, a drunken exchange woke me. I sat up and listened. It sounded like the male guests could not find their room. Their voices slurred as they stumbled and corrected each other.

My door rattled and fear leapt to my throat.

One man huffed at the other, "No, that is not it. Our room is over here."

I lay, frozen to the spot, until it grew quiet. Loud snores finally convinced me the men would not move until morning.

At a cock's crow, I woke with a start, dressed and decided to leave before breakfast. I put my things together and had reached the door when I heard quiet sobbing. It sounded like a woman or young girl. I opened the door a crack. In the dim morning light, almost hidden in a small, windowless cove, the young girl who had served dinner knelt on her knees with her hands over her face.

I tiptoed over and knelt beside her. "I heard you crying. Can I be of any help?"

Her head jerked and she clutched her throat. "Oh, I am so sorry. I did not mean to wake you...or anyone. No. I am fine. I am sorry I disturbed you."

She started to rise, but I put my hand on her arm. "Please do not worry. You did not wake me. I was up and ready to leave. Sometimes, it helps to share your problem with a total stranger, someone you will probably never see again. I will listen if it would help."

The girl drew out a cloth and wiped her nose. "I do not think anyone can help me." Tears streaked her cheeks. "It is my father. He..." She covered her face, again.

My thoughts leapt to my own father, his cruel attitude, and his refusal to see any good in me. I put my arm around her shoulders, and she leaned into me and cried.

Through shudders, she moaned. "He thinks it is all right to touch me in ways meant for a wife. He is getting bolder all the time and I am afraid he, he will..." She broke down again I ached for her. "Can you tell your mother?"

Her head shook. "She would not believe me. She is such an unhappy person. She would take her frustrations out on me... usually does."

I pointed to my face. "Listen, I understand. My father did not touch me like that, but he was cruel and considered me evil because of this blemish." Her eyes shot to my veil, so I lifted it for her to see.

"And my mother..." I shook my head. "My mother beat me for every little thing that went wrong. In her eyes, it had to be my fault."

Surprise dropped the girl's chin as she drew back and stared at me "What did you do? Did you leave home?"

I told her how my father farmed me out, and how I had to make my own way in the world. "But you know, it is better than a life in a household of hate and being mistreated in one way or another."

I put my hands on her shoulders. "You do not have to accept this unjust conduct. You are a strong young woman. I encourage you to go out into the market and find someone who could use your help with their children, or in a shop, or even cleaning or cooking. You deserve a better life, and you owe nothing to those who abuse you."

Hope bloomed in her eyes. She stared as if a vision opened before her. "We have a distant cousin with a large house and a lot of children. She is of a higher class than my family, but sometimes my mother has let me go help her for a day. Our cousin always says she wished I would stay."

Her face lit up and she jumped to her feet. "I am going to do it! I am going to leave here and ask my cousin if I can live with and work for her. Thank you! Thank you! My plan is to go right after I serve breakfast!"

With that, she hugged me and went down the stairs. I followed her down and decided to eat since it was almost ready. When the girl finished setting the food on the table, she gave me a shy smile. I returned it and marveled at how good it felt to be a blessing to another needy soul.

Chapter Thirty-Six

Most of the shops were open by the time I left the inn. I looked for ones that sold yarn or meat, in hopes my experience would impress and convince them to hire me. It was mid-morning when I reached the city end of the market with no prospects. I sat on a bench near the Peirene fountain. What should I do?

A small man with a clay tablet held to his chest approached, followed by two women. "You there, are you looking for work?"

For a moment, I was not sure he meant me, but he stepped close and stopped beside my bench. "Yes, I—"

"Good. Good. My master has a large villa in Delos, but he lacks enough servants and slaves to work the concinum he plans to host. It will be a feast celebrating Poseidon's annual festival. The deipnon is tomorrow night. He will pay you, well."

Suspicion gripped me, tightened by stories I had heard of misuse of help by wealthy or high positioned officials. "I have never heard of Delos. What kind of work?"

"The usual. Cook, clean, or serve meals."
"Where is Delos? Is it part of Corinth?"

"No, it is an island in the Aegean, not too far out."

He seemed sincere, so I agreed to go, grateful for the opportunity. Maybe, it would lead to a permanent position. He found a few more unemployed women and gestured for us to hurry. At a small inlet away from the busy port, he led us to a skiff that could hold all six of us. Two oarsmen waited beside the boat. They helped us wade out and climb into the vessel. It rocked with each addition, and I was glad the sea was rather calm. After we passed a string of small islands, I began to wonder just how far Delos was, but the rowers soon pulled up to a beach on a beautiful island. Interspersed with sandy beaches, rocky cliffs sprouted waterfalls that plunged to the sea.

We wound through streets where large houses, with gorgeous views, sprawled over the island. Each boasted of two stories with large courtyards and gated stone fences that encircled their whole expanse.

The man, we followed, pointed out a striking limestone building. "This is my master's villa. He has many slaves." His tone suggested pride in his master's wealth.

I stared. My original neighborhood would fit inside this vast estate.

"There is to be no loud talking, and never question the orders of the main steward."

He ushered us in through a side gate, toward an outbuilding. People bustled with their assigned preparations. Two slaves, in skimpy loincloths, passed with a large boar that hung from a spit on their shoulders. To one side, women cleaned and chopped vegetables. They lowered their eyes as a man, with a wreath around his head, charged past. He, continually, barked orders over his shoulder to three or four others who hustled to keep up with him.

The one who had recruited us said in a hushed tone, "That is the head steward. He has to make sure the bakers and wine stewards, those in charge of the meats and side dishes, are all fully prepared. Now, how many of you have had experience baking bread and pastries?" Along with one other woman, I raised my hand. "Good. You two come with me and the rest of you wait here. He took us into a large room with many tables and ovens.

A rotund, pleasant-looking woman wearing a long cover, glanced our way and sighed. "Oh, help, at last!" She grasped one corner of her apron and pointed at a counter.

"There are more of these, over there, if you want one." She wiped her brow and looked as if she expected us to jump right in.

"Now, I need one of you to make bread." She looked at me. "Are you sure you can handle those large flour bins? You are not very big."

I assured her I could. She shrugged and showed me where the ingredients were stored. "We need two dozen loaves for the feast. You must get the dough set today, so we can bake it fresh tomorrow."

She left me and returned to the other woman. Several hours passed before she said anything other than to check on my progress. My stomach grumbled and I wondered if we would be fed. I debated silently whether I dared ask, when a young man arrived with a tray of pita bread, meats, cheeses, and fruit. He, then, handed us a dish to put our food on. I caught him watching me. I smiled, thanked him, and he blushed.

The woman, in charge, moved among us. "You may sit over there and rest a short time while you eat."

I helped myself, relieved to get off my feet. Soon, the young man gathered the leftovers and disappeared. We worked for another five hours. I had met the quota and the woman seemed pleased. She motioned to the other woman, and we followed her to a lower level that opened to a part of the estate hidden from public view.

She opened the door to a small room with two cots against the walls. "You two can share this room. Supper will be ready, shortly, out in the courtyard."

I learned the other woman's name was Leto. She was several years older than I. Leto told me she had lost her parents and a brother years ago in an earthquake. Pain spilled with her words. "I had no one and had to make my own way in the world."

I asked why she had not married.

Leto's gaze drooped. "With no father to make arrangements, it is not easy to find a suitable match. A man, who will accept a girl like me with no family to vouch for her chastity and standings, is rare. I had little chance of being betrothed... unless I was willing to marry someone in a much lower class."

We joined the rest of the help and ate a generous dinner. Later, I lay on my cot and wondered what Pavlos felt about my being of a different class. He came from a family of landowners while I was of the working poor. I turned to the wall. That would have been one more hurdle for his father to leap. I had made the right decision.

The sound of soft snoring told me Leto had fallen asleep. I was relieved that I would not have to explain why, I, too, was alone with no family or position. Exhausted by the vigorous expectations of the day, I fell sound asleep. The next morning, a loud clang woke us. We dressed quickly and joined the staff, in the back courtyard, for breakfast. Soon, the woman in charge of baking gestured time to get to work.

All the bread I had made had risen beautifully and I was charged with baking it. The woman pointed at the ovens. "Be very alert and watch it carefully. "We cannot have burnt crusts for the master's guests."

With so many ovens, I finished just as the young man arrived again with lunch. The man who brought me to the estate, entered shortly after and began a lively conversation with the woman in charge. Their voices grew louder until she finally said, "All right, take that one over there. She seems able to handle things."

She had pointed at me.

The man came and looked at me as if for the first time. "We need more girls to serve the food tonight. Have you ever helped with that?"

"Only to the families I have worked for, not a big group."

"I think you can learn. Come with me."

He took me to the servants' quarters and introduced me to the woman in charge. "This is Eunice. She has not served at a banquet before, so you will have to teach her. Sorry, it is the best I can do."

"Hello. My name is Zona." She looked me over. "Well, you are young and attractive. That will help if you make a grave blunder, but why do you wear that veil?"

I wondered why my appearance mattered, but before I could answer she reached over and lifted one end. "Oh..." She let it fall. "What a shame. You have a lovely figure, and gorgeous auburn hair." She frowned and her lips twisted to one side before her face brightened. "Listen. We need servers so I am going to use you, anyway. I will make sure your costume matches your veil. It could present a fascinating, mysterious look." She gave a sharp nod. "Yes! I am going with my instincts."

She led me to a place that was set up as if for guests and pointed at a horseshoe arrangement. "Here is how the couches will be placed in the triclinium. The host will sit at the end of this large dining hall where all can see him. The couches are low so you will serve from behind. The guests will recline on their left arms and eat with their right. The most important are to be served first... with the best of everything."

I began to wish I had not been assigned to this task. "How will I know which are the important ones?"

The woman's jaw fell, and then she snickered. "Oh, you will know! Believe me. You will know. Aristocrats, wealthy men with specific monetary holdings, government officials, and those who hold important positions–all will be here. The guest with the highest status will sit on the host's right and the second highest on his left. Like the proprietor, they will be dressed in jewels and elegant clothing, illegal for lower classes to wear."

"Illegal?"

She nodded. "Look for the tassels on the hem of their garments. Nobility and even royalty wear them as a symbol of their social standing, identity, and authority. All other guests will be assigned a specific place. The more important they are, the closer they will be seated to the host. From there it will descend, according to class."

I must have looked baffled, so she tried to explain. "Look, I know this is all new to you, but the whole point of the deipnon is to display the hosts' wealth. It is an elaborate expression of his social standing, meant to enhance his personal status and significance. The gathering adheres to a strict, class-conscious Roman tradition. You may even see shopkeepers and landowners seated at the farthest end." As if to remind herself, she added, "but they are more likely to be seated in another room where there is even a possibility of some of the poor having been invited to display the host's generosity."

I nodded and hoped I would be assigned the smaller room.

Chapter Thirty-Seven

Zona gestured toward a door. "Come, I need to find you a suitable costume."

We entered a room filled with clothing made of imported silk. Tunics, so short I wondered if they would cover my torso, lay beside wispy shawls and elaborate headpieces.

"These are what the master requires his servers wear." She held a pale blue tunic up against me. "No, you will look better in a bright color." She rummaged through the pile until she found a reddish-orange colored dress. She held it up under my chin. "Yes, perfect. The color blends with your veil and highlights your hair."

I did not know what to say. To me, it looked garish.

"Here, take it into that dressing room and try it on."

I did as I was told. The tunic fit my frame, but as I suspected, it barely covered my backside. I caught a glimpse of myself in a bronze mirror, fastened in a stand, and gasped. The neckline plunged nearly to my navel. Hopes of a respectable, permanent position faded like morning fog off the Gulf.

Zona tapped on the door. "How does it fit? Do you like the color?"

She flung open the door and studied her choice. "I was right. This dress was made for you. Come on out and I will find a headpiece to go with it."

She charged out the door, but I hesitated when she realized I had not followed. "What is it? I pointed at the front. "It is...the dress. It is cut so low."

"Oh, they are all like that. Do not worry. You will not look any different than the other girls. No one will think anything of it. Now, let us find a simple topper."

I wanted to run, to resign and leave, but no other work had opened. I needed the money. To my relief, she passed up those with elaborate feathers and found what she wanted. "Those are for the dancers, but here, this is exactly what you need." She placed a band on my head.

Its colors matched my tunic, with gold threads running throughout. It crossed the middle of my forehead, with a gold charm of Poseidon that dangled just above my nose.

She smiled. "See, it goes right over the tie on your veil and completes your costume beautifully. Now, change into your clothes, but take these with you. Do not go back to the bakery. When the head steward gives the signal, report here. People will start to arrive at dusk, but we will not serve until two hours of mingling over wine and appetizers are over."

I took the costume to the room where Leto and I slept. It was late afternoon, too early to dress, but time enough to bathe. I found the tubs set aside for servants. I filled one with warm rainwater from the barrel, took it back to the room, and soaked. I had just dried off when Leto returned.

Her brows pinched when she saw me. "Where did you disappear all afternoon? I never saw you after lunch."

I told her about being chosen to help serve and showed her my costume. She held it up and stared. "Wow, what a beautiful tunic. But is that front not a bit low?"

I grimaced. "Yes. I have never worn something like this, but I decided to bear it for the few hours required to serve." I finished drying my hair and emptied the tub. When I returned, Leto was packing her things. "Are you leaving?"

"Yes. They said we could sleep here tonight, but I would rather go home."

"Where is that?"

"I live in the house my parents owned when they were killed. The earthquake only damaged part of it and friends helped me repair the rest. Sometimes relatives come and stay a day or two, but mostly it is only me." She smiled as if a thought surprised her. "If you ever need a place to stay, come see me."

She gave me directions and we said our goodbyes. I decided I had better get dressed. A horn blasted within the hour, and I made my way to the servers' area, awed at the number of girls all dressed in similar costumes. Zona met us and began to assign stations. Each girl was responsible for two couches. Some were sent out, immediately, to serve appetizers or pour wine.

I still hoped to be assigned to the smaller room but was given two couches down from the second honored guest. I worried about bending over the couches in this costume.

To prepare us, Zona announced the four courses. "To honor Poseidon, Corinth's most honored god, a cream soup of octopus, potatoes, and leeks will be first. A salad of greens, fruit, and cheese with a vinaigrette dressing will follow. Now, the main course is lamb with tiny potatoes and roasted pork with baked vegetables. As you would expect, bread will accompany each course, and dessert will be a peach cobbler with clotted cream."

She searched all our faces. "Any questions?" I wondered why we needed such detailed information but said nothing. When no one responded, she went on.

"The guests will have already drunk a lot of wine, but be sure to fill their cups the minute they empty them. Remember, do not serve your guests until those closer to the host in front of you have been served. Put out the bread for wiping fingers, immediately. And be quick to dispose of any they toss aside. Be very careful not to spill food on anyone or on their tables. The soup will be hot, so be watchful as you place it before them. Guests' sudden, unexpected moves are likely because by then, most will be drunk. Just make sure each guest has everything he needs, especially the wine."

I looked around at the other girls. They talked and giggled over things they had previously experienced, things I was not privy to. My stomach churned but none of them seemed concerned.

Chatter ceased when Zona tapped on the table with a small mallet and added more directions. "The salad should not be much of a challenge, but do inquire whether the guest prefers you to pour the dressing or wants to do it himself. Plates that hold the main course will have been filled for you. Remove the cover after you place it on the guest's table. If he is not in his seat, leave it and watch for his return. By the time the dessert is served, do not be surprised if many are out of their seats. Each will watch for an opportunity to speak personally to the host."

I made a mental note of all she said and hoped it would go smoothly. Zona clapped her hands. "Everyone to their stations. It is time. The drinking and mingling has finished."

All the servers walked, demurely, to their assignment. I followed, determined to not let my nerves show. The banquet room took my breath away. Beautiful columns lined the perimeter, with gorgeous lamps hung between them. The walls were covered with frescos. Each displayed a scene that reflected the host's wealth and position. On the floor, mosaics of dolphins and sea creatures swirled in patterns and colors that complimented lush draperies which hung from the windows.

My first couch held an older man, probably fifty or over. His cup was empty, so I hurried to the krater to fill it. He nodded, as I sat it in front of him, but did not look at me.

I hurried to my second couch, surprised at the youth of the next guest. How did he come to be important enough at his age to be seated so close to the host? His cup was full, so I turned to see if the soup had arrived.

At that moment, the host approached his elaborately decorated couch at the tip of the semicircle. All the guests stood and applauded.

He looked young too. Amazing! I guessed he was barely over twenty-five. He was dressed in an elegant tunic, popular with the Romans. It swept down his chest on one side, to a jewel studded cummerbund at his waist. A gold pendant hung from his neck and rings shone on his fingers.

He gave a welcome speech and invited everyone to enjoy the feast. I was impressed with his calm, controlled manner of speaking. He obviously had not drunk as much wine as his guests, who staggered to their couches. The soup arrived and I made sure bread was ready for my guests. A sigh of relief rose as I, successfully, set the soup on their tables and both men began to eat. As soon as they finished, I retrieved their bowls and replenished their wine. When I bent over to set down the older guest's cup, he grabbed my arm and pulled me close, his eyes on my plunging neckline.

He pressed his lips to my neck and slurred. "You are a beautiful girl." The heavy smell of his wine laced breath turned my stomach. I pulled away, shaking. What should I do? He laughed and picked up his cup. I managed to calm myself just before the salads were ready.

I served the younger man first, though I knew it was not correct. Finally, I took a deep breath and when the older man's head was turned, I placed his salad on his tray and quickly backed away.

I managed the main course the same way, relieved to avoid a confrontation. The younger man smiled and thanked me when I served his dessert. Again, I watched, ready to place the older man's last course when his attention was elsewhere. I had nearly set it down when he turned abruptly, and the plate landed in his lap. I thought I might faint.

Zona saw the accident and hurried over with a towel and apologies for my clumsiness. I tried to help, but she turned and told me to leave. The snarl in her voice discouraged any thought of explanations.

Chapter Thirty-Eight

I looked back in time to see the older man on his feet, while Zona brushed his toga with her towel. He did not look as upset as she was. When she finished, the younger man I had served beckoned to her. They talked, briefly, before she returned to the spot where she kept a keen eye on all the servers.

I did not know what to do or where to go. An area a few steps from the entrance was clear of people, so I leaned against the wall and rehearsed my defense. It would not matter. It was not hard to discern that Zona was not one to listen to explanations or excuses. My insides finally settled enough that I decided I should go find my things, change my clothes, and leave. The costume needed to be returned to the dressing room, and to find the steward who held my wages might be difficult while the banquet continued into late hours.

An ensemble of acrobatic jugglers rushed past me toward the banquet hall. I ducked out of the way, then stepped over to the entrance and watched them perform. The guests applauded their fascinating antics. They were as amazed I was at the acrobats' ability to balance themselves in strange poses without dropping their props.

Meanwhile, about a dozen young dancers filled the area behind me, ready to enter. Each wore a scanty white tunic that covered even less than mine had. Their feet were bare, and perched on their heads were the feathery headpieces from the costume room. Behind them, a group of musicians gathered.

One lugged a large, triangle-shaped apparatus with strings across two sides. Two more carried lyres, one with three strings and the other with seven. A muscular youth hauled a round, flat device, along with two leather covered mallets.

Oblivious to the commotion, soft sounds wafted from a boy as he fingered a long horn with holes carved from one end to the other. I was sure he was not yet ten years old. To my surprise, he and a young girl accompanied the troupe. She toted a ram's horn in a sling over her shoulder and a small flute carved of bone in her free hand.

The lead dancer gave a few last-minute instructions to her crew and signaled the musicians to begin. Each stepped up and followed her into the banquet hall. The music rose and the dancers swayed as they twirled long scarves in front of the guests.

Most of the girls who had served alongside me left before the entertainment began. As they passed, they glanced at me with pity or contempt. Amongst the group, chuckles sounded over shared incidents, and compliments flew on a successful night,. None bothered to console me. Their comradery heightened the lonely void in my own life and left me wishing I, too, had close companions to share my joys and sorrows.

The dancers went through well practiced routines. Wine flowed freely. Its unlimited supply coaxed uncharacteristic, loud, or boisterous responses from the normally, dignified guests. More than one dancer had to free herself from an overzealous admirer. The host rose and mingled, casually, with his guests. He lingered long enough to give a slap on the back or laugh at a slurred joke, before he moved from one group to the next.

The dancers exited but the musicians stayed, their tempo and velocity competing with the revelry as the symposium began in earnest. Mesmerized by this world, I did not know existed, I stayed and watched.

From a door opposite mine, six female companions entered. Each looked no older than I, maybe younger. Phoebe had told me about them, how they were trained in coarse practices to please men. With disgust that oozed from her tongue, she called them Hetaeras. The girls went to the center of the room, tilted their heads in a provocative manner, and let their capes slide slowly to the floor. The guests roared their approval.

Moments later, a sultry melody rose, and everyone's attention turned to an equal number of handsome youths that entered through the same door. They strutted seductively toward the girls, confident their bodies raised them above the class of less-gifted slaves. Their loin cloths covered little below their navels.

The girls each approached a youth. Her fingers trailed across his chest as she circled him. As one, the nearly naked young performers began to move in time to the music. Their bodies gyrated in front of and against one another. The lewd performance brought their audience to their feet. Some raised their arms and imitated what was demonstrated before them.

I felt sorry for the girls assigned to keep the guests' cups full of wine. Most had to ward off unwanted, sloppy kisses and blatant groping. When the young entertainers dropped most of their scanty costumes, I turned away, ashamed to even watch such debauchery.

As I turned away, I buried my intentions to justify myself to Zona. What did it matter? This was not the kind of place where I wanted to stay. A wrong turn on my way to my room ended before an open doorway that looked into another room full of guests.

A woman rushed up to me. "Oh, I am so glad Zona sent you to help us. Two of our servers became ill and we are so shorthanded. Here, take these meals to that far table and hurry back for more until they are all served."

Before I could explain, she shoved the plates at me and left. I shrugged and did as she asked. The men in this room were not dressed in the finery of the last. Their couches were in rows and each two shared a table.

The first man to receive his food nodded, "Thank you." I was so surprised I forgot to acknowledge his kindness. Many had not been served, so I pitched in and quickly brought as many plates as I could carry. Their fare was different, not fancy nor built around high-priced meat. Cuts from the boar, I had seen roasting the day before, were surrounded with root vegetables and there was no salad.

All but a few had kept their wine consumption under control and their entertainment was simply quiet music, much more to my liking. When all had received their final course, I headed for the door, feeling good about helping a much humbler group of guests. Before I could leave, to my surprise, the host entered the room. I joined the rest of the servers off to one side.

"Gentlemen, I thank you for coming. I hope you were well fed and taken care of. I wanted to show you my appreciation for your good service to the needs of my estate. Many of you have, diligently, supplied my head steward in a timely fashion and have been quick to respond to any urgent needs. Please, enjoy yourselves and drink freely of the wine."

The shopkeepers and merchants applauded as the host backed from the room and left. Once again, I was impressed with his manner of speaking and controlled demeanor. The room soon buzzed with expressions of gratitude for a customer willing to acknowledge their part in his success. I, finally, found the hall that led to the outside room where I had left my clothes. Footsteps sounded behind me and someone called my name.

"Eunice, it is I, Zona."

I sighed. I really was too tired to listen and hear how my failure reflected on her.

"Wait up. I want to talk to you."

I steeled myself, ready to get it over with. "Look, I am sorry, but—"

"No. No, I need to apologize for being so harsh and embarrassing you in front of the guests. The young man you served told me how that older man had accosted you. I should have let you explain."

Her humility drained my defense. Anger and frustration seeped from my heart like the last drops of water from the rain barrel I had emptied. I fumbled for words.

"I... it is all right, Zona. You were under a lot of pressure to make things run smoothly. Thank you for taking a chance on me...I mean with my veil and all."

"Eunice, you did very well. And my assistant, who ran the room for the lesser guests, told me how you pitched in and helped though it was not your responsibility. You are a good worker, and we were blessed to have your help."

I blushed at her praise. There it was again. Someone was telling me I was a blessing. My thoughts ran to Thera and to the yarn merchant's wife. Why was it so hard for me to believe?

"Thank you, Zona. That is very kind of you." I turned to leave. "Perhaps we will meet again sometime."

"No, that is partly why I wanted to find you. I would like you to stay on and be one of my regulars. The host and his family, constantly, invite groups to dine with them. Usually, the crowds are smaller than tonight, but they entertain most days. You are perfect for the job." Here was the offer I had hoped for. Sadly, I knew I could not accept it.

Chapter Thirty-Nine

There was no way Zona would understand my reluctance to live and work in such a decadent place, so I made up a story about how my family needed me.

"Well, if things settle down, come back and I will find a place for you."

I thanked her and went in to pack, suddenly aware of how late the hour was. I had no idea if a boat would be available to ferry me back to Corinth. Would they operate in the dark? I plopped down on my cot where I resigned to spend the night. In the morning, I would find the man in charge of wages. Surely, he would know when the boats ran.

The day had been long, and I fell asleep immediately, surprised at how quickly morning came. I joined the servants for breakfast, now a much smaller group. The woman in charge of the bakery told me where to find the man who dispensed wages.

He shrugged. "There will not be a boat out until mid-afternoon. Most of the temporary help left in the late afternoon, yesterday."

Now what? I decided to explore the island. When I passed all the villas close to where I had worked, I found a path I hoped would take me up to a cliff that overlooked the sea. My heart still longed for the sound of the waves and the smell of saltwater, an out-of-the-way place like the one I often visited as a child.

Instead, the path led to the island's trade center and main port. Wealthy buyers swarmed the area, determined to be first to buy the best goods. Ships named for cities, I had never heard of, unloaded their cargo on the backs of slaves. Sometimes, they were the cargo. Chained to one another on the deck, they waited, probably headed for the booming slave market in Corinth. Their hopeless eyes haunted me.

I came upon an area filled with temples. One after another, they stood clustered and hushed, like old women gathered for no reason but to pass the time of day.

Activity blossomed outside one whose sign read, Temple of the god, Serapis. The temple itself was smaller than most. A spring ran through its courtyard that contained three small altars and a moneybox marked, donations.

I thought that odd. Did the patrons have to pay to attend? Several other buildings were within the low wall that surrounded the complex. Slaves butchered animals within that area. This banquet hall was larger than the others.

Through the open doors, I could see marble benches lined up on walls where guests could recline, drink, and eat the newly sacrificed meat. I wondered if young girl or boy prostitutes served at their parties, too.

The smell of roasting meat filled the air and tweaked my appetite.

A well-dressed man approached the cooks. "We have enough meat for sacrifices and tonight's festival, so take the rest to the agora. It will sell well in the market during festival week."

A slave stood upright and rubbed his back. "Master, will there be plenty for those who attend the synagogue? They always ask if it has been bled out or sacrificed to our god."

The overseer assured him they had enough for those who asked, and those who did not inquire about how it was handled. "And remember, this temple is a fusion of Egyptian and Greek deities It links our countries and was raised to honor the god, Serapis. We cannot bow to the requirements of every other god."

I passed other temples, amazed at the number on this small island. Along the way, I came upon the Jewish synagogue the slave mentioned. It triggered a memory of Alistar in his father's meat stand, where I had been taught about the restrictions of Jewish people. I wondered, again, why anyone would care if their meat came from animals sacrificed to a god. Clouds covered the sun and warned me I had better get to the shore if I wanted to get to Corinth before dark.

The boat looked ready to pull out just as I arrived. Most of it was loaded with packages of assorted sizes and boxes filled with fresh produce. An oarsman motioned for me to hurry, so I took off my sandals, pulled up my tunic, and waded out to climb into the boat.

The oars began to flap and soon we were on our way. I looked back at the island with regret. It could have been a permanent place... no more need to wander and look for work. I loosed a sad sigh and chastised myself. No. Be glad you saw what you did before you committed to staying.

For the first time, I noticed the only other passenger. He was sitting sideways looking out over the water. He wore the fine clothing of the aristocrats and wealthy people I had seen at the banquet. I surmised he was a guest from Corinth, about to return home after a night of celebration.

He turned and caught my stare. I froze. It was the host of the Concinum.

He looked away and turned to one of the oarsmen. "The sky looks dark and those waves have increased. Are you sure we can make it to Corinth before that storm reaches us?"

The head oarsman grunted, "Plenty of time, plenty of time."

The second rower glanced at the sky. He did not look so sure. We started out. Coming to this island had been my first time out on the water. I had no idea if we were in danger. The feel of the wind against my face brought a surge of doubt. Without warning, a wave hit the side of the boat and swept over our feet.

The head rower barked to his assistant, "Put some muscle into it." Both strained against the oars until their arms and chest muscles bulged.

The host did not raise his voice, but spoke in that same calm demeanor. "I think we should turn back."

The head rower smirked. "We are over halfway." I wondered if he worked for the host. Surely, he would have turned back if he did.

The wind increased and fear raised a lump in my chest. I could not take my eyes off the angry-looking waves that washed into the boat and soaked our sandals. I clutched my shawl. What if we tipped over? I had never learned to swim. Few people, I knew, did more than wade in the ocean.

Dark clouds raced until they were directly over us. The wind grew so fierce I could not hear what the host suggested, but I saw where he pointed. We were close to one of the small islands we had passed on the trip to Delos. When the head oarsman nodded and directed the boat to shore, I released breath I did not know I had held. The oarsmen jumped into the water and steadied the vessel enough for the host to climb out.

He held out his hand to me and I clutched it as tight as I could. I was nearly out when a wave crashed and hit the side of the boat. I flew into the water, gasping and sputtering, sure I would drown. The host grabbed my arm and helped me gain my footing in the rocky bottom.

He held on and led me to shore, despite waves that nearly knocked both of us down.

The oarsmen pulled the boat clear of the water and hurried over to check on us.

"Anyone hurt? Are you all right?"

I nodded but could not stop shaking. The water was not extremely cold, but neither was it warm. A flash of lightning lit up the sky, followed by a loud burst of thunder.

The host eyed the sky. "I believe we will be safer away from the water. Let us go wait it out under those trees."

Once again, he took my arm and steadied me through the rocky ground. My clothes were soaked and his finery, ruined. The rain came in torrents that bashed through the branches above us, leaving little cover.

Each of us huddled on the ground and shared a common wish for a fire to warm us. I was fascinated by the man who had hosted the enormous deipnon and the symposium that followed. He obviously had great wealth and standings, yet he could not have been more concerned for the safety of one of a much lower class.

Just as quickly as the storm came, the clouds raced toward the mainland and the sea settled.

The head oarsman stood. "We have enough time to make it to Corinth in daylight. Everyone ready to leave?"

I did not relish another ride in that boat, but the island we had sheltered on was not inhabited and there was no choice.

Once again, the host steadied me through the rocks and into the boat. He never spoke directly to me, and I did not make small talk or ask questions. When we reached the shore, an oarsman helped me wade to dry land. The storm had moved north and left everything wet, but solid ground beneath my feet was a comfort.

As soon as the boat was pulled from the water, the oarsman bid us goodbye and began to unload their cargo.

The host hailed a carriage, the minute we reached the road.

As he started up the steps, I spoke up. "Sir, I just...just wanted to thank you for your kindness."

He turned toward me, nodded briefly, and climbed up behind the driver. His carriage turned toward the city and left me to wonder if he would have behaved in the same manner if his peers were around. No matter. I was thankful that in a crisis his true nature came out. His carriage disappeared and I doubted I would ever see him again.

There was nothing left to do but to start for the market. As I walked, I treasured the glimpse of humanity that I had seen buried inside someone of wealth and power, despite nothing to be gained by his choices.

Chapter Forty

Wet, cold, and with nowhere to go... was this to be a pattern for my life? I thought about Leto's offer to come spend some time with her. Though we had shared some of our lives, I hardly knew her. I tucked her offer into my maybe someday when I am not so needy, docket, stored in my head.

On the road from the inlet on the Saronic Gulf, I came to the temple of Isthmian we had passed on our way to Delos. It was well off the Lechaion road. A huge statue of Poseidon, trident in hand, stood in front of the large columns with a plaque that dedicated the temple in his honor. Other buildings surrounded the temple, including a Roman bath. I had heard tales of a beautiful, mosaic floor within.

It was late afternoon, and no one was around, but soon the temple and the nearby stadium would be hubs for hundreds of visitors attending the Isthmian games.

The statue's eyes seemed to follow as I passed. I shuddered at tales of the god using the trident to shatter objects that invaded his territory. I hurried on. Did he really have the power to command earthquakes like the one that killed Leto's family? Were all gods cruel?

Before long, I reached the Lechaion road. It was paved with stones and much easier to traverse than the muddy ruts, I had dodged, along the way. With nearly five miles to go, I was grateful for a merchant that happened along and offered a ride. He said he preferred the less hectic pace of evening, and seemed happy to find company.

By the time the road opened into the agora, all the shops were closed, and the booths tied up for the night. I thanked him, profusely, for the ride and he went on his way.

I looked around and remembered how being caught sleeping in a booth had opened a door to selling wool for the owner. My hand rose to my veil as I recalled his kind suggestion for a way to hide my blemish.

It was nearly dark when I knocked at an inn, not far from the disgusting one I had used before going to Delos. I fumbled through my soggy bag, relieved that the wages I had earned, and the statue of Grandfather's foal had not been lost when I fell into the sea. I hated using my small savings to sleep but could think of no other solution. Surely, I would find work in the morning. To pay extra for a tub of hot water was well worth it. I laid all my clothes out to dry and let the soothing bath warm and comfort me.

The market was abuzz the next morning. Men talked about the exciting games that were about to begin, and women and servants were busy buying all the goods they would need for celebrations or feasts.

Pregnant with pride, one vendor explained to a foreign customer, "You know, these are the second most popular games in all of Greece. Athletes must take an oath to follow all the rules of competition. But these young men are dedicated, willing to train for ten months. That means no wine, no meat and no sex." He winked at his audience. "And they work tirelessly to win the victor's crown. There is no second or third place."

As I moved on, he continued to urge the stranger to go see the temple for himself, adding that it and the stadium were not far by carriage.

I wracked my brain, trying to sort out which shops would need additional help because of the expected influx of people. That, undoubtedly, would include the wealthy landowners whose homes circled the city's perimeter, but I wanted no part of that scene again. The memory returned of how my brothers anticipated their plans to go to the games with our father. Their disappointment revived, afresh, the pain of the loss of my little sister.

I found my way to the fountain and ate the bread and cheese I had purchased. Inns would soon overflow with guests, and already more people flooded the city streets. Food prepared to eat on the spot would prosper, and the sale of meat would soar, as always, at festival times. I stopped at each possible shop or booth but found no one who needed help.

An older woman, who carried a basket of vegetables and fruits, heard me inquire and stopped me before I left. "You, there, I need someone to accompany my daughter to the games. Would you be interested?"

I stared. What could she possibly mean? Women did not go to the games. I frowned, "The games?"

"Yes. She is our only child, and my husband is not able to leave home or be alone for long periods. She is too young to go by herself, only eleven summers."

"But women... girls do not—"

"No, she will take part in the musical contests. She sings and plays the lyre. You could come with me right now and meet her."

"Well, I—"

"I will pay you well. The musical rivalry is always held the first two days and is over before the athletes compete, so it will not involve many days."

I hoped to find something more permanent, but at least I would have work, and it might be an enjoyable experience. "Yes, I could do that. I have no experience with music, but I used to look after my little sister, and we should do fine together."

The woman gave a satisfied nod, and I followed her to a nearby neighborhood, glad it was not in the upscale portion of the city. We entered a modest home, similar to the captain's From another room, a weak voice called, "Zoe, is that you?"

"Yes, it is, and I found the answer to our prayers." She motioned and I followed. We went into a sitting room where an elderly man sat on a large settee, wrapped in blankets and propped with pillows. "This is Adrian, my husband." She glanced at me. "What did you say your name is?"

"It is Eunice, and I look forward to meeting your daughter."

Zoe looked around. "Where is Calliope?"

"She is in her room practicing. Been there the whole time you were gone."

"All right, I will get her." She left, and I stood there feeling awkward.

Adrian broke the silence. "So, tell me, Eunice, do you live close by?"

What should I say? Would they change their mind if they knew I had no place to call home? "No, I do not really have a home. I usually stay with people I work for, but right now I am between jobs."

He did not reply. Maybe it was a mistake to have been honest.

Just then Zoe returned with a young girl, a mere child. She was very small for her age with big brown eyes and dark hair. She smiled and came over to me.

"My name is Calliope. Mother tells me you will accompany me to the games. I am so happy she found you. I did so want to enter the competition."

I was awed at her manner and poise at such a young age. She spoke like someone much older.

I smiled. "I am Eunice, and I look forward to going with you."

"Calliope, take Eunice to your room and play for her. I want her to see how talented you are." The girl blushed but nodded at me.

In her room, she picked up her instrument with the love one might give a pet kitten. I was mesmerized when she began to sing and accompany herself with her lyre.

"That was beautiful. How long have you played and sang? You seem so young to have such ability."

"Thank you, Eunice. I think I was born with the lyre in my hands and to sing along just came naturally. Come, let us see if mother has dinner ready. Are you hungry?"

As we ate, the conversation that flowed was uplifting. I was so impressed with this little girl. The gratitude she demonstrated toward her parents for their willingness to let her pursue her dream was impressive.

Zoe brightened when I offered to do the clean up after dinner. Calliope helped and we joined her parents when we finished. Zoe smiled at me.

"Eunice, we would be pleased if you would be our guest while we work out the details of how to get our daughter to the competitions."

Calliope nodded her approval, but my glance fell on her father. Adrian did not look so sure.

Chapter Forty-One

We had only two days to prepare for the journey. Zoe was very organized. She arranged for a carriage to take us to the stadium each day, and spent hours perfecting special costumes for her daughter.

Calliope asked, "Mother, if we finish early the first day, could Eunice and I take a tour of the Isthmian temple? I have never seen the inside of it.

Zoe cocked her head. "You had better wait and see how late it is. I want you home before dark."

I took over the cooking and Zoe openly expressed her gratitude. On the night before we were to leave, I lay and stared at the ceiling. How I appreciated this safe place and the opportunity that found me. Zoe was easy to please and Calliope a delight.

I became as excited about her venture as she was. Adrian was a puzzle. More than once, I caught him staring at me, his expression one of suspicion. Except for him, I wished they would ask me to stay and work for them.

It was early when I awoke, but Calliope was already whirling throughout the house.

"Mother, we need to hurry." I fixed the breakfast, and everyone ate when they were ready. I carried Adrian's tray and sat it on the table beside him.

"Good morning, Adrian. It looks like a great day for Calliope's venture."

He grunted thanks but did not look at me.

Did he ever leave his couch? Could he walk? I had never seen him in any other part of the house. Zoe called out, so I unloaded his breakfast onto the table and left.

"Are you ready, Eunice? Calliope is dressed and anxious to start out."

As if on cue, her daughter entered the room. Her mother had fixed her hair in an upsweep that, ordinarily, would have been out of place for a child so young. She twirled for me to see her costume. It was a deep pink tunic, trimmed along the shawl with cream colored lace.

I clasped my hands in front of me. "Calliope, you look beautiful! The judges will choose you, if only, because you look like royalty and could not possibly lose."

She grinned and squeezed herself with her elbows. "Mother, is it time? Is the carriage here?"

Zoe opened the door. "Yes, it is here. Do you have everything you need?"

Calliope nodded and picked up her lyre and a small bag. I grabbed the parcel of food, I had packed for our lunch, and the money Zoe had given me to pay the drivers and anything else that came up.

Calliope ran over and hugged her father. "Pray I do well, Father, and that I am not nervous." For the first time, I saw him smile. Hugs were given and we were on our way. Calliope chatted the whole ride to the stadium. I hoped her energy would not wane before it was time to perform.

We were almost there when I noticed that Calliope stared at my veil. She blushed and looked away.

"It is all right, Calliope. See?" I raised my veil so she could see my hairy cheek. "I was born with a blemish and when I was a few years older than you, hair began to grow out of it. I wear this veil to keep people from being offended by what they see."

"I think you are beautiful. I do not care what..." She did not finish, and I let it drop. I could guess who would vilify me to her.

The driver dropped us near the entrance. It took a while to find exactly where we were to go. A kindly looking man, with a ribbon-like badge across his toga, welcomed us and pointed to the waiting area.

Moments later, he joined us. "I need some information about your daughter."

Calliope looked at me and giggled, but neither of us corrected him. A pang of sorrow hit as I realized I would never take Rose to such a special event.

The man noted her age and what kind of talent she intended to bring. Musicians of all ages lined up to register, so he did not linger but directed us to the proper area for her age.

We entered where a sign read, Ages 10 to 12. Again, an arena worker affirmed Calliope's age and talent. He said we would be in the second group to perform and showed us where we could sit and watch the performers until her turn was announced.

The stadium filled with people eager to cheer on family members. Female relatives of children and women, eager to perform in the musical division themselves, were welcomed. However, they would not be allowed entrance once athletes took center stage.

A hush fell as the man in charge took to the platform. "Thank you for coming. To honor our god, Poseidon, please stand and join us in song to highlight his might and power. Everyone stood and soon, voices rang with a tune familiar to most. Even Calliope sang, but my family did not believe in gods, and I had never heard it.

A few tributes to the god were given, by important looking men, before the competition finally started.

The man announced, "It is time to hear from our youngest contestants." Will all of those aged six to nine please fill the benches before me."

About twelve children answered his call. One little girl looked back at her mother, turned, and dashed back to the safety of her arms. The crowd cooed and laughed. I looked at Calliope. She twisted her hands.

I put my arm around her shoulders. "Do not let that unnerve you, Calliope. She is very young to be out there alone, but you are older and have practiced for years. You will do fine."

Calliope's smile was tentative, but she relaxed some.

One after another, the youngsters sang or played their instruments. Some did very well and some simply froze under the pressure of an unfamiliar venue.

I chuckled as it became obvious which woman's child performed. Each face, of the nervous mother, took on the appearance of a female bear ready to protect her cub. Applause for the brave little stars was great, generated by relief or love, if not talent.

There was a short break after which the judges announced the three who would perform again, the following day.

We were there for two hours before Calliope's group was announced. I accompanied her down into the area where we were to sit. When they called for the contestants to come forward, she stood and looked at me, surprisingly hesitant.

"Calliope, you have practiced and worked hard for years. You are very talented, and you can do this."

She gulped and nodded. I hugged her, then watched her hurry to the front with the others.

She called back, "Please pray for me, Eunice." There was no time to tell her I had no god to pray to.

Another young girl patted the empty seat beside her and motioned for Calliope to come sit with her. Their heads drew close as they waited and whispered mutual fears about what to expect.

Now, I was one of those doting "mothers." Of the twelve in her group, Calliope was number five. I wished she were first so she would finish before nerves overtook her.

These children were eons ahead of the first group. A boy played a beautiful song on his flute. The girl Calliope sat with had a rich voice of amazing range. Her rendition of a well-known song left chills for one so young. The next two performed well and all were graciously applauded.

I could not take my eyes off Calliope. Was she nervous? Could she handle being in front of such a big crowd? I whispered, "Whatever god she prays to, please help her do her best."

To my relief, as the judges called her name, a confident smile spread over her lips. She picked up her lyre, walked to the front and began to accompany herself to a song I had heard her sing many times. Its message was of quiet love and trust,as well as of joy and thanksgiving. I soon became the proud mother that could finally breathe again. She finished and I joined the crowd that showered her with appreciation.

I wanted to hug her, but she had to return to her seat and wait for the rest of her group to perform. Some had amazing talents, but I was sure Calliope had topped them all. My skin prickled with anxiety as we waited while the judges compared notes. I wished I could squeeze her hand during the announcement.

Everyone stood as the man in charge announced the first name, then the second. "Oh, please," I muttered, not sure who I was addressing. He paused and every head turned in his direction. Finally, he called Calliope's name. I had to sit before my knees failed me.

Lots of moaning swirled from disappointed parents, but I only heard Calliope call my name before she jumped on my lap and hugged me.

"Eunice, I am in! They called my name. I get to come back tomorrow. Is it not wonderful? Thank you for praying. One minute I was not sure I could do it and then a peace came over me and I knew you had prayed for me."

I was about to tell her I did not pray to anyone, rather it was her outstanding performance that deserved credit, when the man with the ribbon-like badge approached us.

"Young Lady, I want you to know that the three names of those who will come back to perform again tomorrow were called at random. You did a great job and I look forward to hearing you sing again."

Calliope beamed and I thanked him. We found a quiet place outside in the shade and ate our late lunch."

She pointed at the sun. "It looks like we will have time to visit the Isthmian temple."

I would have preferred to go back in and listen to some of the older youth and adults. Visiting the temple of yet another god did not appeal to me, but I did not want to disappoint her. "Is he the god you and your family pray to?"

Calliope's head lurched. "Oh my, no. I have just heard it is so beautiful and I would like to see it."

I wanted to ask more but it did not seem appropriate to grill a child.

Chapter Forty-Two

The day was so beautiful we decided to walk the short distance to the Isthmian temple. I slung my bag over my shoulder and carried Calliope's lyre part of the time. It was a delight to watch her prance along the road and point out each butterfly and pretty flower.

The broad, rectangular temple could be seen almost immediately. Its low, limestone block walls were surrounded by heavy columns that stood higher than the roof. We passed the Roman baths. Today, they were deserted but would bustle with athletes in a couple days.

Patron god of Corinth, Calliope read off the plaque in front of Poseidon's statue. "Why do you suppose he wanted his temple here in Isthmian?"

I repeated something I had heard. "Maybe because he lives under the sea and Isthmian is close to the ocean."

"But Eunice, why would Corinth choose him over Aphrodite? Her temple is right up on the AccuCorinth."

"Well, Aphrodite is the protector deity of our city, at least that is what is believed. I really do not know much about gods, Calliope."

She sighed. "Father has taught me some. He says the temple of Apollo, that is built on that rock out-cropping and overlooks the Lechaion Valley, dominates Corinth." She wrinkled her nose. "I wonder what that means? Do you think it is..."

I was relieved when we arrived at the entrance and her questions faded. No one was around to give us directions or guide us on what there was to see. A large map of the temple's inner design hung on a wall just inside the door. It highlighted the altar, main meeting room, the area where tributes to the god were displayed, and more.

"Come on, Calliope. We can find our own way." I pointed to the map, "See? Let us start with the altar."

We found the sacred shrine behind two large carved doors. It was dark and gloomy inside, but our eyes soon adjusted to the few oil lamps placed before the altar. An image of Poseidon in a fresco hung behind a low railing.

I heard a noise behind us and expected to see a temple guard, but nothing moved. The god looked so angry and evil, I was glad when Calliope seemed anxious to leave the room.

Down the hall, we found a room filled with hundreds of tributes to the god. Statues, paintings, frescos engraved on slates, and handmade objects hung on walls or sat on shelves. Scrolls from high officials, and even an Emperor, glorified the god.

All were unrolled behind roped off areas to keep them from being touched. Many of the sculptures represented sea creatures that swarmed Poseidon's underwater domain. Carved images of the god in various poses abounded, his trident always in hand.

Calliope wandered before she stopped to stare at the small images. "Where do you think these came from, Eunice?"

I had no idea, but they reminded me of things my father had shaped for his customers. "Perhaps, someone molded them from clay and then fired them in a kiln."

Calliope turned a replica of a dolphin over in her hands. "I would love to own one." When she reached to replace it, the delicate figurine slipped and fell to the floor.

We both stared at the object, now minus its tail and one fin. Instinctively, I glanced around to see if anyone had observed the mishap.

Calliope turned white and began to cry. "Eunice, I am sorry. I did not mean to drop it. It was as if... as if it jumped from my hand."

I put my arm around her. "Do not cry, Little One. It was an accident." I looked around again, not sure what to do. Who could I tell? We still had seen no one. I picked up the pieces and put them in my bag. "Maybe we will find someone who can tell us what to do."

Calliope had been reluctant to leave before the incident, but now stayed close to my side, edgy despite my assurance I would make it right. "I know we promised to be home before dark, but I want to take a quick peek at the famous mosaic floor. Are you all right with that?"

She looked uneasy but jerked a quick nod.

I chatted as we left for the center of the temple. "Someone, at a place I once worked, told me the main room was often used by wealthy people to hold a concinum... parties to entertain their friends." I hoped to erase the frown on her face.

Ornate double doors, down the center hall, opened to the banqueting room. The walls were a rich blue, painted to resemble the ocean on a sunny day. Frothy-looking waves were scrolled across the bottom, and etched into each corner of the ceiling were downy white clouds. The entire length of the ceiling had gold chandeliers with tall white candles that swayed slightly as we shut the door. Velvet couches lined the walls, but the beautiful floor dominated the room and instantly drew our attention.

Both Calliope and I gasped softly at the sight, hardly aware of the pristine marble entry and ledge that surrounded the mosaic. Fashioned in multi colors, sea creatures and emblems from the deep swirled around diamond shapes and circles. An image of Poseidon, stretched out in a relaxed pose, ran along both sides. The pattern was so intricate and imaginative that every few seconds we discovered and pointed out new things embedded in the design.

We had not been there long when we heard someone shouting from the far end of the room.

"This is the realm of Poseidon. You are trespassing and I command you to leave at once."

Calliope spun toward me, alarm written on her face. We both stared as a strange figure approached. I grabbed her hand and pulled her toward the exit, but before we reached it, the man blocked our way.

He was naked except for a loin cloth that ran across his lower body. On his head was a metal crown with peaks that resembled his trident. His costume was almost a replica of the one worn by the statue in front of the temple. In his hand, he held Poseidon's familiar weapon.

I tried to sound calm. "We were just leaving."

Hidden behind me, Calliope grabbed my arm and whimpered.

The man did not move. His eyes grew wide and strangely wild as he raised his trident and pointed it at us. He railed with a loud voice. "You have intruded into Poseidon's private chambers. He is the great god of the waters and has the power to destroy mere mortals and send them to the bottom of the sea."

"But we were—"

"There is no excuse for your intrusion." He stepped closer, raised the trident and continued his tirade. "You have been found guilty. The evidence is in your bag."

At his threat, Calliope gasped and clutched my tunic.

I tried not to cower. "We are so sorry about the dolphin figure. It was an accident. I wanted to make it right, but no one was around."

He began to rant again. I glanced around. Was there another way out of here?

From behind the door, a woman's voice called, "Justus? Justus are you in here?"

I turned to see a matronly-dressed woman hurry toward us.

"Justus, what are you doing? Have you harassed these guests?"

The man pulled the trident to his side. His lips puckered like a child caught being naughty. The woman gently took his hand. "Come Justus, it will soon be dinner time."

His head fell to his chest, and he quietly went alongside her.

She turned to us as they left. "I am sorry I was not able to show you around. I am the only one here today, and there was much to attend to."

She smiled at Justus. "He really is harmless. He just has days when he thinks he is Poseidon, in need of defending his territory. Please shut the outer door when you leave, and it will lock."

I reached for Calliope's hand, and we were out of there before I thought to tell the woman about the broken figurine. I shrugged. Surely, Zoe would know how we could replace it.

We walked toward the Lechaion road and had not gone far when a carriage approached. I signaled and the driver helped us climb aboard. The ten miles back to Corinth and home went quickly.

The minute we entered the door, Calliope called out, "Mother, Mother, you will not believe what happened to us."

In breathless wonder, she relayed all we had been through. Adrian listened. He did not say a word but eyed me with an accusing stare.

Zoe held her daughter close. "Oh, my poor baby. You must have been so frightened.

"I was. But Eunice was not. She stood up to the man and tried to reason with him. I knew she would not let him harm me."

Zoe smiled at me. I shrugged and shook my head.

She turned her daughter's face to hers. "But, Calliope, tell me about the contest. Were you nervous?"

"Oh Mother, I won! I mean I was chosen to come back tomorrow.

Zoe hugged her again. "Oh, wonderful! I am so proud of you!"

"I made a new friend. Her name is Deidra. She was in the contest, too. And Eunice helped me."

She ran over and took my hand. "I asked her to pray for me and she did and I was not nervous after that."

Zoe looked at me. "That is wonderful. You will have to tell us about your god, Eunice."

I nodded and hoped the subject would be forgotten by morning.

Chapter Forty-Three

Once again, Calliope was up and anxious to leave before the day started.

Zoe rolled her eyes as I entered the kitchen. "That girl wears me out...but how I wish I could be with her at the final competitions." Her eyes welled and she slumped toward the window.

It occurred to me that I could stay home with Adrian and free her to go. Silently, I raised every argument to assure myself that it would not work, but the reality was I did not want to be in his presence any longer than necessary. In the end, my conscience wore me down.

"Zoe, this is a big day in your daughter's life. You should be there to enjoy it and cheer her on. I can stay and take care of your husband. You should go."

She spun around and looked at me, without any attempt to hide the fresh tears on her cheeks.

"Oh, Eunice, that is so kind of you. I understand why Calliope has come to love you so much. You are a special blessing that has come into our lives, but no..." she choked and cleared her throat.

"I... I mean Adrian...Adrian has special care needs that compel me to never leave his presence for more than a short time. He is not a happy person, and I could not subject you to the misery he projects to everyone except Calliope... even me. And there are other issues he has forbidden me to mention."

I tried to assure her I would be fine, but soon realized my proposals only spawned more stress.

Calliope bounced into the room. "Is breakfast ready? Eunice, you are not dressed!"

I assured her I would be and finished preparing breakfast.

Zoe picked up Adrian's tray and mournfully announced, "Here is your breakfast, Adrian."

He snarled. "Did you make this or that woman?"

Zoe hushed him. "We both had a hand in it. He grumbled something about being on guard or careful, but I was not sure what he referred to.

Back in the kitchen, Zoe's crumbled expression caused my heart to go out to her.

The carriage arrived and Calliope and I were on our way. Before we turned off the Lechion way, a contingent of Roman soldiers blocked the road. Some rode horses, others walked. Behind the initial group, a carriage large enough to hold half a dozen people moved at a leisurely pace. The shades were down so we could not see who was inside.

Our driver was forced to pull onto the side of the road to make room for them to pass. It took over a half hour for the last of the entourage to clear the road ahead of us.

Calliope fidgeted. "Eunice, what if we are late? What if I miss my..."

I touched her arm. "No, do not worry. We left in plenty of time. Remember how long we waited for your group to perform, yesterday?"

I asked the driver if he knew who was in the carriage and why they were headed toward Corinth.

"Cannot tell you Missus, but probably some men from Athens. Must be important to merit special transportation and the protection of the Roman army. This is only the second year the games have resumed after the city's reconstruction, and you can bet some of the higher uppers want to be there."

He snickered. "They will stay in Corinth at night...better accommodations and nightlife, if you know what I mean."

I thought of the temple prostitutes and shuddered. The faces, of the girl who urged me to join them and the young man the captain brought home, flashed in front of me. Corinth would live up to its reputation and outdo itself with drunken, lewd parties in the week to come.

We arrived at the stadium in plenty of time and were seated well before the youngest contestants began their routines.

I glanced at Calliope, relieved to see she seemed at peace. We applauded along with the others as a boy of seven, who played a miniature harp, won the contest.

The judges placed the crown of celery leaves on his thick curly hair. He jerked a quick bow that caused his trophy to slide to his feet. Unconcerned, he reached down and plunked it back on his head. Everyone laughed and clapped again.

Calliope's eyes shone when the master of the ceremonies announced her group would be next.

She called back, "Do not forget to pray for me, Eunice," and found a spot by her friend, Deidra. They huddled again and shared little girl whispers and giggles.

Deidra was called right before Calliope. As if accompanied by a symphony, her powerful voice echoed in waves over the stadium. The audience affirmed their appreciation with lengthy applause.

Calliope was next. She picked up her lyre, gave me a quick wave and walked to the front. Halfway through her song, a string on her lyre broke. An audible gasp whooshed through the audience.

My insides collapsed like a wind-whipped canopy. I did not care who heard me. "Oh, god she prays to, please help her."

Calliope paused and swallowed her distress. She laid down her instrument and finished her song. The crowd gave her a standing ovation. She gave a slight bow and sat quietly through the final contestant's rendition of a hymn to Poseidon. She did not look as disappointed as I was.

The other two contestants had been excellent, but I hoped the poise Calliope showed under this unfortunate setback would improve her standings.

I watched the judges deliberate and compare notes, look at the contestants, and compare some more. Their faces showed signs of disagreement, but the spokesman finally stepped up to announce their decision. In the end, Deidra received the honor.

Calliope hugged and congratulated her friend, picked up her lyre, and headed for the exit. I expected tears when she reached me.

I drew near but the crowd swarmed Calliope. Each wanted to encourage her. They praised her performance and how she persisted and finished, despite her instrument's failure.

A lady who towed one of the previous day's contestants said, "You should have won."

Another added, "Oh my, yes. "Your gentle expression of the lyrics was beautiful."

The father of the harp player joined the crowd around Calliope. "Young Woman. That was a very brave thing you did. In my mind, you are a winner."

Finally, the way cleared and I reached her. My eyes filled, but she beamed.

"Oh Eunice, you must have prayed, or I could not have finished. I am just sorry I do not have a winner's wreath to take home to my family. "

Before I could assure her that her courageous response to the mishap was greater than a garland, a young voice called out.

"Calliope, wait up." Deidra ran up with her celery wreath in front of her. She tore the crown in two. "Here, you deserve this as much as I do. You were amazing!"

She placed half on Calliope's head and the other half on her own. They both laughed at the torn strips that dangled down their faces.

Calliope squeezed her friend and released the tears she had held. "Deidra, you have ruined your prize. You deserved this honor. You are so talented. How can I thank you?"

Behind, the girl's mother smiled broadly. "That is my girl. She always wants everyone to win."

For a few minutes, the girls chatted about the stress and pressure they had felt before Deidra's mother tugged her arm. "Time to go, Dear."

Calliope fell into my arms and wept happy tears. "Eunice, was that not wonderful? Deidra and I intend to keep in touch."

I was too moved to speak, amazed at the depth of compassion and selflessness in these two young girls. I tried to picture myself at their age but quickly dismissed the painful memories it evoked.

Calliope fingered her half of a crown as we rode home in quiet contentment. Already, the celery leaves had grown limp, but I knew she would cherish it forever.

Zoe listened to the whole story and shook her head. Pride shone from her eyes as she listened to Calliope dwell not on her loss but her joy in her friend and the girl's generous gesture.

Adrian's eyes were closed, but I suspected he was awake.

Calliope walked quietly over but left, thinking he was asleep.

Zoe fixed dinner and we all retired early. In the night I needed a drink of water, so I rose but did not light a lamp. On my way back, Adrian called out to me.

I stopped outside the alcove where his couch nearly filled the space. "Yes, can I get you something?"

"I need to talk to you. I do not like the influence you are having on my family."

My heart began to race. What had I done to irritate him so?

He sat up and looked at me. It was dark but I could see he scowled. "Are you one of those from the group Zoe meets with... the ones that proclaim a new god?"

I was so taken aback I did not answer right away.

"Zoe has come to think this god is the answer to everything, but I know different. Poseidon is the official god we worship here at Corinth."

I was stunned by the animosity behind his voice. Did what he believed bring such anger into their home? No wonder Zoe said there were issues. If Poseidon was his god, it certainly had not given him the prosperity and protection promised, and certainly not the peace his wife and Calliope had.

I inhaled strength enough to answer him. "Adrian, I do not have a god, but from what I have seen in Zoe and Calliope, maybe you should reconsider what god you serve."

"That is enough, young woman. I knew there was evil behind that veil you wear. I want you out of my house, first thing in the morning, and do not come back... ever."

Chapter Forty-Four

I crawled back into bed, but sleep taunted like a puppy whose ball had scrambled out of reach. I would have to leave, but how did I explain it to Zoe and Calliope without setting them against the ruler of their house? They had not asked me to stay. Maybe, it would not be an issue.

You are a special blessing... no wonder Calliope has come to love you. Zoe's words rose and brought pain to my heart. I thought of Calliope's confidence in prayers I had lifted to her god, with no idea who he was. For the first time, I wanted to hear about this god, but the opportunity was lost. How I would miss her.

Before sleep came, I concocted a story about my need to go home and check on my family. I rose early, tempted to sneak off and avoid an unpleasant confrontation or sad goodbyes.

Calliope peeked in my door and noticed I had gathered my bag and cloak.

"Eunice? What are you doing? Why have you packed your things?

A wedge formed between her brows. "You are not about to leave... are you?"

I related the tale I had settled upon. To my surprise, she burst into tears.

"But Eunice, I do not want you to leave. I love you."

I thought my heart would break. She sounded so much like my little sister, Chara, on that fateful day when she begged me to take her with me to the market. I clutched Calliope to my chest, tempted to confront Adrian and expose his false assumptions.

Zoe hurried into the room. "What is going on? I thought I heard Calliope cry out."

Her shoulders drooped as she listened to my explanation. She grimaced. "I am so sorry you have to leave, Eunice. I hoped you would stay on with us. I have so appreciated your help with the house and with Calliope. But if your family needs you, I know you must go."

I wanted to withdraw my lie but could think of no other way to avoid sowing discord among these I had come to love.

Zoe insisted I have breakfast. It was not easy to ignore the smirk on Adrian's face as Calliope continued to lament my decision.

I turned my back and answered a few questions about my family. I hid the reality of my past life by highlighting our nearness to the sea and my grandfather's great influence on my life. Calliope still moped as I hugged her and bid them goodbye.

The sun was bright, and blossoms had burst on every tree, but their cheer eluded me. I tried to imagine a fulfilled future with people to love, who would love me in turn. My hope never rose above the dust stirred by my feet.

All the pleasant places I had settled into, after I left home, had been torn away by relentless circumstances. The orchard with Thera and the twins had held hope, until Yorgos brought home a new wife, . Peace in the home of the wool merchant's family had disappeared once his income faded and necessitated I leave. The promise of a family to call my own, at the meat merchant's home, had evaporated and Phobie's inn, sold for her much needed benefit, left me devastated. And now, I was forced to leave Zoe's family, because of an angry man who saw me as a threat.

Thoughts, of the different places I had lived, revived disappointment in loves I assumed would last forever. I could picture each one... Yorgos, who never knew I loved him, Alistar with his lack of backbone and integrity, and dear Pavlos, whose loss I still mourned.

My mind drifted to those who took advantage of me or tried to... my own brother, the worker at the sheep farm, the man who bought Phobie's inn. Why did evil dwell in so many? I had seen it in my father, who purposefully spearheaded rejection of me throughout my family. I thought about Rose, who perished because of the worst decision of my life, cast aside in a permanent cessation of my doing. Was I not as evil as they?

I passed through the city, alone again, a misfit in one of the most affluent cities in Greece, and the most wicked. I thought about the class system I had witnessed at every turn. Despite no possibility of rising to a higher plane, most everyone seemed to accept his status.

This included those at the bottom of the ladder. Slaves and the poor suffered the most, treated as non-persons by those who looked down on them. Daily, the weak, the sick, and the hungry lined up for the grain subsidy, doled out by the city. This meager provision was meant to keep the many from starvation and to stave off riots.

I skirted the area the citizens boasted as being Greece's largest slave market, grateful it was not open. Seeing people treated as property, with no rights, frustrated my helplessness of no way to intervene. Many passed on the days it operated with hardly a glance. Could I ignore human decency, look the other way, and embrace this accepted pattern of life?

How I wished Grandfather were alive. I would run and hide in his loving care and shut out this world I had somehow become part of.

The agora was crowded, and the market still hummed with people excited about the Isthmian games. Women raved about the poetry and drama competitions they planned to attend. The long-anticipated athletic competition, that followed, inspired wagers and arguments among the men.

The man, who owned a tailor shop, announced to any who would listen, "Dulacus will win the chariot race. Wait and see. He has practiced for years, and this is his time."

The shop owner across the agora challenged, "You cannot be sure of that. Anthony is a lot younger, but he is natural. Nobody controls a chariot or brings out the best in a horse like he does. "

Before I made my way around the crowd, two more men took up the argument. I turned toward the fountain. Did it really matter? Was life more than games or pleasure? I sat and watched the water reach for the sky, hesitate, and fall back into the pond. Its journey seemed as useless as mine.

A cloud passed and the sun filled the droplets with sparkling light. I could not have explained why, but it was as if something or someone smiled on me with a message, "It is going to be all right."

I pulled out the food Zoe packed for me and ate a little, scattering crumbs to sparrows bold enough to hop within range. I knew I should start to inquire of the merchants, but I could not bring myself to take the first step. How could I present a confident, positive front when I had nothing to give and had lost hope of finding a satisfactory position that lasted?

I threw the remains of my pita to the sparrows, disgusted at how they greedily gobbled as much as they could before the rest of the flock discovered the feast. They were so like people.

The large carriage, Calliope and I waited for on our last trip, passed down the agora. This time the windows were not shaded, and I saw four or five men in expensive clothing climb out near the Bema.

Each hurried under the roof to get out of the heat before he climbed the few stairs.

Erastus, the director of public works who oversaw the games, all public facilities, and the agora rose and invited them to sit on seats reserved for visiting dignitaries.

I had seen him once with the man they called Paul. The overseer had a kind face, and one time had even asked me how I fared. People began to crowd the area, curious about who they were and anxious to hear of any new happenings or announcements.

I decided it might be a good time to interview the shops I stood and picked up my things.

"Miss, wait. Could you help me fill these jugs from the fountain and take them to the men on the podium? I will pay you for your time. I need to hurry. It is hot and, already, they are complaining of thirst."

The driver of their carriage held out a coin well worth my time. I nodded, picked up three of his vessels, filled them, and said, "Here, give me the rest and I will come right behind you."

He agreed and I followed him to the back of the podium. He took the first vessels to three of the men and returned for the rest. "If you can, please wait a moment until I return."

He was not gone long. The pompous speeches that boomed from the Bema were full of self-importance and drivel. Even the crowd had diminished considerably.

The driver was back in minutes with a question. "Are you looking for work? I ask because I brought these men here from Athens and they are staying at a nearby inn. The owners are swamped and unable to do any extra laundry. Would you be interested? They pay well and it will only be until the end of the games."

"Yes, I am looking for a new position. I could do it, but I have no place to work out of so I —"

"Oh, that will not matter. The lady at the inn said you could go there in the afternoons when they finished with the tubs and hang the laundry there to dry."

It was not what I had in mind, but I had learned to take work when it was offered. The man gave me a drachma in advance and told me which inn needed my help. I watched him leave and wondered where I might find a place to sleep.

Chapter Forty-five

I decided to locate the inn where the men from Athens registered. Maybe laundry awaited my attention. Not surprisingly, the establishment was in the best part of the city. I knocked on a service door and waited. The woman who answered looked exhausted. Her hair had come loose from her bun and some of the wisps stuck to her forehead. A dark smudge remained where she swiped at the sweat that poured down her neck.

"I am sorry. We have no empty beds. Perhaps you could try..."

"Oh, I am not here for a bed. I was hired to do the laundry for your guests from Athens. I came to see if there are clothes waiting to be washed, or if—"

"I do not know anything about that. I am just the cook. Wait a minute and I will ask the owner."

When she did not return for what seemed a lengthy time, I stood. Should I leave? Loud voices, that came from inside the door, stopped me.

"I am tired of your excuses. You are lazy and completely unorganized. No wonder the meals are never ready on time." The nasal whine threatened from a woman who sounded much younger.

The cook reasoned, "But Misses, I told you this job is too much for one person, especially when the inn is full. I cannot shop and bake bread and pastries and prepare all the food for so many. There is not enough time in a day. You need to hire a girl to help me."

The younger voice continued to berate until an inner door slammed. Had the cook left? I would not have blamed her. Why did those who considered themselves of a higher station treat those they deemed beneath them so unkindly?

A woman in a silk tunic draped in gold chains called out and motioned to me. "You there." She looked me over and lifted her chin. "Cook said you were here about doing some laundry. Is this for some men from Athens?"

I nodded. "Yes, their driver said—"

She snapped, "I know. I know. You will find the tubs in that small building behind the house. I will have my servants put the men's laundry in the tubs when the maids finish with them, and you can use what you need. There may be some in there now. You will have to look" She turned away and added over her shoulder, "They have paid me for the privilege, so I expect it to be done properly."

I felt like a worm the woman would not hesitate to step on. It was still early afternoon, so I began to sort the clothes. When I had hung the last of the undergarments and togas and emptied the water, the cook joined me. Her red cheeks and puffy eyes attested to what had likely transpired between her and the owner.

She asked if I knew how to cook and if I would be interested in assisting her while the games were on.

I asked the obvious question. "Umm, I could not help but overhear the owner's tongue-lashing. Are you sure she is open to hiring help?"

"I put her on the spot. I had begun to pack and leave when she realized she would be in a bad way with no cook and an inn full of people. It was her idea to ask you."

She assured me I would have plenty of time for the laundry. I agreed and told her I needed to find a place to sleep and asked what time she wanted me here in the mornings. She said I could sleep in a little cove off the pantry no one used.

We cleaned and tidied the kitchen after dinner, did some prep work for breakfast, and stopped for the night. Endless clothes to scrub, plus the commitment to help cook and serve, made the days fly.

The men from Athens were served meals first, in a smaller, intimate dining area. The rest of the guests dined at the typical long table in the parlor.

I marveled at how the hostess hovered over the five men, eager and attentive. Her eyes darted from one to the next, like a bird that hoped a few crumbs might fall.

Each night she dressed in a fancy chiton, her dark hair braided or swept to one side of her face. Except to express their wants, none of the five paid her any attention or acknowledged her presence. All her efforts to be accepted on their level accomplished nothing. She, too, was subject to the system.

The morning I prepared to leave, the cook touched my arm. "Oh, Eunice, I wish you could stay on and help me. We worked so well together." I had hardly seen the owner, which was fine by me. I did not want to work for her even if she offered, though it left me with no position to count on.

The cook handed me my wages. We shared a warm hug, and I wished her well. Back in the city, the streets were much less crowded, now that the games had finished.

I passed the many temples along the way. Did the gods, they served, really dwell within those structures like people claimed? Did the elaborate rituals, sacrifices, and feasts maintain the harmony their followers craved from their deity? And were their fears of reprisal relieved, or did they win the favor they sought by their service and offerings?

I thought of Phobie and of Zoe and Calliope. The hunger in their souls seemed satisfied by their trust in a god they deemed bigger and more powerful than themselves. He seemed a different kind of a god, one they were confident loved and cared about their needs.

Sadly, I identified more with the emptiness apparent in the captain's life. Why did the god, he trusted, let him die alone and helpless? Was he really punished because of his lifestyle, or did he not sacrifice enough or pay the proper homage? Did ones welfare depend on whether he pleased the god he chose to honor? What good were these gods if they were not available when a person needed their intervention? Yet, the loyalty and devotion of their followers was evident in all they said and did.

Questions swirled without answers. Would I ever understand?

Chapter Forty-Six

I headed for my favorite bench by the fountain. As I bent to brush off some bird droppings, coins jingled in my pouch. The sound was a comfort. It was enough money to live on, until I found a new position. Too soon, contentment drifted like an elusive thought that teased and hovered just out of reach. I did not mind a life of service to people, but once again, I found myself bereft of hope for much of a future.

Before the persistent emptiness pulled me into self-pity, I decided to pursue work with some of the merchants. Just ahead, the long line of people awaited their daily handout. I paused. Would I not qualify for the same reasons? No job? No place to stay? No family to help me through? Faces wrought with anger or despair stared, as I approached. Pride moved me on. I was not where they were...at least not yet.

I had never been in this area before, and when I reached the halfway point, a little girl pointed at me. "Mama, look. That lady has a mask on."

The woman's face turned red. She pulled her daughter close, "Hush, Child. It is not nice to point."

A burly man, with unkempt clothing and a straggly beard that bore evidence of yesterday's dinner, stared and spoke in a loud voice. "She is right. That woman has the evil eye and she has covered her face to try to hide it."

People turned to see. Women pulled their children close, gestured, and whispered among themselves.

Another man agreed "Yes, that is an evil eye. Stay away or she will bring a curse upon you."

A woman screeched, "Get away from us!" Others joined her fear and called out insults and threats.

The man with the beard picked up a stone and threw it at me, and before I could react, rocks flew from several directions. For a moment, I was so shocked the connection from my mind to my feet seemed to have been severed. I could not move. I stared back, unable to process their cruel intentions. Children delighted in this distraction and eagerly scoured the ground for rocks. Some bounced at my feet, but others hit my legs and arms.

A piece of broken granite, thrown by a youth in filthy clothing, hit me in the chest. The blow unhinged my stupor. I pulled up my tunic and ran, mindful of rocks that bounced behind me. The echo of death threats and footsteps pounded in my ears. When the outcry diminished, I looked back, relieved to see Roman soldiers. It had not taken long for fear of the authorities, and their lack of tolerance for riots, to quell those determined to reach me. Taunts that rang in my ears, finally, faded. It took much longer to dwindle from my fractured soul.

Sobs tore at my chest. Would the soldiers follow me... blame me? How could those people be so cruel? What did I do to deserve their ire? I worked my way down a narrow alley between a Roman bath and the palestrae. Neglected ceanothus bushes, behind the wrestling school, assured me the area was not used. I crawled beneath them, cried, and shook for hours.

Had I deserved this attack? Is this what I was... evil? I could not reconcile what had happened. Deep within, I heard my mother and my brothers scream their mutual conviction that I was born evil. For the first time, I began to question myself. Maybe I was evil. Maybe that was why I had nothing and no one in my life.

It was hours before I dared pursue a different path back into the agora to buy food. Already, the shops were closing. I glanced around and a knowing, deep in my soul, hit with the same force as that piece of rock: there would be no place for me in decent society... now or ever.

But what did it matter? My desire to pursue a respectable life had died, buried under an avalanche of rejection. No one cared and I had lost all hope of change.

I bought some food and took it back to my hiding place. I ate, then spread my cape under one of the overhanging bushes and lay down.

Through branches thick with purplish-blue flowers, I stared at the stars. Tears trickled toward my ears until sleep shut out my misery.

For almost a week, I followed that pattern: go out when people were few, buy food before the vendors left, fill my water jug at the fountain, and bring both back to my desolate burrow.

My funds began to run out. What could I do? I could not stay here indefinitely. To ask for work at the shops made me quiver. Was there something I could sell? Nothing I owned had any value.

Before I dismissed the possibility, I remembered the statue of Aphrodite. It had traveled with me since I left the captain's home. I pulled it from my bag, unwrapped and inspected it. My many moves had caused no damage, or even scratched its perfect surface. Now, where might I find a buyer?

Going out into the crowded agora terrified me. Markets that sold such things were plentiful, but would they see evil when I approached?

Would they scream threats and stir people to attack me?

There were moments when I knew my reasoning made no sense, but I could not bring myself to believe another assault did not await me.

The temple prostitute I had met, before I found work with the captain, came to mind. Maybe if I sat on that same bench away from the agora, she would see me, and I could ask her. Surely, she would know of someone who honored Aphrodite and would want such a beautiful statue.

I waited, until dawn was but a few hours away, before I made my way down the alley and to the spot where we had first talked.

For two nights, I shivered on the bench. When drunken men staggered my way, I ducked behind a nearby flowering oleander bush. Desperation and hunger motivated me to try a third night. Hope leapt to my throat when I saw a girl approach. I wanted to shout. It was her!

She smiled at me. "Hello. Are you not the girl I talked to here once before?"

I jumped to my feet. "Yes, I hoped you might come by again."

"You did? I had the impression you disapproved of my mission to serve Aphrodite."

"I am sorry, I—"

"What are you doing here? Are you still looking for work?"

I was not sure how to answer her. I pulled the statue from my bag. "I am out of work again, but I have this statue and I thought maybe you would know someone who might want to buy it."

Her glance at my clothes and hair brought a frown. I held up the statue. She took it and looked it over.

"My, this is beautiful. I believe the overseer of the temple, where I serve, would love to display it. The sun will soon light the horizon. Why not come with me, and I will show it to him."

I wondered where her temple was. I had climbed the Acrocorinth and seen the ruins of the original temple, but knew a couple of smaller ones had been built to continue Aphrodite's worship.

Part of me hesitated to step into one, but I dismissed the thoughts. Who was I to say what was acceptable?

"Yes, thank you." I gathered my things, grateful I had brought them with me.

She smiled. "I will show you where I live, and you could bathe there if you like."

My face flushed as I imagined how I looked and smelled after over a week without a place to bathe or wash my clothes.

I followed her past the Apollo temple, beyond the ones that honored Dionysus and Hera, to an area where a shrine to Aphrodite clustered with several smaller temples.

She stopped before a two-story building with tall pillars on each side of the entrance. Near the roof, a scroll depicted a woman in a flowing gown. It had been carved into the exterior. Foam covered waves lapped at her feet and one arm reached past her head, as if she directed her chosen flight.

An older man with a gold and purple cap on his head, stood when we entered.

"Welcome Zylina. Were you able to honor our goddess with a sacred marriage tonight?"

She nodded and pulled some coins from a pouch. I watched in awe as she proudly dropped what she had earned into a box with a slot on the top. They clanked against those already deposited. The man smiled and she beamed like a victor at the games.

His eyes swept my rumpled tunic. "And who have we here? A new follower of Aphrodite?" Zylina turned to me. "I do not know your name."

"It is Eunice " Should I show him the statue?

She introduced me. "Eunice has a beautiful statue of our goddess, she is looking to sell. Would you like to see it?"

The man nodded, his face a picture of doubt. I unwrapped and held it up, then watched for clues of what he thought. He looked it over for several minutes.

His brow flinched as he looked back at me. "This is a very special likeness of our goddess. May I ask how you came to own it?"

What should I say? I kept it after the owner died with no heirs to claim it. Would he consider me a thief? I told him the truth, that after the captain died, I had to leave when his rent was due. "He had no heirs, and because I had not received my wages for nearly a month, I felt justified in keeping this as partial payment."

"Well, I believe this statue would have compensated you for several months. It is an exquisite likeness of our goddess, and I would love to have it here to inspire everyone who honors Aphrodite. Let me look into its true value and I will tell you what I find in a day or two."

I nodded and Zylina motioned for me to follow. I picked up my things and stepped into the heart of a temple that heralded the immoral lifestyle of Corinth.

Chapter Forty-Seven

Zylina led me into a large room with a marble altar swathed in silk draperies. Candles flickered in brass lamp stands. Each multiplied the eerie glow on the carved statues of the goddess.

I turned from those that showed her in lewd embraces with her many lovers. While Zylina bowed at the altar to recite rote homage to her goddess, I stood aside and waited.

The quarters where she slept were small. Four bunks were crowded into a space that left barely enough room to pass through. I wondered where the thousand other prostitutes, who serviced the goddess, lived.

"This is it, Eunice. None of the others are back, so you can undress here. Our tub is behind that curtain, but there is not much room or a place to put anything in there."

I thanked her, eager to bathe and put on my only other tunic. The water felt wonderful. I wanted to linger but felt I should finish before her roommates returned. I dumped the water after I washed my dirty clothes in it and rolled them in the towel she had given me.

As I pulled a comb through my wet hair, Zylina said, "Eunice, you would make a lovely addition to our efforts to glorify our goddess. Would you not like to join us? It would end your ongoing struggle to find work and a place to sleep."

Thoughts of what else it would include made me shiver. "Zylina, I do not think I could do that, and besides you have seen my face. I doubt your overseer would want someone like me to represent your goddess."

"Well, lots of girls wear veils. The thing is, you have to see yourself as Aphrodite's partner in marriage. When you entice a man to cohabit, you must believe in your heart that you honor our goddess as you enter a realm of intimacy. It is the same as when a wife honors her husband's wishes.

I listened and tried to grasp the validity of what she believed.

"And I doubt anyone would notice your face with your lovely figure, your beautiful brown eyes, and that gorgeous hair."

"Besides that, Zylina, I am not a virgin. There was a time when I lived with a man I thought was going to marry me."

With a brush of her hand, she swept aside my confession. "Oh, that. Few of us were before we entered Aphrodite's service. Well, maybe ones whose families brought them here immediately after the start of their menses. It is true men want to marry a girl with the flower of her innocence in tack, but it does not matter here. We are engaged in an act of marriage to honor our goddess of virility, love, and fertility."

We talked for a while before I picked up my bag. "I should probably leave. I assume this is your time to sleep."

"Why not nap too?" She pointed at the bed next to hers. "You can use that bunk. The girl that slept there has not returned for three days. By late afternoon, dinner will be ready and you can eat with us before you go."

The warm bath and sleepless nights persuaded me. I would leave before Zylina began her nightly ritual.

It felt good to lay in a bed instead of the hard ground. As I drifted off, I wondered what happened to the girl whose bed I lay in.

"Eunice?" A voice called me out of a hazy dream. "Dinner is almost ready. Are you awake?"

I opened my eyes. Zylina stood over me in a fresh tunic. It was not like the ones I had seen on priestesses in the early mornings or after a night in the city. The ones who plied their trade in the daytime wore simpler tunics.

Layers of white folds fell from her shoulders, across her bosom and wrapped her tiny waist. Her sandals were of gold leather with straps that criss crossed up her calves.

I yawned. "I am sorry. I did not mean to—"

She laughed. "Do not worry. You must have been tired to sleep so soundly. Come, let us go down to the dining room.

"You look beautiful. Is this a special costume?"

"Yes. On the night of the new moon, we celebrate the birth of our goddess of beauty and pleasure. We take candles and incense with us to intensify passions."

Such uninhibited assent amazed me. Eager to change the subject, I asked about her roommates. "Did they come back this morning?"

She assured me they had and were already at dinner.

We entered a large area with plenty of seating. As soon as we sat down, a worker brought us a plate of fish and vegetables. Watered wine was passed, along with rolls fresh from the ovens.

Bits of upbeat conversations surprised me... subjects one would hear discussed among any group of young women. At a far table, seated by herself and looking forlorn, a young girl pushed food around on her plate.

Back in the room I asked Zylina about the girl.

"Oh, you mean Lycia. She is new. Her father recently brought her as an offering to our goddess. She was not happy about it. We heard her cry for her mother the first three nights and she still has not fully entered into our purpose. It happens, but she will get used to it in time. We all do."

Zylina introduced me to the two girls who shared her room. Sidelong glances swept at my veil, but they did not ask about it. I gathered my things, prepared to leave when Zylina said it was time.

"Eunice, would you like to come with me? You could see what —"

I shook my head. "I do not think so, but I will walk back to the city with you."

Zylina cocked her head, her lips pursed. I could not read her expression. "All right. But it will be dark soon. Why not stay and sleep here? That bed is still empty, and we can check with the overseer about your statue when I return in the morning."

My instinct was to refuse, but I had nowhere to go and I needed to be back in the morning. What harm could it bring?

Before the sky forewarned of dawn, I heard someone prowl about in the darkened room. My heart raced. I did not move but squinted and saw a woman searching through the parcels on two of the beds. She did not take anything, just rifled through each bag, then replaced the contents.

She started for Zylina's bunk but tripped over a leg of the bed and fell. Caution aside, I sat up. My eyes adjusted and I stared into the face of a terrified soul that probably reflected my own.

"Can I help you? Have you lost something?"

She rose from the floor. "Please, please, do not tell anyone I was here, I did not mean to—

"She sounded so frightened, I wanted to comfort her. "It is all right. I would not, normally, be here either. What is it you look for?

She burst into tears. "It is my daughter's things. This was her room before, before..."

I waited while she calmed down. "This is the bed of a girl who has not been seen for a while, perhaps it is her things in the pouch under the bed. Did she send you to get them?"

The woman sobbed, hardly able to speak. "She cannot send anyone. "She is dead!"

It took a while, but I finally learned the girl's body had been found beaten and dumped in a field not far from the temple.

Occasionally, word spread through the city that one of Aphrodite's prostitutes had been found dead, probably killed by a drunken suitor. I pulled out the pouch and handed it to her mother.

"I am so sorry about your daughter. Take her things with you and do not worry. No one else is around and I will not tell anyone you were here."

She left and I lay awake. I shivered at the thought that I lay in the bunk of a girl who had met a vicious end. To shut out a scenario of what probably happened was impossible.

My imagination played and replayed the horror. Thoughts of the young woman who cried for her mother, returned. What was I doing here?

Zylina returned just after dawn. She looked worn out. As she drew close, I noticed a tear in the front of her special tunic and some marks on her neck.

She tossed some things on her bunk and motioned for me to follow. We went to see the overseer about my statue, but he was not there. Zylina frowned. "I think we may have to wait a while. Let us go get breakfast and we will try again."

The overseer still was not there when we arrived the second time. I insisted Zylina get her rest while I waited in the courtyard.

Time dragged as I sat on a bench by a small table. Should I have let the man take the statue? I had almost talked myself into going over to see if he had arrived when he walked through the outer gate, accompanied by a Roman soldier.

Chapter Forty-Eight

The director of the temple smiled. "Good morning, Eunice, this is Captain Blaylock. He would like to ask you some questions."

I gasped and jumped to my feet. My mind scrambled for possibilities of what this might be about. Was I responsible for the near riot among the people lined up for food? Had I trespassed by sleeping behind the palestra? Nothing made sense.

The soldier stepped closer. He looked vaguely familiar, but in their helmets they tended to look alike.

He cocked his head and stared at me for a moment. "Miss, I need to find out how you acquired the statue you brought here yesterday."

I opened my mouth, but fear wrapped my tongue and refused to release it.

The overseer spoke up. "Do not be afraid. He just needs to verify how you came to own it."

The soldier pointed at the bench. "Please, sit back down and I will join you."

I willed my feet to move and both men sat across from me.

"Now, tell me exactly how you came to own this statue."

I found my voice and related the same sequence of events I had explained to the overseer.

The captain squinted, noting everything I said. "What was the name of the officer you worked for?"

At the mention of the captain's name, the soldier's head rose sharply. He did not acknowledge it, but suddenly I realized he was the soldier who had brought me the news of the captain's death. I repeated what he had told me that night, and how I learned that the captain had no family in Greece but might have had some in Rome.

I explained, it was strictly a working relationship. "I shopped and cleaned and had meals ready for him. He never talked to me about anything other than what he wanted me to do or his expectations. Most nights, he would leave after dinner and not come back until early morning."

"When did you first see the statue?"

"I had not seen it at all until after he died. I cleaned the place before I left and found it stored in a cabinet that I never had occasion to open."

The soldier eyed me for a moment, then spoke kindly. "Well, Miss, I am sorry to have to tell you that this valuable statue was stolen over a year ago from a collection of artifacts from Aphrodite's original temple. We do not believe you stole it and there is no way to verify how it ended in the captain's possessions."

He stood and addressed the overseer. "It belongs to the city of Corinth and will have to be returned to them."

He nodded at me. "Thank you for your time."

The overseer followed the soldier out and handed over the statue. My head fell into my hands. I wished for a moment I had sold it in the market. But of course, it was not mine.

Now I had nothing of value to sell, no money, and no prospects of work. I thought about the place where I had hidden. But then what? I could not chance a search for work in the agora, and to line up for food with the poor was out of the question.

The overseer called as I shut the courtyard gate. "Wait a minute. I am sorry for the way this turned out, but I suspected from the start that it was an ancient treasure. Why do you not join us and become a worshipper of

Aphrodite? She is the goddess of love, and she will put her seal of approval over you and take care of all your needs."

A picture of the hurt young girl flashed before me. It faded to Zylina's torn tunic and the marks on her neck and settled on the face of the distraught mother who gathered her dead daughter's things.

But my terror at being attacked in the market, and my vulnerability to it happening again, rushed a tsunami of panic to my chest. The rush drowned the imminent danger and degradation from my brain.

Why not join them? Nothing I could foresee, in my future, held any promise of change.

I heard myself say, "Yes." The word echoed, as if it bounced off the image of Aphrodite above the entrance and back in my face.

The overseer explained there would be a ritual of purification and dedication to which I must submit. He added that I would be assigned a mentor to prepare me for my mission.

I was ushered into a room behind the one where I first saw him, and introduced me to the woman in charge of recruits. The overseer left and the woman asked me to sit while she filled out a list to give to my mentor.

After a short interview, she excused herself. I sat in numbed silence, amazed that no attention was paid to why I decided to join them.

She returned with a much older woman whose jowls hung nearly to her shoulders. They pulled the bags beneath her eyes past her nose.

"Sabah will be your mentor. Follow her lead and you will be one with us in no time."

The aged woman nodded at me and took me into a small cove where she went over Aphrodite's history, her birth, her lovers, and her legacy. For one so old, her enthusiasm surprised me.

Most of it I had heard since I moved close to the city but had given little thought to its importance. I marveled at the woman's zeal and dedication to the goddess. Had she herself served as a prostitute in years past?

She spent several minutes emphasizing the mystery of marriage that honored the goddess with each intimate encounter as Zylina had explained.

I fought to dismiss the memory of my brother's demeanor when he raped me. Would this be a similar experience? Could I go through with it? Hopelessness overruled my desire for a less dismal choice.

I thought of the young women chatting in the dining area, awed at their cheerful outlooks. Would I ever be like that? Would I ever get used to it, as Zylina had said?

Sabah stood. "The offerings you receive, for this labor of love, will keep our temple strong so that Aphrodite will be forever honored. The purification and dedication ceremonies will be held tomorrow night.

"Come, I will show you where you can put your things until you are assigned a room. Meanwhile, you need to spend time in worship of the goddess and to prepare your heart for a life of service to her."

She showed me to a room not unlike the one Zylina lived in, then encouraged me to spend time in the courtyard until the late afternoon meal.

I wandered about and thought about the instructions the mentor had given me. Guilt pulsed. Most were here because they worshipped the goddess. My motive was simply I had nowhere else to turn, but no one seemed to care.

When a gong announced dinner, I went in with the others, not sure where I should sit.

"Eunice." I turned and saw Zylina stand and wave at me. She caught up and smiled. "You are still here. I hoped to see you before you left. Did the overseer buy your statue?"

She led me to a table, and I filled her in on the discovery that the statue had been stolen.

"Oh, Eunice, I am so sorry, you must have been so disappointed. But wait, why then are you still here?"

I told her about my decision. To my surprise she reached over and hugged me. "I am sure this was not an easy decision, but I believe—"

I held up my palms. "I know. I know. I will get used to it."

She laughed. "You need to ask if you can be assigned to the bed next to mine. I heard about the death of the girl from our room. It is too bad. She was very beautiful."

It struck me as odd that Zylina mentioned only the girl's beauty. Had her roommate not been a close colleague, a daily companion? Perhaps she had not been there long. I tried not to think about it.

I told her that the ceremonies were tomorrow night. "Is there any way you could come with me? I know you leave about that time."

"Oh, I will ask. They are fine if we leave a little later or do not go at all, some nights. I am so happy for you. It will be great to have you with us."

I turned in early. I wished I were as sure as she was. We had breakfast together the next morning and while Zylina slept, I spent time going over all the things Sabah shared with me. She met me in the courtyard, in the late morning, and quizzed me about Aphrodite's history and background.

I passed her test, and she smiled. "Here is a copy of the oath you will need to recite, by heart, at your confirmation. I will be there with you tonight." She reminded me of the hour and left me to practice on my own.

Over and over, I read and recited the words. *Oh, goddess of beauty and love, source of virility in men and fertility in women. You, who authored the passions of marriage through your loyal priestesses and priests, accept this honor bestowed by your humble servant and sanctify my efforts to be a tribute to your glory.*

Right after dinner, I went to the room where my things were and changed into the costume given to me for the ceremony. It was a drab covering of heavy cotton that slipped over my head through a slit in the center. The ugly garment fell to my feet with no adornments and no sash.

When we met, I asked Zylina, "Why would they want me to wear such a thing?"

"Oh, it is part of the ritual. You wear it until..." She put her hand over her mouth. "Woops, I am not supposed to tell you any more than that."

My face fell, but she grinned.

"Do not worry. It is not bad. Come on. It is nearly time."

Chapter Forty-Nine

Sabah waited for me at the door of the temple. Zylina squeezed my hand. "I will sit in the spectator section to cheer you on."

Sabah's face glowed with anticipation. "Are you prepared?"

I gulped at the knot that bulged my throat and nodded. She led me into the room and walked me up to the marble altar. I looked around, disheartened to be the only candidate. All eyes would be on me.

The temple overseer entered from a side door. He was not in his usual clothing but wore a red velvet robe with a crown of fabric that matched. It had gold rings that circled into a pointed spiral.

He expounded on the virtues of Aphrodite, her history, her love of beauty, how she was formed by the gods from the foam of the sea, and of her many conquests. My mind wandered to what Zylina had almost revealed.

In a loud voice, he said, "Daughter of Aphrodite, is it your wish to dedicate yourself to our goddess, to uphold her mission to bring love to all who seek her favor? Are you prepared for a life of service to her?"

I ignored the bile that accumulated in my mouth and nodded.

The overseer pulled a scepter from the sash on his robe, raised it to the ceiling and touched the top of my head. He nodded at me and announced. "We will now hear the oath from our inductee's own lips."

My heart raced with such vigor I could hardly speak. I took a deep breath and began. "Oh, Goddess of Beauty and Love, source of, source of..."

Someone whispered, "virility in men and fertility in women."

"Virility in men and fertility in women." I finished strong with, "and be a tribute to your glory."

A flash of doubt swept the overseer's face. I held my breath, but seconds later he nodded his acceptance, and I released my breath.

He pointed at the altar. "Please bow before our goddess and be purified of all other desires."

I glanced to each side, climbed the two steps, and walked close to the statue. I bent on one knee as my mentor suggested, not sure how long I should stay in that position. My eyes were closed, when a huge torrent of cold water unexpectedly gushed from above and drenched me from head to toe.

I yelped and shot to my feet, wiped the water from my eyes, and searched for my veil. It had been swept off my face and onto the floor. As I picked it up, I heard a loud gasp.

Someone cried, "No! No, this cannot be!" I looked. It was Sabah. As she rose, her head shook, and she wrung her hands like one who had witnessed a tragedy. Her mouth opened but she seemed unable to get out what she needed to say. I fingered my veil, but it was too soaked to reattach.

The overseer rushed over, his face wreathed with irritation. Sabah's head still shook as she motioned toward me. Were they upset that something broke and water had flooded the altar?

He looked where she directed, annoyed at the interruption until his focus settled on my face. Anger rushed up his neck and turned his face red.

"You!" His eyes pierced mine. "How dare you! What kind of deception is this? What made you think you could offer a blemished vessel to represent our beautiful goddess?"

His shouts filled the room. "Your face is the epitome of evil and I command you to come off that altar and leave our temple grounds, this very moment. Did you really think you could hide such an emblem of evil from us?"

His words scalded my inner being while my outsides shivered, cold and wet. All the breath left my lungs, and I began to shake.

With a mutual show of contempt, he and Sabah turned their backs on me. I looked for Zylina, but it was dark where she waited and I could see only her form.

Why had she led me to believe my disfigurement would not matter? Surely, she was not ignorant of the standards set for those who represented Aphrodite.

I pulled up the hem of the sack-like tunic and ran down the steps and out the door. I passed Zylina on the way, but she lowered her head and did not look at me.

In tears, I hurried to the room where I had left my clothes, quickly changed and left. I ran, with no destination, until I was well away from the temple. On a secluded bench, I sobbed at the overseer's words that still rang in my head. *Your face is the epitome of evil... the epitome of evil.*

I could not escape his cruel tirade. His words racked the depth of my soul. I had been rejected and driven off because my face attested to evil. I sniffed back my tears and stroked the hair on my cheek. Was I truly evil? People seemed to think so.

I found my spare veil at the bottom of my bag. Maybe I should not cover my face. Maybe I would do better if people saw me for what I was. I snuffed at the staccato-like shutter that remained in my chest and put on the veil.

Nothing in the area that surrounded me looked familiar. Had I been here before?

In the near distance, I heard an uproar. Drunken voices rang with zealous songs and curses at any who tried to quiet them.

I kept very still as two women, heavily made up, approached, relieved when they did not notice me. Their tunics barely covered their backsides and plunged to their navels in the front.

Zylina had explained that sometimes she and the girls from the temple provided services upstairs in the many brothels above public drinking houses.

It hurt as I pictured her lowering her head as I passed. Maybe she would not have shunned me if we had been friends longer. Does loyalty to a god come before people?

The hour grew late, and I did not know what to do, or where to go. Things had quieted to almost complete silence, so I decided to pass the public houses and see what was on the other side. Maybe I could find a place to sleep.

A voice called as I neared the end of one building. "Hey Girl." A stocky man with a short beard bent to wipe down some outside tables. "You do not look like the regular girls. What are you doing here so late? Do you not have a home?"

He did not appear to be a threat so I stopped where I was "I...ummm, I—"

"You sound like you could use a glass of wine. Come sit for a while."

We sat across from each other at a small table set for four. He said his name was Pekka and asked about my plans. At first, I pretended to have somewhere to go, but after several glasses of wine, I told him my name and confessed I needed a job.

He spoke about a recent disagreement with his worker, who had left, and asked if I could cook or had ever served tables.

He urged me to come look around, so I followed him into the deserted building. The heavy smell of smoke, spilled wine, and spoiled food buffeted my senses.

Besides the few tables outside, there were six or eight inside. The floor was sticky with spilled wine, and trays of half eaten meals were everywhere.

"I know it is a mess in here. I cannot keep the customers fed, their cups full, and find time to clean. Come see the kitchen."

We started for the door, but I staggered and slipped on something stuck to the floor. Pekka turned at my cry and caught me. He pulled me close to his chest and whispered in my ear.

"Eunice, we would make a great team." I was so dizzy I could not walk or think straight.

"You need to lie down." He carried me into a nearby room.

I do not remember anything that happened after that until the cackle of a rooster announced dawn. I sat up, aghast. I had no clothes on! Where was I and who was the man beside me? A moan rose from my throat as my mind flashed to hours of drinking wine with Pekka.

He heard me, reached over and pulled me back down beside him. As if in a fog, I heard him tell me how wonderful I was and how beautiful. In a panic, I reached to check my veil. It was gone.

"Do not be afraid or alarmed. I do not care about the blemish on your face, I want to take care of you. We can work together, and you will be safe.

My head ached and my mind refused to believe what I had allowed to happen. I jerked free and found my clothes, went outside, and heaved until I doubled over from the strain.

Chapter Fifty

I returned to the barroom to find my things and leave.

Pekka had risen and stood by the door. His head drooped. "I am sorry about last night, Eunice. I had not planned to take advantage of you. It is that I became so enticed by the sensation of you in my arms, I lost control and well... I am sorry.

I really think we could make a go of things if you decided to stay. I would pay you to clean, prepare food for my customers, and help me serve at night."

I walked past him, not unmindful of what else he would expect. He did not follow me or say any more, for which I was grateful.

Thoughts of last night's brooding returned. Cast aside because of my blemish, once again labeled evil, and disappointment in one I thought a friend overwhelmed me.

In truth, distress over the temple's rejection had already evolved to relief. I would not have to lie with a different man each night to contribute to Aphrodite's treasury.

I picked up my things but paused. Maybe it would not be so bad to stay and work here, even if it meant I would have to endure

Pekka's ardent desires. Basically, he seemed to be a decent, hardworking fellow, and I was desperate, with nowhere to go and no prospects.

Pavlov's face loomed before me. My eyes welled as I shook off the impossible hope of ever being with the man I truly loved. I would make this work. I saw no other choice.

For three months, Pekka and I worked side by side. It took days to get the place clean and acceptable. I prepared food for the crowd I would serve that night.

Late in the evenings, customers grew rowdy. I tried to ignore the stream of women, Aphrodite's servants and other prostitutes that traversed the outer stairs.

I stayed in the kitchen and Pekka supplied the never-satisfied demand for more wine. He tried hard to defuse arguments or complaints with a joke or a free drink, desperate to prevent a brawl.

Occasionally, a patron asked about my veil. Mostly, I ignored them. One man who showed up every night, engaged me in meaningful conversation between orders. He said his name was Attis. I enjoyed his view on things I knew little of.

He had no use for the many temples and their gods, with which I readily agreed. Several times he declared, "Corinth is the crossroads of the world, Eunice." I wondered what he meant.

On a particularly hot and muggy night, an argument broke out among those at the outside tables. The squabble stemmed over which athlete, in the recent games, was the most talented.

Men took sides. One pushed his table into a man who disagreed, which led to a fight. Eagerly, all the drunken patrons joined in, some who had no idea what the fight was about.

It did not take long for a Roman squad to show up with their no-tolerance policy for street brawls or disturbing the peace. They rushed in with clubs and beat those that were not fast enough to escape.

When things were under control, several men had been arrested and Pekka's public house was in tatters. The next day, he was served a notice that his business had been permanently shut down.

Pekka was distraught. Nothing I said encouraged or helped. One morning I awoke, and he was nowhere to be seen. He did not show up all day or into the night. I stayed, sure he would be back, but after several days there was no more food, and no sign he would return. I needed to move on, but where? I had very little money. My skimpy wages had gone to replace my badly worn tunics.

I finished getting my things together and was ready to leave when Attis showed up. "It looks like you are about to leave. Where is Pekka?"

Attis knew about the fight and the Roman order to close, but not about Pekka's disappearance. I explained and he too seemed puzzled.

"So where are you off to?" I hung my head. How I hated to admit I had nowhere to go.

"Listen, I have a big house with many rooms. Why not come stay with me until you figure out what to do?"

I chewed my lower lip. Could I trust him? He was probably my father's age. I would probably be safe. My options were nil, so I decided to take a chance and see what it led to.

Maybe, I could earn my keep if he let me cook and clean for him. He was comfortable to be around, considerate and respectful.

I had been in Attis' beautiful home, about a week, when I awoke one night to find he had climbed into my bed. I shot up and pulled my blanket to my chest.

"Do not be afraid, Eunice, I would never hurt you." I tried to get up, but he held onto one arm and pulled me to himself. I remember my surprise at how strong he was for a man his age.

I tried to free myself. "Attis, please, let me go, I do not want..."

He would not stop and when he finished, he left me crying into my pillow. I packed my things and left that very night. As I looked back, months later, I realized I would have been better off there with him than with the next few men who took me in under the pretense of needing a housekeeper.

It seemed, if I were to survive, I was destined for a life of being used or abused. I did not think anyone would ever care for or protect me until I met Pandaros.

He found me asleep on a bench in a city park hardly anyone ever visited. Rays of sunshine flickered across my face and stirred me to a new day.

Before I opened my eyes, a shadow blocked the light. I heard someone cough and shot to my feet. A Roman soldier assigned to monitor this area could find me and turn me in for vagrancy.

A man with a walking stick stared at me. "I did not mean to frighten you. Why are you asleep here in the park?"

It was not a reprimand, more a gentle inquiry. I smoothed my tunic and picked up the bag I had used for a pillow. "I was just on my way. I became lost and it was late, so I..."

He shook his head and disbelief poured from his eyes. "Look, I am out for my morning walk and I always stop here to enjoy some breakfast. Sit down and let me share it with you."

I do not know why I stayed. Maybe, it was the kindness that spread with his smile. We sat for over an hour, munched on his biscuits and honey, and shared our lives like old friends.

Once again, I experienced the freedom to speak of things with someone I knew I would never see again. He said his name was Pandaros and it just so happened that his housekeeper had left to get married. He asked if I would be interested in working for him.

My mind spun like a child's top. It reeled with all-too-recent memories of past positions that soon lost their promise. But, as we conversed, flags of caution faded. I felt it was worth a try and followed him to a modest house in a well-kept neighborhood. He showed me to a spare bedroom. I was relieved it was not the typical nook behind the kitchen.

"Come into the kitchen when you are settled, and I will show you where things are."

I put away my meager possessions and hung my only other tunic before I peeked around. His bedroom was next to mine and a parlor and dining area covered the rest of the main floor. Some narrow stairs led to a second story, but I had no idea what was up there. A deep cough hurried me to the kitchen. I hoped he was all right.

He smiled. "There you are. Let me show you the stove." With great care, he detailed how the damper worked and where the staples were kept.

To my relief, he told me about a small local market area where I could buy whatever was needed.

"Just make yourself at home, Eunice. I need to rest a while, but you can call me when lunch is ready.

I assured him I would manage just fine, and he left for his bedroom. I found some eggs and pita bread and went to work. Was his cough related to why he rested so early in the day? I stood outside his door and told him lunch was ready. In minutes, he joined me and insisted I eat with him.

We settled into a comfortable routine, and to my relief, he never entered my room. Each morning at dawn, he set off with a pouch of breakfast fixings for his walk.

Occasionally, his two sons and their wives stopped to check on him. The women ignored me or looked past as if I were not even there.

Pandaros always seemed relieved when they left. We often sat and talked, for hours, after lunch. He told me about Amara, his wife, who was the love of his life. He explained she had died many years ago. His eyes lit up when he mentioned her name, and such devotion brought tears to my eyes.

I told him about my family's abuse over the blemish on my face, and of Rose and my deep regrets over her needless death.

He reached over and patted my arm. His heartfelt sympathy spread a soothing balm over the tender spot her memory always evoked.

One sunny morning, he was up early. He declared it was a perfect day to visit the Acrocorinth, and asked if I would go with him.

I did not want to return to the place I had last spent with Pavlos, but he was so excited I did not have the heart to refuse. We started out early and stopped to rest whenever coughs overtook his enthusiasm. At the top, we stopped and ate the lunch I had packed.

"What is it, Eunice? You look like your thoughts have taken you far from here"

I covered my face with my hands. He was silent but soon coaxed me to share my pain, and I told him of my lost love.

"You are a noble girl, Eunice. Most people in your position would have ignored the upheaval it would likely have brought Pavlos' family and latched onto an easier life."

His eyes brimmed with compassion and for a moment, his face became that of my grandfather's. We arrived home tired, but content.

That night, Pandaros' coughs invaded the dark. The sound lingered like a guest who had long since worn out his welcome.

The next time his sons stopped by, I tried to stay out of the way, but overheard them inquire in accusing tones about his routines.

One of them singled me out and grilled me about our relationship. I squirmed but assured him I was only Pandaros' housekeeper. He demanded I detail his father's habits. Was his appetite good and did I see that he rested and bathed regularly?

Obviously, I was not to be trusted.

Pandaros suddenly appeared and brought an awkward silence to our conversation. His son's loud footsteps sounded on the stairs.

A grimace swept Pandaros' face and his mouth fell before he hid his concern behind a cough.

Chapter Fifty-One

I was relieved when Pandaros' sons left. He sensed my discomfort and took time to assure me that he was pleased with my care.

We had been together several months when I noticed he did not always do his morning walk. He said nothing and I did not intrude.

One day, he had not risen though it was already midmorning. Concerned, I went to his door and peeked in. He had not left his bed, and his back was to me, so I could not tell if he was asleep. I whispered, "Pandaros." This was not like him.

"Eunice? Is that you?"

"Yes, I did not mean to wake you but it is midmorning and I wondered if you were all right."

He turned part way, "Yes, please..." and began to cough. He caught his breath, then eked out, "Could you bring me some water?"

His voice was so weak, I was not sure what he asked, but I brought some water to his bedside.

He pushed himself up on one elbow and I held the cup to his lips. Near his pillow a large, brownish-red spot stained his bedding.

"Pandaros, you are ill. Shall I call your sons or find a doctor?"

He laid his head back down. "No, Eunice. I should not have tried to keep it from you. I have seen a doctor, and nothing can be done. I have days like this when it is hard to get around, but most often, I am all right and I try to enjoy the time I have left."

I wanted to weep. He was such a gentle soul and had gracefully accepted, without complaint, that his time on earth was limited.

"I will warm some goat's milk. It is good to sip on and will soothe your throat."

He thanked me and closed his eyes. The next day, he rose as usual but did not continue his walks. For several weeks, he grew worse. I could hear coughs rack him through the night, and would bring him a clay jug to relieve himself when he was too weak to get up.

I helped him bathe, washed his soiled bedding, and dressed him when he was up to it.

The wives stayed away but the sons made their obligatory check on him each week. He never complained or spoke unkindly of the burdensome duty they performed. But he often expressed his appreciation for my staying and taking care of him.

One night, I heard him slowly work his way up the stairs. I had never had an occasion to venture up there and had no idea what motivated him to take on such a strenuous effort, especially in the dark.

I debated whether I should offer to get what he needed or just let him be. He did not stay long and when I heard him back on the landing I relaxed, grateful he had not fallen on those steep stairs.

His cough grew worse, and a few days later, we both knew he would not live long. He called me to his bedside and handed me a pouch, heavy with coins.

"Eunice, you have been so good to me, and I know my time is almost gone. I have dug into what my sons left of my treasury. I want you to have this so you can buy a small house of your own and never be without a home again."

I started to object, but he cut in, his voice insistent. "Now, listen to me. I want you to pack up and leave in the morning, before my sons discover some of my money is missing. It is mine to do with as I please and I want you to have it."

"But Pandaros, I cannot take—"

"Yes, you can. You have earned it, and have been like a loving daughter to me. If you care for me, you will do as I say. The man I hired to take care of my property is a good friend. He has witnessed a letter, I have written, to notify that this gift I have given you was of my own free will and desire. He will come in the morning and notify my sons you are gone. He will tell them that I will need their help."

I knew he spoke the truth, so I packed my things and was ready to leave at dawn. I stopped at his door to say goodbye, but he had not moved. Through tears, I kissed his forehead and whispered my gratitude.

Miles away, in a different section of town, I stopped by a small fountain and tried to come to terms with whether it had been right to receive his gift.

I sobbed, no longer able to hold back my grief at the loss of another friend, who actually cared about me. The sun's rays hit the shimmering droplets that cascaded up and over the base of the fountain. I did not understand it then, but a peace I could not fathom filled my heart.

I found a little house that was perfect for me. It was simply one room. It included a small kitchen and sitting room that opened to a tiny cove. big enough for my bed mat. I had enough money left over to keep me for several months, but no way to earn more. The people in my new neighborhood were poor and could not afford a maid or a cook.

I did not venture out much in the daytime, haunted by the fear someone would notice my veil and accuse me of being an evil threat.

At dusk, one evening, a man approached as I returned from our small market with a loaf of bread and vegetables. The purchase had emptied my purse. He was dressed in finery, too expensive to be part of the neighborhood.

He called out to me. "You there. I have some vintage wine. We could find a place to share it."

I knew his intentions and started to walk away but stopped. I lifted my chin. Why not? I was used property with hair growing out of my face, unlikely to find someone who would ever want me for a wife, and I needed some money.

I invited him into my house but made it clear there would be a price. He left shortly after and I finished the wine. Perhaps it would lull me to sleep, and I could forget that I had sold myself for a few coins. When that ran out, I lingered by the market and found it easy to find men who had money to pay for my favors.

The time came when I needed food but could find nobody to service. I was too frightened of crowds to leave my area.

Before I gave up and headed for home, two men approached me. They were not unfamiliar, often accused of theft by the market vendors or abuse from anyone who challenged them.

I put my head down and tried to pass, but they blocked the path. They proposed a scam wherein I would be the bait to catch any man who looked like he carried a hefty moneybag.

I refused and tried to leave. One grabbed my arm and twisted it behind my back. I cried out in pain.

The other man pulled my head up by my hair, "You had better come along, or you will hurt a lot more."

The first one shoved my arm further to make sure I knew they would carry out their threat. They hustled me to the outskirts of the city where a dark alley separated a temple and the palaestra.

I was terrified by what they might do, so I followed their instructions. A short way into the passageway, at their signal, I kneeled and I pretended to cry, loud enough to attract the victim.

The man stopped and looked in my direction. He stepped closer and asked if I needed help. In the moonlight, a handsome face, clouded with concern, stared back at me.

My conscience pricked. I did not want him to be killed or injured. As quietly as I dared, I whispered, "Sir, you are in great danger here. Please, you must leave this area, immediately. It is not safe for you to be here."

It was too late. He never heard the two ruffians sneak from behind nor saw the club they smashed against his head. As if in slow motion, he slid to the ground.

The men pulled off his money belt, tossed me a few coins and ran off. My breath caught as I looked at the blood that streaked from his wound. It was all my fault. What had I done?

He tried to stand but collapsed in pain. I wiped his head with my covering, "I am so sorry. They forced me to do it. They said they would kill me."

I doubt he heard me. He mumbled something but the words were jumbled and made no sense. I helped him to stand. He swayed and I was afraid he would fall so I steadied him with my arm around his waist.

"My house is not too far, please come with me and rest until you are able to leave."

He was too disoriented to object, so we slowly made our way to my house. I took clean rags and washed the gash on his head and secured it with cloths, just above his ears.

I asked his name.

He frowned. A strange expression crossed his face. He opened his mouth but said nothing. For a moment he stared beyond me, then shook his head.

"I do not know... I do not know who I am!" Panic streamed from his voice. "Do you know who I am?"

My heart ached at the desperate expression on his face.

"No, my name is Eunice. We just met. But please, lie down on that mat and rest till morning. You have had a severe head injury and I am sure you will remember in the morning."

Like a lost child, he nodded his gratitude and let me help him to my bed mat.

Chapter Fifty-Two

I thanked the neighbor who allowed me to sleep at her house, before I went back the next morning. I expected my unplanned guest to be eager to leave. The coins, his attackers tossed, bought some food for breakfast... it was the least I could do.

He was awake but looked pale and shaken. "I do not know where I am. Do I know you?"

"You are in my house. We met last night." I ignored his gaze that fixed on my veil. "Are you hungry? I bought fresh fruit and some bread and cheese."

He did not answer so I sliced some of each and took it to him. He winced when he tried to sit. I grabbed his shoulder and steadied him. "Does your head throb?"

He nodded and massaged his temples. "Do you have some water?"

I hurried out to the cistern and brought him a drink. He mumbled his thanks and drank it down. His eyes pleaded for answers. "Do you know what happened to my head?"

What should I say? Obviously, he did not remember anything about last night and I could not bear to tell him of my part in the scheme.

"I was nearby when I saw two men attack you and steal your money belt. After they left, I ran over to see if I could help.

He stood and frantically searched his waist. "I have no money! But I, I..."

I gently helped him back to the mat, afraid his legs would fail him. "Please, do not push yourself. You have had a terrible injury to your head and rest will help. You are welcome to stay as long as you need to."

The next day, his dizziness had faded enough that I offered to take him to the nearby areas and see if anything might trigger memories of his past. Nothing looked familiar. We soon returned. He did not resist my suggestion to rest.

He raised his hand and covered his forehead. "I am so sorry to put you through this. I have no way to repay you for your help... and for feeding me."

I was taken aback by his humble demeanor and appreciation, so different than most of the men I had known. He never asked how I supported myself, for which I was grateful. It was obvious by his clothing and his manner of speech, that he was a man of substance.

"I am sure you will pay me back when your memory returns, besides, I owe you."

"Owe me? Why would you owe me?"

I was sorry that slipped out. I cared what he thought of me.

"Oh...I just meant I saw what happened to you and any decent person would want to help." I quickly busied myself with the food I had bought. "Have you any memory of family...a wife?"

His eyelids drifted downward, and he sighed. "I cannot tell you how many times I have tried."

I finished my preparations for the lamb stew and held up the pan. "I am going outside to cook this. Just rest. Maybe you are trying too hard."

My veil caught on the door and tore it from my face. The slip exposed the bristling, black hairs that covered the ruddy section of my cheek. I saw his reaction but did not stop or explain. What would it matter?

I had retrieved my veil and when I returned an hour later, he stirred. Eyes half-closed, he pushed himself upright. "Daphne, what is it you ordered for dinner? Is that my favorite?" He looked around, blinked several times then grimaced.

I smiled and hurried over to him, genuinely happy he remembered something. "Now, who is Daphne?"

He straightened. "She is...she is..." He shook his head, his eyes moist. "I do not know who she is. It is like this cloud came and covered a picture that had been clear seconds ago." He groaned. "It is worse than not remembering at all."

"No. No, it is not worse. Something came back and perhaps the next time it will stay. Come, let us sit by the bench and eat."

By the third day, his cut had closed, and his head no longer ached. With him beside me, I bravely ventured out. We wandered around different parts of the city. Surely something would jog his memory.

"This street has many inns. You do not talk like a Corinthian, so maybe you stayed in one. Let us see if any look familiar to you."

We walked slowly. He gazed, intently, at each one. Where the inns ended, he stopped and leaned onto his knees. A minute later, a strange look flooded his face. I grabbed his arm."What is it? Did you remember something?"

He straightened, "I... I do not know. Something came into my mind...a familiar voice, but I do not know who it is or what it meant."

"What did it say?"

"It said, 'Trust me, Nicanor.'"

Her brows flinched. "Trust me? Was that all?"

"It called me Nicanor. Do you think that is my name?"

"It could be. It is a nice name. For now, let us assume that it is."

He shrugged and his tone was bitter. "Let us go. I do not see anything here that looks familiar."

"All right, but there is a section of the city we have not explored. Shall we try it?"

We stopped in the market and bought buns and cheese with money my neighbor lent me. We ate as we walked. The bustling part of the city gave way to neighborhoods.

Nicanor scowled. "I do not think anything here is going to help me."

We cut to the next group of homes, and he stopped.

"Wait." Singing came from a courtyard. They stepped closer and listened.

"Do you know what this is? Have you ever been here?"

I shook my head. "I have never been here but I used to live with a woman named Phobie who was part of a group that brought news of a new god to Corinth. She said they did a lot of singing when they met. The meetings she attended were in homes in this part of the city, and this could be one of them.

I am not sympathetic toward, nor do I worship any of the many gods in Corinth, but do you think you might have been part of that?"

He stared, lips pursed, brows touching. In time, he dropped his arms and shrugged. "I do not think so. It is just that the music seemed... like something I may have heard before."

"We could go in there and ask. Maybe they —"

"No, I would not know what to say. It is probably just my longing for... for whatever. Come on, let us head back."

We worked our way home. And, after a quick dinner, I bid Nicanor goodnight. The forlorn expression on his face led me to try to think of a way to bring him some comfort.

Who was Daphne, the name he had spoken while half awake? A part of me wished I were her, permanently connected to this admirable person who stumbled into my existence. He was not Pavlos, the love of my life. But he was a decent, well-mannered man, I could respect and serve well.

And who, I wondered, was this voice that called him by name and said to trust him? Was it a god he once worshipped? I thought about the music he found familiar. Could he have belonged to that same sect? And why was he reluctant to pursue a chance to find out if there was a connection?

I arrived early the next morning with buns and boiled eggs for breakfast."Did you sleep well?"

He grunted a pleasantry but offered nothing more about the names he spoke or the voice he had heard.

"I have to be gone most of the day. Sometimes the manager of the palestra pays me to clean the floors."

"Can I help? I used to..." He stopped, unable to verbalize thoughts from seconds before.

"No, you just rest. I will be back by dinnertime. Will you be all right on your own?"

"I will be fine. You have done so much for me. I do not want to interfere with your life."

I left what remained for his lunch, assured he would not wander far from the neighborhood. The rundown buildings and squalor in the streets surely were a poorer part of a city than he had ever known, and more prone to trouble.

I shrugged. Maybe he would find something to pass the time. I thought of those thugs and hoped they hid out in the daytime.

I released a deep sigh. Or maybe he will sleep, if he can escape the confusion that taunts like these pesky flies.

It was late afternoon when I brushed through the door and called out, "I am back."

He stirred and rubbed his eyes. "Where have you been, Daphne? Patharus expects..."

I dropped my parcel and knelt beside him. "You have remembered something! Who are those people...and who are you?"

Chapter Fifty-Three

Nicanor sat, after we finished dinner, arms folded and head down. I put my hand on his arm and let my shoulder brush his. "Try not to be discouraged. It will come. You are welcome to stay here while you wait."

I finished my work at the palestra, put on a fresh tunic, and treated my hair with a flowery scent. My face was but inches from his. We sat in silence. I moved a little closer. Perhaps he would see me in a new light and desire to find comfort in my arms.

He straightened, brows pinched, and hopped to his feet.

Disappointment slipped in a sigh. I bid him sleep well, gathered our dishes, and left without a word.

Back at my friends' house, I decided to try a bolder attempt to reach Nicanor. If his old life was gone, maybe he could build a new one with me. We had gotten to know each other under difficult circumstances, and while he would not ordinarily choose me, maybe now he might.

I changed into a sheer nightdress, entered my house quietly and shut the door behind me. My wispy tunic shimmered in the sparse moonlight that shone through my small window. It hugged my figure and plunged nearly to my navel.

Nicanor woke when I lowered myself to the mat. "Eunice? What...?"

I ran my hand down his chest. "You seem so lonely. I have come to bring you the comfort I know you long for, and —"

He pulled my hand from his chest. "No, this is not right. I owe you much and I will repay, but this cannot be."

I huffed and stood. "Am I not enough? Is it my face that offends you?"

He rose beside me. "Eunice, you would be more than enough for any man...a blessing to whomever you choose."

"But not you!" My voice strained and became a screech. "Of course, not! What man wants a girl with a beard on her face? I thought you were different but you are like all the rest. You are —"

He grabbed both my hands. "Eunice, stop it. Just hours ago, I had a dream, and all my past life came back! In the dream there was a large house with many rooms and a young woman moved toward me. I called to her, Daphne, it is me, Nicanor. She waved and I could see she was about to leave on a trip. I called again. Daphne, wait. I will drive you to Neapolis."

I tried to free my hands, but his grip grew stronger.

His eyes pleaded with mine. "Eunice, listen. My past pelted me like an unexpected spring hail. I knew that woman was my wife, Daphne. I must find her so we can get back to Philippi. That is where we live.

God called her to go back to Delphi, her homeland, and I came to Corinth to meet her here. Our plans were to return together, and I now know the voice I heard was the Lord telling me to rest and trust Him."

My hopes dwindled as repressed anger spewed throughout my being.

Excitement shone in Nicanor's eyes as he shared his awakening. "I wanted to leave right after it happened and get back to the inn and find her, but dawn was a good way off, so I lay back and reveled in the joy of memories of who I was."

He laughed, "I mean who I am, and what my former life has been. I must have slept until I heard the door open.

He pumped my hands, "Eunice, I remember who I am! Nicanor is my name, and I am married to a woman named Daphne whom I love very much. She is sweet and gentle, kind...like you. He dropped my hands. "I cannot be untrue to her."

I could not deny his joy and relief, but neither could I embrace it. He did not deserve it, but vengeance spilled from my lips. "Sweet? You think I am sweet? You do not remember that I told you I was paid to lure you off the street so those men could rob you...do you?"

His face fell. "You did that? Why?"

I yanked the veil from my face and screamed, "Look at me.". Would any decent man marry me? I have to sell myself to live. Even the men I service do not know what is behind my veil." Her voice caught... at first"

"Eunice, true beauty is not from the outside. Inside, where it counts, you are beautiful. God loves you just the way you are and has a better plan for your life than this."

"God? Which god? I searched for what it meant to worship a god, and it brought me nothing. Nothing! Even the temple of Aphrodite rejected me. No one has ever loved me, including my parents. They put me out as soon as I became a woman." I fell to my knees and sobbed.

He pulled me up. "Please, let us sit on the bench. I want to tell you about Jesus, the true God who created you and loves you dearly."

The sun twinkled through the window by the time Nicanor finished telling me about Jesus. I listened, as tears welled again and again.

"But I have lived in wickedness. Surely, He could not love and forgive me. And how can a god, I cannot see, make a difference anyway?" Where is His temple? I have never seen one that honors a god named Jesus."

"He does not live in man-made buildings. Your heart becomes His temple when He comes into your life. He uses His powerful Holy Spirit to change your outlook and your situation for the better. He has given us hundreds of promises of His love and help that we can stand on and claim as our own.

"Eunice, Jesus knows all about what you have been through and all your bad choices. Still, He loves you. All He wants is for you to believe He is God's Son and ask Him to be your Lord. He will forgive your past and transform you into a new creature in Christ...brand new, top to bottom."

I hung my head, my voice so muffled, Nicanor had to lean in to hear me. "Are you not angry with me for what I caused to happen to you?"

"No. We all make bad choices, sometimes. But my God requires that we forgive others as He has forgiven us. And Eunice, I truly forgive you."

I burst into tears again. "Please, I hate my life. I want what you have. Do you think your God will let me make your Jesus my God too?"

Nicanor led me in prayer and when we finished, for the first time ever, I had hope. "Thank you. I cannot explain it, but I feel different... peaceful inside."

He gave me a brotherly hug. "Eunice, there is so much more for you. Now listen. I want you to go back to that house where we heard the singing. A woman named Chloe lives there. I know her well, and you will love her and she will love you and help you. Tell her all about how we met and that you have become a believer. She will welcome you with open arms and help you find a new life."

Chapter Fifty-Four

I was not surprised that Nicanor was gone after I had changed and returned. I had so many questions. I wished he were still here. Is prayer just talking to God? How do I hear His answers? How can I be sure I have really changed?

I sat on the bench where he told me about this Jesus, and reflected on Nicanor's assurance that I was now a child of God, reborn into His kingdom. Chosen, he said, called to be a part of a family that would never reject me.

Could it really be true that there was a God who loved me despite my imperfect face and dark past? My mind reeled with all Nicanor had explained. To believe this Jesus was the Son of God, the ruler of the whole world, who would forgive all my sins simply because I asked, was amazing.

Somehow, I knew it was true... a gift... a blessing I could never deserve.

"Jesus." I whispered His name several times. It brushed like a soft breeze and coated my lips like a soothing balm. My gaze lit upon my bed mat, for months a source of guilt and shame. I waited for the usual condemnation to squeeze my chest, but the voice of harassment was silent. Instead, a burst of freedom overwhelmed me with joy.

I gathered my things, determined to go and find the house where a woman named Chloe lived. A cold wind blew as I opened the door. I shut it and went to fetch a shawl I had not worn since spring. I wrapped it around my shoulders.

As I started to leave, the wind whipped with a furry, and seemed to carry a message of condemnation. I backed inside. *Who do you think you are? Everyone knows how you have lived. Do you really think this woman will welcome someone with your past?*

The uplifting joy I had felt buckled beneath the weight of the bona fide accusation. I cried out, "No! Nicanor said Jesus washed away my past."

Well, that might be true of some sins but think of how you have lived. Do you really think that can be forgiven in one brief night?

I slumped back onto my bed mat and held my head. Had it all been too wonderful to believe? I searched the pocket of my shawl for a cloth to wipe my eyes. All I found was a tiny slip with something written on it. I pulled it out and half-heartedly looked to see what it was. My breath held and my heart raced as fast as it had when I ran from the crowd in the marketplace.

Tears of joy ran as I laughed and jumped to my feet. "Phobie's note! It is the slip Phobie gave me the last time I saw her."

I picked up my things, rushed through the door and headed for the neighborhood where Nicanor and I heard the singing. No wonder I had not been able to find that slip of paper from so long ago. My newly found God knew I would need it today, to confirm His love and care. I pictured Phobie writing Chloe, after she encouraged me to seek her out. How I wished I had listened back then.

I found the right neighborhood but had no memory of which house the music had come from. I circled the area a couple of times before I spotted a gardener at work in a courtyard. I called out, "Excuse me. I am looking for the home of a woman named Chloe. Would you happen to know which house is hers?"

The man did not look up or respond. I shrugged. Maybe he could not hear. A boy, about fourteen, came out of nowhere. "I heard you asking about Chloe's house. Follow me and I will show you."

It was not far. I waved my thanks as he pointed to a house with a large courtyard and left. I gulped. No one I had ever known lived in such a lovely place. The house and the gardens were beautiful, groomed to perfection. A curved path of hewn stone led to the front door. I looked for a back or side entrance like I normally used, then said to myself, "No. I am a new creation. I can go to the front door."

I was only part way up the path when a woman came from around the back of the house. Her hair was tied in a kerchief and her apron streaked with dirt. "Can I help you, My Dear?" I assumed she worked for the family, so I asked her if this was Chloe's house.

"Well, actually it is God's house, but I live here."

"Do you know if Chloe is home?"

She laughed. "I am Chloe. What can I do for you?"

Her humility swamped my bravado and buried thoughts of my being worthy of anything on my own.

I stammered, "My friend... I mean a man named Nicanor... told me about Jesus and said I should come here and that you would help me come to know Him better."

Her brows raised and her lips stretched a smile. "Oh, yes, Nicanor. A fine young man. I have not seen him in over a week. Do you know if he left for Delphi to find his wife?"

"Well, he had an accident and I... I mean he was attacked and I... oh, I should not have come." Tears of shame pooled at the memory of what I had done. I turned to leave. "I am sorry to have bothered you, I—"

Chloe laid the late summer flowers she carried on a bench and took a hold of my arm. "Please do not leave. Come in and have a cup of tea with me. I have some nut cakes I would love to share with you."

She seemed so sincere, I wiped my eyes and followed her into the house. It was beautiful inside too, with lush carpets and lovely frescos on the walls. She led me to a sunny cove, where there were windows all around, and invited me to sit while she heated some water.

Before long, I had poured out the whole sordid story.

Chloe listened. At first, sympathy streamed from her eyes, but they lit with joy when I explained how Nicanor had told me about Jesus and prayed with me to become a follower.

"But I struggle to believe it. It all seems too good to be true, and I hear a voice that denies it is true for me."

"Eunice, you must practice believing that you truly are forgiven. Remind yourself a dozen times a day until your heart refuses the lies of the enemy that accuses you. He is a liar, you know."

"Oh Chloe, I want to trust and believe it. Nicanor told me a little about my enemy, but I have so much to learn. How will I ever — "

She reached over and touched my arm. "My Dear, I think we can help each other. This big house of mine has lots of rooms, same as the Father's house that awaits us in heaven. So, mine too, needs to be ready for those who gather daily to celebrate Jesus. There is a lot to do. I would love to have you move in and stay with me for a while. We can help each other."

I felt as I had when I fell into the water and the wealthy owner from Delos rescued me.

"Really? You would let me stay with you? Oh, Chloe, I can clean and cook and work in your gardens or..."

Chloe laughed. "Hold on, Eunice. I am not hiring a housekeeper. I have invited you to stay as my guest. We will get to know each other, and I will teach you what I know about our Lord. I do not doubt for a minute that you will be a big help. All right?"

I floated back to my house to gather my things and inform my friend that I would not be around for a while if she needed a place for her guests to stay. As I closed my door, a distinct knowing this would never be home to me again, settled in my heart.

Chloe had a lovely lunch ready when I returned. She pointed at a settee. "Put your belongings, for now. We only have an hour or so before people will arrive.

Chapter Fifty-Five

I had no idea what to expect. Exuberant singing was all I remembered from the time Nicanor and I stood and listened to the music.

I followed as Chloe laid out cups to dip water out of several large vessels. We arranged the benches that were close to her house in a semicircle, but she explained many would bring blankets to sit upon or simply stand around the perimeter.

By early afternoon, dozens of people had gathered. Chloe introduced me to as many as she could. To my surprise, many hugged me or kissed my cheek. A woman pulled Chloe aside to talk privately. Tears flowed as she whispered in Chloe's ear. With one hand raised and the other on the woman's shoulder, Chloe's lips moved, I assumed in prayer. The woman found a seat, just as a man with a lyre stepped to the front and began a song of joyful praise to the Lord. I wished I knew the words so I could sing along.

The music evolved to a worshipful chorus. People closed their eyes and raised their hands as they ministered to the Lord in languages I had never heard.

My heart joined with theirs as murmurs of grateful praises poured from my innermost being. I did not want the moment to pass, but as if a signal had been given, a hush fell over the crowd.

A loud voice rose from those standing at the back. I listened in awe as a man spoke as if the words came right from the mouth of God. "I have welcomed you into My kingdom of grace and mercy, forgiveness and unconditional love. Do not doubt My power to erase the sins of your past, but believe I have cast them into the sea of My forgetfulness. Enter into My rest by faith and refuse to entertain an evil heart of unbelief. You are My beloved. Trust My love."

I felt I could not breathe. The message was aimed right at me! Surely, Chloe told the man of my struggle to let go of my past. My breath released as the words soothed my heart.

Before I could wipe the tears from my cheeks, another voice rose. It was one of the women Chloe had introduced me to. Boldly, she began. "Thus saith the Lord, I am the God who sees all and I exhort all who are called by My name to lay aside thoughts of vengeance toward our Roman oppressors and trust Me to bring about the justice you long for."

Cries of "Thank you, Jesus and praise the Lord," rose from every corner of the courtyard. I felt like I was a float in a sea of love as songs, again, rose all around me. Some people were so excited they jumped, or danced, or shouted praises to Jesus.

Another loud voice said, "Hear, hear. Yes, give Him praise. Shout your love and thankfulness."

The people roared a welcome. I looked to see who spoke and felt my knees grow weak. It was the man the Jewish leaders wanted to remove from the Bema, the day Spiros and I returned from a delivery into the city.

Later, when I had briefly stood and listened to him in the market square, I had felt the man's eyes hover over me. My breath caught. I now believed, with all my heart, the message he shared that day.

He raised his hand, and everyone grew quiet. "Friends, may God's grace and mercy abound in your hearts and toward one another."

I sat on the grass, mesmerized by the wisdom and understanding that poured forth as he taught the ways of Jesus and how we were to apply it to our lives. When he finished with a prayer that the Holy Spirit would enable each of us to walk in victory, the two hours seemed like minutes. I made a mental note to ask Chloe about the Holy Spirit he spoke of.

The speaker, referred to as Paul, did not linger but the people did. Many shared their joy in the encouragement they had received, or prayed in small groups for whoever had needs.

When the last person left, Chloe and I sat in the last of the sunlight and enjoyed the peaceful cry of martins as they dove for insects. "Well, Eunice, how did you like the meeting?"

"Oh, Chloe, I..." My throat constricted and tears choked my words. "I... I did not want it to end. Like a sponge from the Gulf, my heart soaked up every drop as I tried to absorb all Jesus has accomplished for me. I have never felt such love... from people and from the Lord. It left me with even more questions, but the presence of God assured me He was right here with me."

Chloe rose and held out a hand. "Let us go scratch something up for dinner and I will explain whatever I can."

We talked the whole time we prepared dinner, as we ate, and while we cleaned up. I asked her if she had shared my story with the man who seemed to know about my struggles. And then, I questioned what Paul meant by the Trinity and the Holy Spirit.

Chloe laughed at my first question. "Oh, Eunice, no. Of course not. But I believe God inspired him to speak because God knew you needed that assurance."

Her lips twisted as she thought how to answer the second. "Well, the Trinity is somewhat like our human makeup. We have a spirit that is reborn when we receive Jesus as our Lord, and Savior. We have a soul that is our personality, emotions, will and so on. And we live in a body. They are all different, but all are you. The godhead is similar.

"God is our Father, the great I Am, who created the world. Jesus is His Son, who sacrificed His life so we could become a child of God. The Holy Spirit is the power of God sent to live within us to help us live our lives in victory. All are different but all are one God."

The candles had burned low when Chloe showed me to a room and bid me goodnight.

In the dark, I rehearsed all she had taught me. I fell asleep, determined not to forget to ask about things I still did not understand.

Chloe was already in the kitchen the next morning when I rose and went downstairs.

She turned from the eggs she had boiled. "Good morning, Eunice. Did you sleep well?"

"Oh yes... fine... once I managed to stop replaying the wonder of yesterday."

She smiled and nodded. "Eunice, you are a delight. Did you know your name means joyous victory? Your parents must have been so..."

The look on my face squelched her thought. "I am sorry. Did I bring up something painful?" I had not thought of my family for a long time. I brushed off her question and busied myself setting the table. Soon, we enjoyed the eggs and her specialty, biscuits baked with cheese and ham and smothered in butter. Chloe did not pry, but she eyed me with concern.

I took our dishes to the kitchen. "What can I do for you this morning?"

"We will just tidy up a bit. The crowds will not be as big today because Paul said he planned to visit other house churches this afternoon."

"You mean there are more groups like those here, yesterday?"

"Oh my, yes. The crowd that meets with my friends Aquilla and Priscilla is smaller. They meet at their leather shop on a street close to the market."

They had to be the kind couple who invited me to stay with them when I had no place to go. "I think I may have met them. Is their home right above their shop?"

"Really? Yes, it is. You may see them tonight. Paul is having a meeting in one of the larger buildings in the city. Would you like to go with me?"

"Oh, I would love to. I cannot wait to hear him teach again."

The gathering was similar to the one at Chloe's house, except the room was stuffed wall to wall with people. She introduced me to Priscilla and Aquila.

Priscilla touched my arm. "I am so glad to see you here. I have prayed for you ever since the day you stopped at our shop."

My eyes welled. "Thank you, I am amazed that someone would care enough to pray for a complete stranger." I had a lot to learn.

Except for a man who looked vaguely familiar, Erastus, the city administrator, was one of the few of high social status. Erastus introduced Paul to the crowd. No one seemed to mind or even be ready to leave when Paul spoke well into the night.

For the next few weeks, I could hardly contain my joy in what this new life had brought into my life. Each afternoon, I reveled in the company of believers and learned more each day. Confidence in my position in Jesus grew each time the truth was shared.

I was busy filling the water vessels and did not meet a young woman Chloe and some others seemed excited to see. At the end, I heard Chloe invite her and her servant to come to lunch the next day along with Priscilla and Aquila. I had gone to the market and was not there when they arrived. Chloe heard me come in and insisted I join them.

She gestured at the visitor. "Eunice, this is Daphne, your friend Nicanor's wife."

My heart fell to my feet and my jaw dropped as guilt and shame bombarded me afresh.

Chapter Fifty-Six

I groped for a way to excuse myself, but Chloe recognized the panic that spread across my face. She jumped up, took my arm, and led me to a chair. "Daphne, this is Eunice, a new believer who is staying with me."

My lips quivered. "You... are Nicanor's Daphne?" I knew she had to be, but I was stunned to see her here and by how lovely she was. No wonder his loyalty to her had not failed.

Her brows twitched as she looked at Chloe, then back at me. "Yes. You know Nicanor?

How did you two meet?"

Chloe grinned. "Oh, Eunice, you must share your story with Daphne."

Priscilla nodded. "Yes, I would like to hear it too."

All the evil I had brought upon Nicanor rushed back and for a moment I could not speak. I swallowed the lump in my throat and tried. "I am so sorry. I never meant to... I mean I was..."

Chloe reached over and put her arm around me. "No, you must not dwell on the past. Remember God has forgiven you and so did Nicanor."

Daphne's brows rose as her lips mouthed forgiven,.

I wanted to run.

Chloe nodded. "Just begin at the beginning, Eunice. Daphne loves the Lord, and she will understand."

I stared at the woman whose husband had brought such change to my life, and she stared back, her face lined with questions.

I squeezed my hands until my nails poked my palms. "Again, I am so sorry. I never meant for anyone to be hurt, I just, just..."

I struggled to make my dire situation clear but fumbled badly. Even to me, my reasons sounded lame. But finally, bit by bit, I blurted out the whole story... my desperate need for money to survive, being forced to help the two thugs, and remorse at what I had done.

"I could not leave him there, bleeding and disoriented. Sorrow, and I suspect guilt, led me to bring Nicanor to my house. I tried to take care of his injury, and then to help him remember his past."

Nicanor's wife leaned forward as I recounted the details. She gasped in horror at the extent of her husband's injury, and groaned aloud at his frustration, when he could not remember who he was. I did not leave out anything, not even my attempt to entice Nicanor to accept me as a substitute for what he had lost, or how he had refused to be tempted.

"So, I am alive in Christ today because of his kindness. I will always regret that I led him into danger but will never cease to thank God that He allowed Nicanor into my life. I am so grateful he insisted I listen, as he told me about Jesus and helped me understand God's love and forgiveness."

For a moment no one spoke. Had I said too much? Despite a random happening, could a wife accept that another woman shared such an intimate encounter with her husband?

Daphne's eyes teared as she rose and took my hands. "Eunice, I am so thankful you were brave enough to tell me about what happened. Truly, I understand. There was a time I, too, was desperate, until I found hope in our Savior. And I am so glad you asked Jesus to be your God... and I am sure Nicanor was too."

Relief freed me to hug her. "Thank you for not hating me. I never met a man like him. The only men I knew were..."

My head drooped then rose to meet hers. "If he were not such an honorable man, I would not have listened as he told me about our Savior. You are blessed to have such a husband."

She smiled and hugged me back. "I know, and I will tell him you said so."

Lunch ended with joyful stories from Aquila and Priscilla's recent gatherings, until Chloe stood. "You must all come back at sundown. We have planned a love feast."

Murmurs and nods wafted as she sent her guests on their way. I helped her clean up and asked what a love feast was.

"Oh, it is another name for a shared meal. People love to eat together so every so often we plan one. Each family will make several dishes, and we put them all together and enjoy fellowship while we eat. Want to help me make up some?"

"Yes, of course. What do you have in mind?"

We busied ourselves with a baked lamb stew and prepared some of Chloe's biscuits to go with it. I peeled apples and folded them inside a pastry dough with cinnamon and butter.

Once again, we put out benches, chairs we gathered, and a long table to hold the food. People began to arrive and add their specialties to the large number of dishes. I carried a tray of biscuits and almost backed into a woman who held a large pot of steaming fish soup.

"Oh, I am so sorry. I should have been..."

She, carefully, sat her container on the table and turned toward me. "Eunice? Is that you? Really you?" She called out across the lawn,

"Calliope, come quick! Look who is here. It is Eunice."

Calliope shouted my name. "Eunice?" She hurried to the table. "It is you! I never thought I would see you again."

I had hardly laid the biscuits down before she grabbed and hugged me. Tears of joy streamed down both our cheeks.

Chloe made her way to my side. "My, my, who are these people, Eunice?"

I tried to explain our relationship while Zoe and Calliope chimed in with their versions of how we came to know each other.

We sat together while we ate and caught up on our lives. Zoe's husband had died during the year since I had lived in their home. His demise had, at last, freed them to be able to celebrate their faith with other believers.

Calliope bubbled with excitement. "Eunice, do you remember how you prayed for me to win the contest? I did not know you were a Christ follower."

"Oh, Calliope, at that time, I was not a believer. But God knew I would be one day, so I guess He honored my request. Anyway, did it not work out beautifully?"

With a mother's pride, Zoe filled Chloe in on Calliope's broken string catastrophe. "But she bravely continued on and the girl who came in first, generously, shared the crown with her."

The meal ended and the praise and worship began. Along with the others, my voice rang with delight as I united with those I truly loved and the joy of praising God together.

I went to the market for Chloe the next day and sat, a moment, by the fountain. The longing I had felt the last time I was there rose, but dwindled with the assurance that even then God had tried to reach me.

The booths overflowed with people who jostled to be first in line. I joined them, thrilled to suddenly realize I no longer walked in fear of crowds. I released a sigh of thanks. God had answered a need I had yet to pray about.

As I returned, I thought about the message Paul preached to the larger meeting in the city. Out of nowhere, I remembered who the well-dressed man beside Erastus was. I had never heard his name, but I recalled his kind speech to the less influential workers at the banquet at his estate on Delos. Even now, I pictured again how he stooped to rescue this lowly serving girl, when a storm threw me into the water.

I whispered the memory, "He must have already been a Christ follower. What a difficult place to live as a believer, surrounded by such evil influences.

Chloe and I had formed a routine. Each time, after Paul or another man spoke and taught about how to become like Jesus, I would ply her with questions. She would listen patiently and explain what she knew. To love and forgive seemed a consistent theme. Why did the command prick at the peace I had found and make me uneasy?

One evening, I brought it up. "Chloe, I know God says all of our sins, past, present and future are already forgiven, but what if you..." My throat constricted, "What if you..."

She laid her hand on my arm. "All means all, Eunice. Whatever torments you is from the evil one, not God. Remember, there is no condemnation to those in Christ Jesus. God has forgiven you completely and sent your sins into the sea of His forgetfulness. Whenever you are reminded of a sin, you have already confessed, just know that prompt is from Satan."

Comfort washed my soul as I poured out that I had caused my baby girl's death. Tears of relief cleansed my heart, and while I would always deeply regret it, peace confirmed I was forgiven, free of the guilt and shame that came with it.

I had hardly wiped my tears when a thought hit with such force, I gasped. I jumped to my feet. "Chloe, I think God has asked me to forgive beyond what I have strength to do."

"Well, Jesus said if we do not forgive others we will not be forgiven. Who do you need to forgive, Eunice? I cannot imagine..."

I sank into my chair. "Oh Chloe, it is my whole family. I do not know if I can. They were so, so..."

"But remember, Eunice, God does not ask us to do anything in our own strength. If your heart chooses to forgive, He will guide you and give you the power to do it."

In bed that night, my family's past cruelties paraded before me without end. The rejection, the rape, the constant belittling, the beating... all marched in unison down the street of my past.

I thought I had successfully distanced myself from my family, vowed I alone would be the guardian of my soul. Never again would their rejection stomp on my heart. Life would work for me not against me. But had it? Had the freedom to run my own life brought the serenity I sought?

I had a roof over my head, but a demeaning life and an empty heart until Jesus came and made me new. Reality set in. For me to forgive my family would be the affirmation of my faith, as I walked in obedience to God's will.

Chloe's wisdom echoed in the darkness. Choose to obey and He will guide you through it.

I turned down my lamp. Could I do it? Could I turn off the pain of my past and humble myself before them?

Chapter Fifty-Seven

For three days, I wrestled with what I knew God had called me to do. Determined, eager, confident... one moment, and dozens of reasons to put it off, the next. Every time I prayed about it, peace confirmed it was the right thing to do. But the third night, I had made up my mind. "Chloe, I am going to see my family tomorrow morning."

To my relief, she volunteered to go with me. It would take less than a half hour to walk to the other side of town. I filled her in with the horror of my home life, how I had lost Chara in the market, the beatings that followed, the rape by my older brother, and rejection because of the blemish on my face.

"So, tell me, Friend... how do I forgive people who have not asked for forgiveness? They will probably curse me and tell me to leave."

"It sounds to me like they should be the ones to ask, but God wants you to clean out all the hateful feelings and resentment you have held against them. Until they come to know the Savior, they probably will not be convinced of or admit their wrongful deeds. Still, to forgive them will set you free of

Satan's accusations so you can love and pray for them to come to know Jesus one day.

I wished I was as sure as she sounded. My heart began to pound when we reached the street where my family lived. I stopped. "Chloe, I do not think I can..."

"Of course you can. First, let us pray." She took my hand, and I clung like a scared child while she asked God to fill me with the knowledge of His presence and give me courage. An amazing peace overwhelmed my fears. "All right, I am ready." I took a deep breath and walked right up to my family home.

My mother answered my knock. I was shocked at how stooped and old she looked. Had it not only been a few years? Her jaw dropped and she squinted. Her eyes darted like a bird that could not decide where to land. Finally, a deep frown swept her face. She lifted her chin and growled like a watchdog. "Eunice. What are you doing here?"

"I wanted to see you, Mother, to — "

"Well, your father is not here. He is at his kiln and — "

I was relieved. His heart was so hardened. "It does not matter. This is my friend, Chloe. May we come in?"

Her hands twitched on the broom she held. She glanced at Chloe and grimaced. "I did not expect company, and I have not finished my chores."

"That is all right." I motioned for Chloe to follow me inside. I had been the only one who cleaned the place since I was six or seven, and it was obvious my mother had forgotten how. She frowned and tossed articles aside as she stomped into the sitting room.

I began, not sure what to say. "Mother, I am sorry I have not been by to see you. I am here to ask you to forgive me for the ill-will I have harbored against you and my father for things that happened when I was a child. I have had a wonderful change in my life, and I wanted to tell you about..."

Her face reddened. It was not embarrassment. I had seen that look before.

Damian, my elder brother, charged through the doorway. "Who is here, Mother? I heard voices." His eyes widened as he looked at Chloe and then at me. He sneered. "So, look who is here. Come back to make amends? Father said you owe him a lot of money."

Adonis, my younger brother, followed him in. "Eunice? That you? Where did you get the funny mask? Is your face still hairy?"

Through gritted teeth, my mother turned to Damian. "Go get your father,"

I had to remind myself why I had come. "That is not necessary, Mother. I just wanted to tell you all I am sorry for any trouble I have caused any of you."

Damian huffed. "So, what is this big change you were about to say?"

I glanced at the door, desperate to leave. What could I say that would break through such hostility?

Chloe gave me a you can do it look so I shot up a quick prayer and jumped in. "I know our family has never been one to follow gods, and I was not either. But recently, I heard about the one true God. His name is Jesus. He paid for our ungodly conduct with His own life blood so we could be forgiven. His sacrifice gives us the privilege of becoming a child of His Father, the God who created the world and all of us. He loves each of us and only asks that we believe."

Adonis cocked his head and stared at me.

Damian stuck out his palms. "Ungodly conduct? Are not you the one who ignored our little sister and let her fall into the hands of some evil monster? And now, you think some god loves you? Hah!"

My mother shot to her feet. "I have heard enough. You are a poor excuse for a daughter. Take your friend and get out of here. How dare you come and insinuate that we are not as good as you are. Who do you think you are? You were never good for anything. Now, be gone before your father comes and throws you out."

Her reaction sucked the breath from my lungs and froze my feet to the floor. Somehow, Chloe helped me out the door and onto the street. Neither of us spoke until we had walked several blocks.

She took my hand. "Eunice, I am so sorry that did not go well, but know—" A voice called from behind. "Eunice, Eunice, wait up." I jerked around. Had Damian followed with orders to do us harm? But it was Adonis.

He tried to catch his breath as he looked shyly at Chloe and at me. "Eunice, I, ummm. I just wanted to tell you that I am sorry for the way I treated you when you lived with us. You never did anything bad to me, but Damian insisted I be as mean as he is, and I was too fearful to stand up to him."

Tears sprang from my eyes. "Adonis!" I could hardly speak. "Thank you for coming to tell me this. It means more than you will ever know."

He shrugged and looked uncomfortable. "And, Adonis, if you ever get a chance, go into the market and listen to the man called Paul who speaks frequently from the Bema. It is his message that changed my life. Believe me, God has more for you than living in such a disparaging environment."

He turned to leave. "Adonis, wait. I have something I want to give you." Out of the pocket in my cloak I pulled the tiny statue of the colt our grandfather had given me. I carried it often to remind myself that someone I once loved, loved me.

"Do you remember how Grandfather would visit and tell us stories about his horse ranch?"

He nodded. "Well, he gave me this statue of his favorite foal to remember him by, and now I want you to have it to remember me. I believe we will see each other again one day."

My younger sibling studied the statue, a moment. His Adam's apple bobbed before he nodded and ran off. Chloe wiped her tears as we started for home. "That touched my heart, Eunice. I am sure God was pleased."

I basked in her encouragement but thoughts of all I should have said to my mother ran rampant, through my mind. That night, I lay awake and rehearsed what had happened.

Gratitude welled for the peace that, for now, I had done what I could. I felt genuine sadness for my mother and even for Damian. They did not know what they did not know, but Adonis' desire to confess his failure gave me great joy and hope. I committed to pray for him daily, comforted that God often begins with just one member of a family.

I did not want to wear out my welcome, but Chloe insisted I stay, that my company blessed her. I smiled at her choice of words. I reflected on the people who had told me I was a blessing, despite the image my family had planted.

I thought of Thera back at the orchard, the wool merchant after I had helped his wife birth her baby, Phobie the day Teris died, and the girl at the inn whose baby I had comforted.

I did not really know what being a blessing was back then and could not see anything good in myself. Now, I knew it was to have peace with God and be in right standing with

Him, ready to do whatever He told me to do. I had learned from my family in the Lord, to accept I was a new creation in Christ, blessed to be a blessing through God's grace.

Still, I grew uneasy about living off Chloe though I did the majority of the cleaning and laundry and helped her with meals.

I had been there about three months and continued to look forward to our frequent gathering of believers. The courtyard was nearly full on a day when I arrived back from the market with the food on Chloe's list. The singing had already started by the time I unpacked our goods and joined the crowd.

Someone came from behind and tapped me on the shoulder, I turned and could not believe my eyes. "Hello, Eunice. "I thought that was you."

I tried to speak but nothing came. Finally, as my glance darted behind her, I whispered, "Frona." Was Pavlos here with her?

Chapter Fifty-Eight

Frona hugged me. "I am so glad to see you and so surprised! Have you become a believer in Christ?"

I nodded, relieved that Pavlos was not with her. "I am glad to see you, too. Yes, Jesus is my God and my Lord. And you? When did you come to believe? I do not remember that coming up when you and..." I could hardly speak Pavlos' name.

She did not wait for me to finish. "No, we were not believers back then, either. A man from the Peloponnese had business here in Corinth, and he became a Christ follower after he heard Paul share the good news from the Bema. He was so excited, he began to tell everyone he knew about the unconditional love of Jesus. We listened to him at a gathering one night and came to believe shortly after.

A male voice interrupted, "Oh, there you are, Frona,..."

I looked up into the face of the only man I had ever loved. He looked exactly as I pictured him, awake and in my dreams. His hair still tangled out of place and the smile that made my heart forget to beat, had not changed.

His voice dropped, "Eunice? I cannot believe it is you."

I strained to hide my tears and nodded. The music had ended. It was time to take our seats. His eyes darkened and held me captive.

"I want to see you after the meeting." His tone almost threatened. "Will you wait for me? Promise not to run off?"

I whispered my promise, and he and Frona left to find their seats.

I never heard a word the speaker said that night. My mind raced down a path so cluttered with possibilities, it shut out every sound but the pounding of my heart. The light that had flashed in Pavlos' eyes when he first saw me, weakened my knees.

It reflected that same hope when he asked to take me home and meet his family. A girl, who had lived the sordid life I had once lived, could never match that brilliant luster.

Promise or not, I needed to disappear. I could not face the hunger I saw in his eyes or deny my desire to fling myself into his arms and never leave. Where could I hide?

Worship resumed after the speaker finished. I slipped through the crowd and dashed through the gate, eager to get away from the temptation to pretend I was all he wanted me to be.

I thought about going to my little house, but I had all but turned it over to my friend, and it was probably being used. I ended up in the marketplace, grateful few people lingered there after dark. The chilly mist that drifted from the fountain soothed my swollen eyes.

Hours later, a glance at the moon's position assured me the meeting at Chloe's would be over and the people gone. I stayed in the shadows as I neared the house. Nothing moved so I entered the gate.

From the side of the courtyard came, "That is a strange way to keep a promise."

I gasped into my hands. "Pavlos. You were supposed to be gone."

He put his hands on my shoulders. "And you were...where did you go? Why did you run away" Do you not know how much I have missed you... longed to be with you again?" His face was so close, even in the dark I could see his brows flex.

"Pavlos, I..."

He pulled me close. "Enough." His voice trembled in my ear.

I knew I should leave, but when his lips pressed mine, I melted into his embrace.

"Eunice, I love you. I have prayed for this moment, and I believe God, in His mercy, arranged for us to find each other again." He looked into my eyes then whispered into my hair, "And your kiss tells me you have longed for and want me as well."

All my resistance drowned in those few words. He loved me. He had said it aloud. He loved me. "Oh, Pavlos, I have thought of you every day since I last saw you, but I..."

"No. No buts, I will never let you go again. I want to marry you and make you mine forever."

We moved to the bench, outside Chloe's side door, and feasted on our long-denied hunger to hold one another close.

I tried to explain why I had run from him before... my concern I would not be acceptable to his father and my desire to not be the cause of dissension in his family.

Pavlos shook his head. "Eunice, my father was set in his ways, stern and unbending. But when I told him about you, that I intended to marry you whether he approved or not, he accepted my decision.

Perhaps old age opened his eyes to what really matters. This is my third trip back since we were together, and each time, he knew I hoped to find you and bring you home. Sadly, he died about six months ago, so you will not get to meet him."

I said I was sorry his father had passed, but he brushed it off with questions I feared would come.

"Where did you go after you left me? Did you find employment in another inn?" What have you been doing since last I saw you?

His concern broke my heart. Panic rushed to replace the indescribable joy I had cherished moments before. How would he react when he heard of the poor decisions I had made... the dark side of my past? I could not tell him. I needed to think, perhaps to disappear for good.

"Pavlos, it is very late. Where are you staying?" I tried to keep it light as I grasped an excuse to avoid what I could not bear to face. "I am sure Chloe is worried about me. Let us meet tomorrow and talk some more."

He told me that he was at the inn where we had met, and agreed to come around midmorning. How I treasured what would likely be our last embrace and hurried into the house.

"Eunice? Where have you been, Child? I was about to..."

I sobbed, "Oh, Chloe." Compassion replaced the concern on her face, and she held out her arms. I fell into them and blubbered an apology.

"I had to leave. The deepest desire of my heart has come to pass, but I have ruined everything. I cannot stay here. I have to leave... tonight."

She insisted we sit a moment. She did not probe, simply stroked my arm. When I finally ceased to shudder, she asked, "Would you like to tell me about it?"

I sniffed. "Did you meet a man from the Peloponnese and his sister, Frona, at the meeting tonight?

"Yes, lovely people. When most of the guests were gone, they came and asked me if I knew you and where you were. They said they were friends of yours and had not seen you for a long time. I told them you live here with me, and they waited quite a while in hopes to see you again. Why did you leave?"

My head drooped. Where should I begin? "His name is Pavlos. He stayed at the inn where I worked, about two years ago. He was on a journey to find new sheep dogs for his father's ranch.

"We struck up an unlikely friendship that quickly evolved into something more. He wanted me to meet his family, but after his sister filled me in on their tyrannical father and the betrayal and loss of Pavlos' first love, I knew I would not be accepted as Pavlos' wife. So, to prevent upheaval in his family, I disappeared. He tried to find me, but finally gave up and went home."

Tears rolled again. "Oh, Chloe, now he is here, determined to marry me. He thinks I am that innocent girl he met at the inn. You know my past... I cannot bear to tell him and break his heart again." I leapt to my feet. "I need to be gone before he comes back in the morning."

"Now, wait a minute." She grabbed my hand and pulled me back down. "Maybe you need to give him more credit. He is a believer, and God can help him understand what a desperate time it was in your life and forgive past mistakes. Eunice, remember, you are a new creation in Christ. The old you has passed away."

I leaned onto my forehead as degrading memories flashed before me. Chloe's counsel seemed a frivolous dream. I told her I would pray about it, and we headed for bed. Instead, I packed my few belongings and waited until I was sure she would be asleep.

By the time I reached my little house, it would be morning. I would give my friend's guests a few hours to pack up and leave, before I resettled into the place where memories of my old life waited to taunt me.

Chapter Fifty-Nine

I slept in my house for two nights... prowled or paced would be more accurate. I vacillated between hope that Chloe would try to help Pavlos find me, and relief that we had never discussed the whereabouts of my house.

My cries to the Lord rose and disappeared like smoke that smoldered off ashen coals, and left me desolate. I repented again of every sin I ever committed, but ugly memories pulled me deeper into despair. God had assured me He covered the most grievous of my sins... the decision to end Rose's life, the times I had sold my body, and the pain I had held against my family. Each had lifted a weight from my heart, but to forgive myself and put my past behind seemed impossible.

Finally, tears over losing life with the man I loved, ran out. I put aside my grief and self-pity and sought the Lord's wisdom.

Echoes of the things Paul taught, or Chloe had made clear, popped in my head like green wood in a fire. Each truth was immediately followed by taunts from the evil one that my sins were too horrific, that I knowingly followed the wrong path and should not expect God to forgive me.

On a long walk the third evening, something Nicanor said filtered through the conflicting voices that sparked my confusion. God loves you just the way you are, Eunice. The blood of Jesus is what has cleansed you of all sin... past, present, and future. There is nothing you will ever be able to do to deserve or earn your forgiveness. It is a gift only God can give.

I fell to my knees on the side of the road, unmindful of who might see me. I looked up into the heavens. Stars dazzled a bright display against the dark. A smaller light, distanced from the moon's dominance, seemed to twinkle with the vigor of a waterfall. It beckoned with a force I could not resist.

It was as if the tiny star could not contain the urgency behind its message meant for me alone. I watched it pulsate as it awakened my spirit to grasp that the Lord knew of my struggle. Even before I was born, He had positioned a part of His creation to get my attention.

I cried, "Lord, I believe it! I receive your forgiveness. Never again, Jesus, will I question Your power to cleanse me of my past. I am so grateful to be called Your child. I worship You. I worship You." I do not know how long I stayed there, swaying in grateful relief and joy in my newly found freedom.

I gathered my things the next morning, informed my friend I was leaving and started for Chloe's. It was late afternoon when I arrived, relieved no preparations were in place for a nightly meeting.

She welcomed me with a hug. "I am so glad you are back, Eunice. To run away from a problem never accomplishes anything." Her tone mimicked one weary of repeating a familiar lecture.

Running away struck a chord. How many times had I reverted to that whenever I found myself overwhelmed with disappointment or rejection?

I had run from the orchards when Yorgos chose a wife I had hoped would be me. I had run from Alistar when he would not stand up to his father and marry me. I had run to an evil midwife to rid myself of the guilt of a pregnancy outside of marriage. I had run from Pavlos to avoid the rejection of his father. Instead of standing up to him, I had run from the innkeeper who threatened to accost me, and now I had run from the man I loved to avoid the painful truth of my past.

I was done running. I would be honest with Pavlos, ready to accept the likelihood he would change his mind and not want to marry me. My heart was about to break, but I would trust the Lord's grace to show me a life that pleased Him. People would likely continue to reject me, but from here on, I would rest in the certainty that God never would.

"Oh, Chloe, I know you were right, but I had to sort it out for myself." I told her how Nicanor's words had helped me to truly believe I was forgiven and to trust God fully. A troubled expression passed from her eyes to her lips before she looked away and sighed.

"Chloe? What is it?"

"Let us sit down, a minute." I followed her into her receiving room.

"Your friend Pavlos and his sister have been here every day in hopes you would come back. They questioned me over and over about why you would have left. It was so sad. They really wanted to be with you."

I tried to grasp why this upset her so. "What...did you tell them?"

Her forehead fell into her hand. "Yesterday, they said they were to sail today and begged me to help them understand.

I probably should not have, but they planned to leave so I gave in to their pleas. I explained how demonic pressures had so overwhelmed you that you could not let go and forgive yourself of the past.

I repeated the powerful testimony that you shared with Daphne, how you were forced to live and of how God changed your life through time with Nicanor. They asked a lot of questions, and I sensed they had not yet learned much about God's redeeming power.

I tried to explain in detail what Christ's victory on the cross brought to each of us, salvation no matter our past."

I was stunned. I wanted Pavlos to hear it from me. I sighed, her heart was right, she had done what she thought would help them understand.

My lips trembled until I managed to eke out what I did not want to hear, "And I assume that was the last you heard from them?" She nodded. "Eunice, I am so sorry, I..."

I swallowed the pangs of disappointment that threatened to buckle my knees. "No. The truth is the truth, and we all have to deal with it the best we can. Pavlos needed to know why I could not marry him, and now he can forget me and move on."

With a heavy heart, I climbed into bed that night, removed my veil and stared at it. Was it part of the deception I had used to cover who I really was? I laid it on the bedside table and blew out my candle.

The Lord whispered words I had heard once before, The Eunice I love is beautiful inside and out, with or without the veil. I drew up my blanket and let the warmth of His words soothe my pain, aware the battle against the lies of the evil one would continue to bring condemnation, but victory in Christ was mine

The next day, I determined to put all heaviness aside as we readied the courtyard for the nightly meeting. I carried a heavy water pot outside as I sang by faith, a song of praise that affirmed God never stops his work in us, but uses all things for good.

"I would be happy to help you with that if you promise not to run away while I do it."

I jerked around. My jaw hung like a broken hinge. "Pavlos! Chloe said you left for home, yesterday."

He took the jug from my arms and set it on the table. "We were supposed to, but neither Frona nor I had a peace about it. We exchanged our passage for next week." He took my hands and looked into my eyes. "Now, I know why."

I backed away from him. "Pavlos, I am so sorry... about everything. Chloe said she told you... I mean, I came back to tell you myself, but...."

He stepped closer, his feelings masked.

I backed some more. "When I saw you at that first meeting, I could think of nothing but how the truth would hurt you. I cannot imagine how you must have felt when you heard it. Please do not think I expect—"

"Eunice, no." He reached out and pulled me close.

My trumped-up bravado to humbly reap what I had sown, disappeared. I could not let him go, now or ever. Between sobs, I whispered, "I am so sorry. If I could go back and—"

He lifted my chin and studied my face. "Eunice, I admit I wrestled with what Chloe told us. It was painful to hear, worse to swallow. I spent a whole night trying to put images of you and... well to put it out of my mind.

"But near dawn, something Paul preached rallied in my spirit. He told of a disciple who refused to eat what he deemed unclean. Three times the Lord told him to eat but he would not until God said, 'Do not call unclean or common what God has cleansed.'" Paul was talking about people, Eunice... about us, you and me... about every sinner's condition before God cleansed and made him new."

Joy rose like an unexpected swell and flooded my heart. I held his face between my hands.

"Oh Pavlos, my Pavlos. Only God could do such a work of forgiveness and acceptance in your heart. I love you so much. I will never deserve you, but I will not ever fail you or run from you, again. I promise."

Once again, those arms I had dreamed of, held me to his chest. I could almost hear Paul's words, and the God of peace will crush Satan under your feet.

As we walked over to tell Chloe the good news, I claimed it for myself, once and for all, and trampled the spirit of rejection that had plagued my life.

The Epilogue

The next day, Pavlos added my name to the roster of those leaving for the Peloponnese. And Chloe, aglow with joy, arranged for Paul to marry us after the next meeting. We spent our wedding night and the rest of the week in a closed-off room in Chloe's house. I had often wondered what was behind that door but never asked.

Her voice was heavy with emotion. "This is where my husband and I slept for twenty years. I want you two to enjoy it as we did."

I was awed by the beautiful draperies and bed covers, the frescos, and the carved statues of birds and flowers.

Chloe had not spoken much of the life she had shared with her husband, but the peace on her face told me it had been a marriage built on love.

The evening before we were to be married, I told Pavlos I needed to go and sign my little house over to my friend. He volunteered to accompany me, but I convinced him I would be back in the morning, and he could use the time to visit the other sheep farm he wanted to see.

His eyes held a teasing twinkle until I assured him I would return.

It was twilight as I passed through the city. I took in everything. Funny how different things look when your heart is not weighed down with worry or sorrow. That is when I found the temple prostitute beaten and whimpering alongside the road.

I took her with me to my little house, cleaned her up and put her to bed. When she asked me why I was helping her, the words of Jesus came back to me. You will be my witness when the Holy Spirit comes upon you.

I shared the story of my life with her... the sorrow and rejection, and the struggle to survive. Her eyelids began to drift, so I tucked her in.

"I will tell you more tomorrow. For now, go to sleep. You are safe here and I will not leave you."

When she awoke the next morning, I fixed some food my friend brought us. The bruised girl was so broken I wondered how best to reach her with the wonderful news that brought new life to me. Her questions made it easy.

"How, Eunice? Your life was even harder than mine. What brought you to a place where you could care about someone as pitiful as me?"

For the next few hours, I told her how God had intervened at the lowest time in my life. I shared how He sent a man, one I had taken part of in an ambush that injured him, and then to ease my guilt, brought home to help him heal."

I grinned. "But I was the one who was healed."

Her attention never strayed as she listened to how Jesus loved her and wanted her to become a child of God. The usual feelings of being unworthy or undeserving of such love, poured from her along with question after question. It was no surprise that I mouthed the same words Nicanor had used to comfort and encourage me to believe.

In the end, she received Jesus as her Lord. I told her we were going to a woman of God who would welcome her and help her grow in this new life.

My feet nearly danced along the road back to Chloe's. "Lord," I whispered, "I have never known such joy. Please let this be an on-going pattern of being used for Your glory."

Characters in Veiled Promises

EUNICE, IN HER EARLY TEENS

CHARA, SISTER, THREE-YEAR-OLD

DAMIAN, OLDER BROTHER, ADONIS, SECOND BROTHER

GRANDFATHER, EUNICE'S MOTHER'S FATHER

YORGOS, ORCHARD OWNER

WIFE, THERA, MOTHER OF TWINS, BELEN AND BEMUS

OPHELOS, YARN VENDOR

CRATHIS, MEAT VENDOR, WIFE, LARNA

ALISTAR AND SPIROS, THEIR SONS

PHOBIE AND TERIS, INN KEEPERS

AELLO, MIDWIFE

ROSE, EUNICE'S DECEASED CHILD

PAVLOS, GUEST AT INN, FRONA, HIS SISTER

AEGEUS AND CYANEA, INN KEEPERS

KYROS, OLDER NEIGHBOR OF ROMAN ARMY CAPTAIN

ZONA, MATRON IN CHARGE AT DELOS

ZOE, MOTHER OF CALLIOPE A YOUNG MUSICIAN

ZYLINA, PROSTITUE OF APHRODITE'S TEMPLE

PEKKA, BAR OWNER

PANDAROS, ELDERLY MAN

NICANOR, VICTUM OF ATTACK

CHLOE, HOME CHURCH LEADER

Carol S. Lacey

Thank you for reading *Veiled Promises*, my fourth novel. I love creating characters and putting them in real-to-life situations. You might also enjoy my *Snare of the Fouler* series, available on Amazon. I started writing as a child, became a busy mom, and at about 60, started writing for Christian magazines, and eventually moved to novels.

Recently, God has opened doors to speak and share about my books and my journey — exciting and scary. If your book club, church group, library or such, are in south-west Michigan and are interested in having me share my story, please contact me on my website, carollacey.com, where you'll also find my blog.

About a month ago 1 Corinthians 15:8 jumped out at me. St. Paul spoke of his being *"as one born out of due time,"* and adds that by

God's grace he is who he is. My Bible's notes explained that when Paul wasn't yet a follower of Jesus, he was like an *"undeveloped, aborted fetus, incapable of sustaining life."*

I too wish I'd been born again sooner, to have been a better daughter, wife, mother, and friend. But Paul knew it and I too know that God's timing is perfect. Eunice had to learn along with all of us, that God has a plan, and He is in control, working all things for our good. That by His Holy Spirit He is taking our once undeveloped souls, minds, spirits and bodies, incapable of sustaining our walk without Him, and transforming us into the image of our Savior, Jesus Christ, enabled to conquer every difficulty.

I wish you peace and joy on your journey, and I would love to hear from you.

Blessings, Carol

Made in United States
Cleveland, OH
11 February 2025

14276413R00272